GHOST BONES

Helen Currie Foster

Alice MacDonald Greer Mystery Series

This is a work of fiction. All incidents, dialogue and characters, with the exception of some well-known public figures, are products of the author's imagination and not to be construed as real. Where real-life historical or public figures appear, the situations, incidents and dialogues concerning those persons are used fictitiously and are not intended to depict actual events or to change the entirely fictional nature of the work. Any legal issues and analyses are fictional and not intended or to be taken as legal analysis or advice. Coffee County and Coffee Creek exist solely in the author's imagination, where they are located somewhere in the Texas Hill Country between Dripping Springs and Fredericksburg.

Book Design: Bill Carson Design
Library of Congress Control Number: 2024911196
ISBN 978-1-7327229-3-4

For Isla, Foster, Lawrence, Emilia,
and Edward

C h a p t e r   O n e

The Role of Love

"No! No! And NO!" Alice Greer glared at the sign someone had stuck in the front yard of her law office in downtown Coffee Creek: RICHARD RILEY FOR STATE REP! She parked, strode through the chilly morning wind to the sign, yanked it out of the ground, and marched to the trash bin. For good measure she ripped the pasteboard sign off the stick and tore it in half. Illegal, without permission!

Another Riley sign was stapled to the telephone pole at the curb. Also illegal, as Riley—a lawyer—should know. With the wind blowing her hair into her face, she reached up and tore it off.

The idea of taxpayer dollars going to pay Richard Riley's salary! Smarmy, arrogant, and lazy, he'd worked briefly as a summer clerk at her old law firm in Austin. Worst of all, he was dishonest, as she learned to her horror when he handed her the law memo she'd requested for a hearing before Federal Judge Edwin Mahan. She'd frowned, reading it: "Are you sure about this case citation?"

"Oh yes. That case wins for us. It's right on point," he'd drawled.

Though feverishly preparing for the hearing, she'd stopped to look up the case herself.

Riley hadn't just misstated the holding. He'd got it backward. When she stalked into his office, he'd admitted he "hadn't read the whole case"—in itself unforgivable. "But it was in the list of cases under the statute..."

If she'd cited that case before Judge Mahan—a stickler for accuracy—she'd have lost all credibility with the court, maybe for the rest of her career.

No way did Riley deserve elected office.

But at least, she thought, unlocking the front door, I don't have to deal with him any longer.

She'd dressed up for today's meeting, this third Monday in January—black jacket and pants, cream sweater, red cowgirl boots. Alice firmly believed boots gave her more swagger, more confidence, and a couple more inches—useful for someone who had to tiptoe to get close to five-foot-six. Walking past the entry hall mirror, she saw the wind had played havoc with her brownish-blond hair, highlighted with talent by her Austin hairdresser. Plus she'd forgotten her lipstick. Brush, tube of red—now she was ready.

Minutes later, Alice looked out her office window to see pulling up, precisely on time, the old blue VW Beetle belonging to Judge Mahan. Now retired, the judge was rapidly becoming her all-time favorite client. He disembarked from the passenger seat, followed by Charley, his elderly brown-and-white basset hound. The Beetle pulled away.

Alice greeted the judge at the front door. He was still tall, slightly hunched, with the lined face and penetrating blue eyes she remembered from law school. Alice bent down and extended her hand to Charley for olfactory inspection, then gently massaged the crown of his head, admiring each magnificent ear. Each time Charley arrived, she saw a few more white hairs on his muzzle.

"Who's driving your Beetle?" she asked.

"Johnny. He's picking up groceries while Central Garage inspects his car."

Alice was fond of Johnny, the judge's only grandchild. After what the judge termed a disastrous freshman year at nearby Texas State—too much partying, then scholastic probation—Johnny had turned it around. Now, a junior majoring in economics, he was studying hard, hoping for an honors degree. Judge Mahan had told Alice that Johnny's mom was dead and that his dad lived in California. Sounded to Alice like the judge had taken over parenting.

"How's his big economics paper coming?"

"He's burning the midnight oil," said the judge. "He's finally got some decent roommates who actually study. He's also working part time, but he needs a little help with the rent deposit till his next paycheck. I'm willing, given how hard he's trying. Where's that red-headed barrel-racing assistant of yours?"

Alice smiled. "Silla's filing papers at the courthouse. She'll be here shortly."

The judge's blue eyes rested on Alice. "Ready to get this show on the road?"

"Ready to roll."

Alice got him seated, Charley at his feet, at the antique tea table by the window in her office, with a view of the back yard. She and the judge had hammered out all details of his proposed gift to the Texas

State ornithology lab. Now she handed him the final agreement. The university officials had already provided signatures, with only the judge still to sign.

The judge leaned forward, long legs folded, glasses perched on his nose, finger moving down each page before he turned to the next. Sun gleamed on his white hair.

I'll bet he went over every court order, every judicial opinion, the same way, Alice thought. Judge Mahan was famously meticulous. She'd once seen him chastise an over-aggressive prosecutor, grandstanding for the press, who'd hastily filed election fraud charges against an ex-con who'd properly registered to vote. Glaring, Judge Mahan had entered a terse order of dismissal: "The government owes its citizens, at a minimum, the duty to present an accurate fact record to the court." Ouch.

He licked a finger, turned to the next page.

Alice wished he was still on the bench, demanding facts, dispensing justice. He'd scared hell out of her in law school, when she made her first moot court argument staring into those unblinking blue eyes. He'd never indicated any approval. "Miss MacDonald, your time is up."

But now she'd made his bird project a reality. She'd been honored when he asked her to visit his place to discuss possible terms of the gift. He'd led her out to the terrace, surrounded by bird baths and bird feeders. "Have you always been a bird man?" she'd asked.

"Nope. Birds are a late-in-life passion. I've pretty much given up on the human race," he'd added, with a small, one-sided smile.

Alice occasionally felt the same.

"Especially after researching our county history," he'd added. "Another project I started, a few years ago."

"It's that grim?"

"You'd be surprised," he'd said. "Partly it's oral history, stories of some pretty rough times."

When she'd asked how fast he wanted the gift finalized, he'd said: "Right away. I don't want to be dead before it kicks in. You know what I'm really hoping, Alice? To be able to visit the lab and the profs now and then and hear what they're up to. Pay to play, sort of."

Now, sitting at her tea table, the judge turned to her. "Ready to sign," he announced.

Alice felt a rush of satisfaction. She'd helped him negotiate his "pay to play." Now he could enjoy it.

Silla burst through Alice's office door, red ponytail bouncing. "Got my yard sign! Gracie Castro for State Rep!" she crowed triumphantly to Alice. Then she spotted the judge. "Sorry, Judge!"

The judge's eyes sharpened. "Gracie's running? Against Richard Riley?"

"Yes," Silla said. "So far neither's got a primary opponent." She grinned. "I'm on Gracie's team."

A pause. "Excellent," said the judge. "I need to keep up."

Apparently, Alice wasn't the only one who lacked confidence in Riley. "Where'd you get your sign?" she asked.

Silla, bending over to stroke Charley's neck, looked up. "At the Camellia, of course. Her committee was meeting there." The Camellia Diner sat across from the Coffee County courthouse, ideally situated for collecting gossip.

Charley leaned on Silla's leg, gazing up with hopeful eyes.

"Hang on, Charley. Just a minute—she's busy," Alice said.

Silla stood by the tea table, watching the judge's pen move, then collected the agreement. "I'll notarize your signature, email this to the university, and take the signed original to the post office at lunch." She swirled out, followed by Charley, his nails clicking on the wooden floor.

"You lucked out when you hired Silla," said the judge.

"Don't I know it! She's saved my bacon so many times. Plus, she gets all the scoop. Knows everyone, finds out everything."

The judge gazed out the window at the pecan tree in the back yard. Yellow leaves littered the grass.

"You like Gracie Castro?" Alice asked.

"She's a good person."

"And Richard Riley?"

He frowned. "I don't—I don't have confidence in him. There are reasons. Possibly just ancient history." Like many judges, Alice thought, he was careful about opining on lawyers.

"Speaking of history, I'd like to read your history of Coffee County."

He glanced at her, then slowly nodded. "I'm flattered. You'll undoubtedly spot errors, and I haven't finished the footnotes. But Alice, I'd like you to take on more work. Will you help me get it published? Can we amend our engagement letter to include your shepherding the book to publication? Cover, copyright, costs, forms, proper format, ISBN, Library of Congress deposit, all the stuff I've never had to do?"

"Published by you, or the Coffee County Historical Commission? Or some other publisher?"

"Me, if the Historical Commission refuses."

She'd never had a client ask for publishing help. Sounded doable. She and Silla would figure it out.

"And one more thing. I've got an archeology project about to get started out at my place. Potentially interesting. My contract's with an archeology team headed by Bobby Bender. He claims to know you."

"We've worked together before, when he was with the Rock Art Conservancy," Alice said, intrigued. "Isn't he also on the Texas State faculty now?"

"Yep. I'm looking forward to watching the dig, but I got to thinking—if something happens to me, I get sick, or whatever—I need to be sure this project gets properly completed. Can you help?" He pulled his phone from his pocket. "I'll email you the contract."

Holy cow. Oversee an archeology project? Surely she could evaluate whether Bender met his contractual obligations.

She opened the email, scanned the short contract. Simple enough, and signed by Dr. Robert Bender, Ph.D., Diplomate, and ABFA, whatever that was. But detail was scanty. "What's Bender looking for, Judge? This just says 'evidence of human history.'"

"He's digging in that rocky ravine, or draw or gulch, whatever you call it, that runs through one side of my property and empties into Blue Creek. Hill Country water's an irresistible magnet for humans. I'm curious about human history."

"Wait just a moment." Alice walked out to Silla, explained the two new tasks, drafted two short new paragraphs, and asked Silla to update the engagement letter.

Silla's eyes were wide. "Archeology? Cool!" In five minutes she darted back into Alice's office, handed Alice the letter for proofing, watched while the judge read and signed the revised letter, and swooped back out.

"What a relief to have you on board," he said. "On both counts." He stared out the window again, then turned to Alice. "Different topic. Do people ever really change?"

"For better or worse?" Alice clung to the slim hope that occasionally people did change for the better, maybe after death, tragedy, or revelation. But generally? "Maybe it's like Maya Angelou put it—'When someone shows you who they are, believe them the first time.' Of course, that ignores the love factor."

"The love factor," mused the judge, a small smile on his face. "I didn't have to deal with that in my courtroom. If you're weighing the scales of justice in a criminal case, you're balancing only a crime and its punishment. Lately, I've thought a good bit about the role of love, its absence, its irrelevance, in criminal court." He looked up at Alice. "Sentencing allows some mercy. I still hope a couple of people I had to send to prison may have changed. The dream of rehabilitation, right?" Then he added, "But as a general rule, believe them the first time. Otherwise, Santayana's warning comes to mind—'Those who cannot remember the past are condemned to repeat it.'"

"And also, 'History is written by the victors,'" Alice said.

"Yes. But occasionally someone can keep the victors from overstating their victory by revealing the real story."

Silla stuck her head around Alice's office door. "Okay, Judge, it's done. I've emailed your signed document to the university." She disappeared.

Judge Mahan leaned forward. "Excellent! Thanks for getting this done, Alice. And thanks for offering to read my draft. I'll be interested in your comments. I may not need your help on the archeology project, but it's good to know you're available."

Needed or not, Alice already planned to invite herself out to the dig. Just for orientation, she told herself. And to catch up with Bender. The judge's phone beeped. He looked down. "Johnny's almost here. Alice, you know David Frohbel in Fredericksburg, right? Muriel's nephew. He drafted our wills before Muriel died, plus a recent codicil. He says you're friends from law school. Can you coordinate with him about the two projects in the codicil?"

"Sure." She liked and respected Frohbel and his wife Isabel.

Silla opened the door. A tall young man followed her in.

"Johnny!" Alice held out her hand to the boy, struck as always by his looks—the thin face with deep-set eyes, like the judge's, and straight blond hair, shaggy around the ears. He was taller than his grandfather, would be a handsome man—but right now he looked uncertain, and, to Alice, so very young.

"Hey, Johnny, how's the job situation?" asked Silla.

"I'm working at the Last Corral in San Marcos as a part-time bartender," Johnny said shyly. "I've got feelers out for a second gig."

Silla said, "You mind getting your hands dirty? On something temporary?"

"No ma'am!"

"The stable where I ride is desperate for an extra hand."

Johnny held out his phone; she tapped in the number. "Thank you!" he said.

The judge rose, pushing up from his chair with both hands, and stood for a moment. Catching his balance, Alice thought, as she joined him by the tea table. He was well past eighty. He gave Alice that small smile. Their handshake became a hug. He hugged Silla too.

"Thank you, Alice. Thank you, Silla. Okay, Johnny, let's go retrieve your car, now that it's street-legal. Then I can get back to the birds. Wish me luck today—an American kestrel's been hanging around, up on the west ridge, in the trees. Gorgeous bird. I'm trying to get a photo with my new camera. It's got an impressive telephoto lens. All I ask is one decent picture, but that bird keeps dodging me!"

The two women watched Johnny, the judge, and Charley make their way down the sidewalk to the judge's car.

"I love that man," said Silla. "Hey, the Dallas paper had a little article today—some guy the judge put in federal prison was released yesterday after thirty-five years. He's got to be nearly as old as the judge, though, so maybe it's okay. And you'd better leave for Rotary right now or the lord knows who you'll have to sit with. And take your jacket— the wind's up."

Mercifully, today was enchilada day at Rotary. Alice grabbed her jacket and hustled out the door. She smiled to herself, wondering if this very afternoon the judge might begin enjoying his bird project. Would he perhaps schedule a visit with experts at the ornithology lab—or finally capture a photo of his kestrel?

Chapter Two

Got To Work Out Some Issues

In the back room at La Tapatía restaurant in downtown Coffee Creek, big pans of enchiladas wafted scents of pasilla, ancho, cumin. The rolled-up tortillas oozed sour cream and melted cheese. Alice's stomach growled as she joined the line of Rotary members gazing intently at the buffet table. She grabbed a plate, then spooned two enchiladas, plus guacamole and salsa, onto her plate, added a handful of chips, and headed to the table where her best friend, Red Griffin, waved at her.

Red was blonde, with an East Texas accent and a strong preference for red clothes, red cars, and red uniforms for sports teams: "Come on, Alice, it's the winning color!" A former high school rodeo queen and CPA, she'd left her job as administrator at a high-powered Houston law firm to create Red's Rescue Ranch in Coffee Creek—a refuge for abused horses. After Jordie died, Red was instrumental in convincing Alice to move her Austin law practice to Coffee Creek. She'd dragged her introverted friend to Rotary meetings and introduced her to everyone in town. Alice knew she owed much of her success in Coffee Creek to her friends—Red, Miranda at Madrone Bank, Jane Ann at the title company.

Today Red had saved her a seat at the table close to the speaker's platform, with Mayor Betty Wilson, Probate Judge Bernie Sandoval, and three of Alice's favorite clients—Bill Birnbach, Bill Benke, and Jorgé Benavides—who owned the Beer Barn, Coffee Creek's beloved dance hall.

In the eighth chair sat a ramrod-straight man, perhaps mid-fifties, with iron-gray hair, freshly crewcut. Everything about him looked crisp, neat, brushed.

"Alice, meet Tim Johansen," Red said. "Tim's chair of the Coffee County Historical Commission."

Alice perked up. "Doesn't your board meet every month in the reading room at the library? I've seen your name on our calendar." Alice served on the library board.

"We do."

"I understand Judge Mahan's working on a history of Coffee County for the Historical Commission."

Tim Johansen nodded. "It's just at the draft stage, though. Plus we've got to work out some issues with the judge."

"Issues?" asked Alice.

Johansen frowned. "Well...some principles...you know, everyone will have access to the history. I mean, we've got some pretty grisly stories in Coffee Creek. Do we want to air all the dirty laundry?"

"History's history, isn't it?" Alice asked. "Aren't you after the truth? The real story?"

"The real story?" Johansen's eyes shifted, traveling around the table. "From whose perspective?"

"What do you mean, whose perspective?" asked Mayor Wilson. "The Indians? And which ones, Karankawa or Comanche or Kiowa or Apache? The Mexican army? Mirabeau B. Lamar, who hated Sam Houston? Sam Houston, who opposed slavery and secession? The slaves who weren't told about emancipation? The white children who were kidnapped by Indians and didn't want to come home? Their parents, who wanted them back?"

Johansen snorted, laughing. "You got it, Mayor. Which stories do we tell?"

"All the stories?" asked Alice.

"What's the truth?" asked Bill Benke. "You've got to include the Czechs."

"And the Germans," interjected Birnbach.

"Don't forget the Tejanos," Benavides insisted. "We got screwed by the Anglos later, but we fought for independence from Mexico."

The mayor waved her hands in the air, her silver hair high aloft à la Ann Richards. She glared over her purple reading glasses. "I represent all of you. And I say all the stories should be in the history. Hear that, Tim?"

Tim Johansen nodded. "Noted."

A cooling off pause. Judge Sandoval looked up from his plate. "Alice, I hear you're going to marry that guy from Fredericksburg. Kinsear, right? Where will you live, his place or yours?"

Alice felt her face redden. "I—we—well, that's not clear yet." Self-conscious, she hid her left hand in her lap, fingering the ring Kinsear had given her just weeks ago at Christmas. It was hard to keep secrets in Coffee Creek. People knew Alice's husband, Jordie, had been declared dead, five years after his helicopter vanished. They also knew Alice had reconnected with law school classmate Ben Kinsear, who'd left New York hedge fund life to come home to nearby Fredericksburg. Bill Benke rescued her. "Hey, Mayor," he said. "I hear you're going to introduce the candidates for state representative, right? Any kind words for either one?"

The mayor waved two index cards. "I can say good things about Gracie. She's done great work as city attorney. Cleaned up our contracts, got rid of our case backlog. Efficient, fair. I hate for her to move on. But she could do even more for us as state rep."

"And Riley?" asked Benke.

The mayor looked down at her index cards. "Well, they moved here two years ago. Riley's wife got active in the annual City food drive. Word is, she's the brains of the outfit, not Riley. But he's got some backers," she said. "Heavy hitters. Like Winifred Hutton. She'll show up today. So Riley could outspend Gracie."

Silence fell. Alice decided not to voice her experience with Riley quite yet, though nothing would change her mind. Meanwhile, she resolved to send money to Gracie.

"What kind of law does he practice?" Red asked.

The mayor lifted an eyebrow. "His website says personal injury and some wills and trust work. I'm not personally familiar with him, though."

All heads turned toward Judge Sandoval.

"Probably not proper for me to respond," he said, forking up another bite of enchilada. "On either candidate, of course," he added. He popped the enchilada into his mouth.

At the podium the Rotary president tapped the microphone. Mayor Wilson rose, muttering, "Here we go."

Alice heard a kerfuffle at the podium. Gracie Castro, dark-haired, dark-eyed, athletic-looking, a quizzical expression on her face, stood staring at the Rotary president. Alice had met Castro—a long-time runner—when Red dragooned Alice into running the first annual Coffee Creek 10-K.

The president covered the microphone with one hand, sending rasps and blips across the room. He leaned over and whispered to the mayor as she stepped onto the speaker's platform. The mayor frowned. She paused, then leaned forward into the microphone.

"Ladies and gentlemen, we're most grateful to Gracie Castro for appearing today. She's been our beloved city attorney for ten years, but now she's running for state rep." Applause. "We expected Richard Riley as well, but his staff just phoned to say he was unavoidably detained, running late. I understand he hopes to arrive soon. Since you're all busy people who've made time in your day for this meeting, let's go ahead and hear from Gracie. And while she steps up here, I'll shortcut to her resume—UT undergrad, Order of the Coif at UT Law, worked three years at the municipal law firm McIver and Dilley before joining the Coffee Creek Law Department." She turned to Gracie. "Okay, Gracie. Show 'em what you got." The mayor stepped to the rear of the platform.

"Thanks, Mayor," said Castro. She swept the room with her eyes.

"I know many of you. I live here; my son and daughter attend city schools; I've got skin in the game. The privilege of working for the City has underscored my gratitude for what we've got in Coffee Creek: good schools, decent roads, great first-response teams. Good government." Again her eyes traveled across the audience. "I'm grateful for what we've built here together—a caring community that supports its library, its schools, its businesses. Our residents know that imagination and good ideas get traction with the City. I want to build that same confidence within our entire state rep district. I've got ideas on how we can do that. I hope you'll give me your vote! Thank you."

Castro smiled at the applause and glanced at the mayor, who'd joined her at the mike.

"Any questions for Gracie?" The mayor surveyed the crowd.

From the back of the room: "Richie Farmer from the *Caller*. How many cases have you actually tried?" Alice peered over her shoulder. She knew the editor of the *Caller* but didn't recognize the young man standing at the back. Brown hair, side part, blue blazer.

Castro leaned forward. "In private practice, about twenty-five. At the City, our three lawyers work as a team"—but here the mayor interrupted.

"Gracie's been our lead counsel on every litigation matter that's gone to trial. Turned out very well for the City. Any more questions?"

People were shifting in their seats, glancing at their phones, beginning to edge their chairs away from their tables. Alice couldn't believe Riley had stood up Rotary. Maybe afraid a reporter would ask him how many trials he'd chaired?—way fewer than Gracie Castro, Alice thought. His website suggested that in the ten years following law school he'd bounced from one small firm to another, then gone into solo practice.

"It's one o'clock," announced the mayor. "I believe we're done." She handed the mike to the Rotary president.

"Thanks, everyone." His voice was drowned out by departure noises—voices, chairs, members—including Alice—leaving their tables.

Then the hallway door opened and Richard Riley made his appearance.

Big grin. "Howdy, folks. Sorry to be late. Unavoidable!" With no explanation forthcoming, Riley began glad-handing his way through the room. Maybe six feet, a little heavier than when he'd clerked at her Austin firm, brush-cut brown hair, white teeth, wide smile. Blazer and blue shirt, red tie. Full candidate regalia, Alice concluded. Just at that moment he lifted his eyes, saw Alice, blinked, and turned quickly away. Hmm—he did remember her—and clearly didn't want to renew her acquaintance.

The mayor pushed her way through the crowd, grabbed his arm. "What held you up?" she barked—loud enough to be overheard. Alice felt embarrassed for him, but hey—showing up late for Rotary?

"Sorry, campaign event ran late, students asking questions," he said, eyes flicking left and right past the mayor.

She still gripped his arm. "Who's managing your campaign?"

"Oh—um, couple of guys. Excuse me! Hey, Winifred!" and he slipped past the mayor to a waiting hug from a woman standing nearby. Statuesque, dominating, a well-kept sixty in a red silk sheath and a vintage leather shoulder bag with a hand-tooled design, she smiled at the crowd while embracing Riley, then pulled him by his hand to meet others nearby. Alice had never met Hutton. She'd heard Hutton was new to the area; according to rumor, she'd bankrolled one candidate in the last school board race—a conservative young man who expressed concern that tenth graders were reading *One Day in the Life of Ivan*

Denisovich and argued the book would prejudice students against the old Soviet system. "All that repression is over," he'd claimed. He'd lost, but not by much.

The mayor joined Alice. "That's Dedra Riley," she said, tipping her head toward a dark-haired pretty woman, maybe late thirties, on the edge of the group surrounding Winifred Hutton and Richard Riley. "In the blue dress with the red-and-white scarf." As Alice watched, the woman's pasted-on smile momentarily disappeared. She rolled her eyes briefly in—what? Exasperation? Frustration?

"She's upset, and I don't blame her," added the mayor. "Her husband cruises in, late to a big event—embarrassing. He hasn't said boo to his wife—he's too busy sucking up to Winifred. Meanwhile Winifred ignores Dedra like she's nothing. Tough duty, and I wouldn't stand for it."

Interesting. "Who *is* Winifred Hutton? Why is she interested in Coffee County politics? And how'd she hook up with Riley?"

"She wants to be a player, like those guys from west Texas," growled the mayor. "Word is, her party suggested she might be able to help them win our state rep seat with some outside dollars. They mentioned Riley, and she liked him. She kept her big house in Dallas when she bought that ranch off Middle Creek Road. Apparently, there's serious family money from land on the Colorado River, in Bastrop County south of LaGrange. Her brother's still in Dallas, but they don't get along—reportedly haven't spoken for years."

"Why don't they get along?"

"I hear Winifred and her brother constantly competed to be Daddy's favorite. The brother's been a hugely successful investor. Now I hear Winifred's trying to develop a chain of jewelry stores." The mayor lifted an eyebrow. "Another thing—my Dallas friends say she's got a hell of a temper. Got kicked out of Hockaday for beating up a classmate. The other girl wound up in the hospital."

Alice knew The Hockaday School in Dallas was a well-respected girls' college-prep school.

"Ouch. That must've mortified her parents," Alice said. "Anyway, why'd she pick Riley to support? What's he stand for? If anything?"

"Whatever Winifred tells him. I hear his last law firm edged him out, and his solo practice got no traction."

"Is she married?"

"Two nasty divorces, no kids."

Alice nudged the mayor, tilting her head at two men by the doorway, arms folded across their chests. "Who are those two guys in the cowboy outfits? Not Rotary members..." Both wore cowboy hats pulled low on their brows. One was fiftyish and barrel-chested, the other maybe forty and bony; neither was smiling. "Are those earbuds?" She'd spotted the little wires running down into the collars of their cowboy shirts.

The mayor scowled. "They showed up with Winifred during Gracie's speech. Winifred calls them her 'hands,' like ranch hands, but I doubt ranch work's what they do. Bodyguards, more likely, given all her money."

Alice wondered what it was like to have so much money you needed bodyguards.

On her way out she tracked down the *Coffee Creek Caller* reporter. "Do you plan to ask Riley how many trials he's chaired as lead counsel?" she asked.

The young reporter glared at her. "You suggesting I'm not neutral?"

"Just curious," Alice said. "Seems like you'd want to ask the same facts about Riley."

Walking to her car, Alice contemplated calling Castro to ask if her campaign was advertising in the *Caller*. But no. Alice had paying client work to do: finish the position statement for the upcoming mediation, due by ten tomorrow morning. Goal: finish her draft this afternoon.

*****

Back in the office Alice stared at her computer screen. "No calls! No emails!" she told Silla. "I promise I won't even look at my phone until I finish."

"Excellent."

Alice printed her draft and carried it, plus the mediation and discovery files, to the conference room. She spread out the papers and grabbed her favorite red pen.

At four o'clock Silla stuck her head around the conference room door, waving a flat leather folder. "Judge Mahan forgot this, left it under your tea table. Plus, the university emailed confirmation that they received the judge's final executed document. I thought I'd take a hard copy and this folder out to the judge. I've always wanted to see his place."

"Great idea. The judge might be glad of some company, right? I'll have this mediation statement ready for you first thing in the morning." Silla left.

Alice dived back into the mediation statement, added a concluding paragraph, revised it twice, then threw down the pen. Done. She heard her cell phone ringing and hurried back to her office to answer.

Silla. Silla, barely able to speak. Silla, as she'd never heard her before.

Chapter Three

Let It Not Be So

"Alice—the judge! He—he's lying in the driveway. There's blood everywhere." A pause, then, "I can't find a pulse. I think he's dead!" She heard Silla take a ragged breath, then another. Then Silla said, "I think he's been dead awhile." Her voice trembled.

"Did you call an ambulance?"

"Yes! Just now."

Alice was already up, grabbing her bag, out the front door, phone in hand—"Call the Sheriff's Department too. I'm on the way."

*****

When Judge Mahan first asked her to come discuss his project, Alice had cruised out to his place on Blue Creek, relishing the long views of hills and water. But now she drove like a maniac, all the while muttering, "let it not be so, let it not be so, let it not be so." She raced south from Coffee Creek till she reached century-old Willie's Store, then, tires screeching, turned west onto the old blacktop called Geisberg Lane, braked desperately to avoid disaster at what was known locally, with reason, as Dead Man's Curve, and hit eighty on the last mile. She managed a hard left onto the judge's long gravel driveway, skidded to a stop at the gate, and punched in 1787—the gate code chosen by the Constitution-minded judge.

The gravel drive ran downhill toward Blue Creek, made a J-curve back uphill, widened into a graveled parking circle, and extended briefly uphill to a classic Hill Country limestone ranch house, wide, one story, with deep eaves and a limestone front porch.

An internal voice said... if he was shot in the driveway, stay out of the driveway. Alice obeyed the voice and rolled to a stop behind Silla's green truck, which sat in the dry grass, the driver's door ajar.

Alice jumped out and ran to Silla, who stood at the edge of the drive, hands tightly clenched on her chest, tears running down her freckled face.

The judge lay roughly in the middle of the driveway, near the stone walkway that led to the front porch, his head toward the garage on this end of the house. He was sprawled face down, left arm flung out, right arm bent, wearing an olive canvas vest over a blue long-sleeved shirt. In a bloody splotch on the back of the vest, Alice could see what looked like a bullet hole. Around the judge's head and torso, in a rough circle, the gravel was stained brownish-red. The edge of the circle looked browner than red. A duck-billed cap lay upside down near his right side.

"How long has he been dead?" Alice whispered.

Sirens wailed in the distance, coming closer.

"I tried to find a pulse," Silla said. "Nothing."

Alice could see Silla's footprints in the gravel near the judge's head.

"I didn't touch anything else," Silla said.

Alice scanned the house. Garage door down. Front door closed. In the grass to the judge's right lay a camera with a black telephoto lens. Had the judge been birdwatching?

Alice felt a shadow pass overhead. She looked up. A turkey vulture—no, two. No, three, slowly circling above.

She shivered, folded her arms across her jacket. The wind was picking up. Above the ridge to the west, the January sun turned the sky a pale orange. Sirens again, much nearer. She realized the various responders might lack the gate code and ran back to the gate. Like most ranchers, the judge had a second gate next to the first—designed for fire trucks. Alice called it a "fire gate." To her relief it was only chained, not padlocked. She unhooked the chain. The gate—probably rarely used—was sunk in some mud. Alice was about to grab it and heave it up when she saw tire tracks in the grass. Had someone just come in, or left, through the fire gate?

Alice dashed over to the keypad, punched in the gate code, frantically tried buttons until she found one that held the gate open, then hurried back to Silla.

Behind her a yellow Coffee County ambulance, siren blaring, lurched through the open gate and raced along the drive, spraying gravel. It stopped abruptly below the parking area. EMTs jumped out and ran toward the body.

Close behind followed a black-and-white Coffee County Sheriff's Department SUV, lights flashing. Two deputies emerged, scanned the area, then walked over to Alice and Silla.

The taller deputy's nametag said Everett Berry. "Can you please show your IDs."

Alice hauled out her wallet, groped for her license, handed it over. Silla did the same.

"Why are you here?"

Alice nodded toward Silla. "My assistant Silla called me. Judge Mahan is our client. She came out here to bring him some papers." Silla was staring toward the EMTs, crouched by the judge. One looked up toward the deputies, shook his head no.

Everett Berry walked toward the EMTs. Alice heard him say, "I'll call the JP." Law required a justice of the peace to decide where a body should be taken after what looked an unlawful death.

It looked unlawful to her.

The younger deputy, grim-faced, notebook in hand, blinked at Alice. "Does the judge have family?" His badge: Gerald Olson.

Alice nodded. She pulled out her phone and tapped the contacts list where Silla routinely entered client information—relatives, phones, addresses. "His son Eric lives in California. His grandson, Johnny, lives in San Marcos." She read off the names and phone numbers.

A Coffee County Sheriff's Department cruiser pulled up, lights flashing. Detective George Files rolled down the passenger side window. "Alice. Silla. Why are you two here?"

Alice couldn't control the tremor in her voice. "The judge is our client. Silla found him."

Files's eyes rested on hers. He shook his head. "I'm sorry."

Assistant Detective Alan Joske—Files's assistant—was at the wheel. "Park here," Files ordered.

Alice didn't think Joske much liked her. At least he didn't seem to trust her. She thought, given her history with Files in the past few years, that Files did trust her—mostly. Of course, even with Files, it was still "trust, but verify."

Files opened the cruiser door, unfolded his long legs, and climbed out, looking at Silla, then Alice. "You two stay here, please," he directed.

He and Joske joined the two deputies near the judge's body. She heard Files tell the deputies to check the premises. "Be sure no one else is here. Crime scene team's on the way." He paused. "But don't mess up any footprints, like on the path to the front porch, and don't screw up fingerprints on doors. Maybe start in the back." They nodded and started toward the back yard of the house.

Files and Joske walked back to Alice and Silla.

"Judge Mahan's a federal judge, right?" Files asked. "Doesn't he have any federal protection?"

Alice shook her head no. "He's not hearing cases any longer. He's—he was eighty-plus. He persuaded the feds to leave him alone. They didn't want to, but he insisted."

"Who got here first?" Files asked.

"I did," Silla said.

"How'd you get in?"

"He gave us the gate code. 1787."

Files made a note, then nodded at Joske, who took Silla out of earshot and began questioning her, taking notes.

"Silla called you?" Files asked Alice. "That's why you're here?"

"Yes. The judge was in our office this morning, signing papers. He forgot his leather folder. Also a document arrived we wanted him to have. Silla said she'd run it out here."

"Were you at your office when Silla called?"

She nodded.

"Time?"

"Silla left the office a little after four. She called me at—" Alice checked her phone. "Four-fifteen. She told me she'd already called the ambulance. I told her to call you all."

"What'd she tell you when she called?"

Alice repeated Silla's message.

Files tilted his head. "How'd you get here so fast?"

She just looked at him.

"You touch anything?"

She gave him another look. "No. Silla told me she tried to find a pulse, but couldn't."

"You haven't notified any family, have you?"

"No, I gave the contact info for the judge's son and grandson to

Deputy Olson."

"Let us take care of that, okay?"

Alice knew that meant don't call them…yet. She nodded.

"Neither of you went into the house?"

"I didn't. I doubt Silla did, but Joske will ask her. I've been here before—once recently to meet with the judge and once when his wife, Muriel, invited me and some other former students to his retirement party." Before Files could ask, she said, "Muriel died a few years ago."

Deputy Olson appeared at Files's side. "Doesn't look like anyone's here. An old dog's inside, whimpering."

Alice had forgotten Charley. "That's the judge's basset hound." Who would take charge of Charley? Her own burros would attack any coyote, any dog—even a feeble old hound. Maybe Johnny?

Another Coffee Creek SUV pulled in. "Crime scene team," Files muttered. They unloaded their equipment, dressed in protective garb and bagged their feet, talked to the EMTs, and began photographing the body *in situ*. Alice watched as they bagged the judge's wallet and phone. One, head down, systematically quartered the grass and the gravel around the body, searching. For a shell casing? Another walked the grass slowly around the parking circle, camera in hand, then farther up the drive to the garage. Checking for tire tracks, Alice assumed.

"One more thing," she said to Files. "It looks like someone drove through the fire gate recently. Maybe didn't have the gate code." Files went to tell the crime scene team.

A blue sedan crunched up the driveway. The justice of the peace emerged. Alice knew him vaguely—middle-aged, gray-haired, gray suit, pleasant smile. He peered at the body from the edge of the driveway, spoke briefly with Files, then conferred with the EMTs and crime scene team. Alice knew the justice of the peace would issue the declaration of death and decide when the body could be moved and where it would be sent. In this case, she was betting Judge Mahan's body would be driven to the medical examiner's office in Travis County for autopsy and perhaps further testing.

The JP nodded at Alice as he backed down the drive and turned around to leave. The EMTs stood by the ambulance, waiting for the crime scene techs to signal the body could be moved from the driveway. Finally, the EMTs began carefully loading the judge's body onto a stretcher.

The bloody circle on the driveway, darker now on the edges, looked like a bullseye.

Files walked back to Alice. "What's the deal with the camera with the telephoto lens? Is it the judge's?"

Alice nodded. "Judge Mahan's a birdwatcher." She paused. "What he hired me to do was help him make a gift to the ornithology program at Texas State. That's why he came to our office this morning—to put his final signature on the agreement and send it to the university. The university emailed confirmation of receipt. Silla was bringing him copies for his file—along with a folder he left in our office."

"All your clients get personal delivery service?"

"He's—he was pretty special, George." She was staring at the house, then at the bloody circle in the gravel in the driveway.

Files followed her eyes. "And you're thinking?"

"How long—how long did he lie out here?"

"Medical examiner and the crime scene team will have to tell me. Looks like he was bleeding out maybe an hour before Silla arrived."

Alice closed her eyes, shook her head. "If we'd decided sooner to deliver the documents..."

"Come on, Alice. Listen, just now you were staring at the house, and the body. What's your thought?"

"He was either just leaving, planning to do some birdwatching, or coming back home afterward. Maybe the latter."

"But not in his car, apparently," Files said. "The deputies say there's an old blue VW Beetle and an old blue pickup in the garage. They're his, right?"

She nodded.

"Where'd he do his birdwatching?"

"Locally, I'm sure, but also out here, on his property—well, you'll see the feeders behind the house."

"And look at the views he's got," Files said, scanning the landscape. "Good bird territory, all these trees." He pointed to the knoll in the west, surmounted by live oaks and Spanish oaks, their branches now backlit by the orange sky. "That'd be a good location."

Alice nodded. Then she wondered: did he mean for birdwatching, or sharpshooting?

"What's over there?" Files pointed east of the driveway, toward the tangled line of shrubs and cedars.

"There's a drop-off that way," Alice said. A gulch? Wet-weather creek? Ravine? Wasn't that the location for the judge's archeology project?

"He have any enemies you know of?"

Alice stood silent. "Sure. Any federal judge does, these days. But he'd really retired, you know? He wasn't still sniffing around the courthouse. He was taking care of his grandson. Working on a history of the county. Birdwatching."

Files lifted his eyes, stared at the house. "A retired federal judge. First appointed when he was forty. How many criminals did he send to prison, over what—thirty-five years?"

"He was fair, George. Strict, demanding, and a stickler for proper procedure. He didn't tolerate prosecutors who hid evidence from the defense, or fudged the facts, or misstated case law. I saw him in action. You wouldn't dare do anything less than your dead level best in his courtroom."

Files lifted an eyebrow. Alice noted the creases on his face looked deeper. She wondered how many deaths he'd seen, how many crime scenes he'd studied.

Joske sent Silla back to join Files and Alice. Hmm, did Joske just smile at Silla? That'd be an improvement, Alice thought.

Alice, Silla, and Files stepped back as the ambulance, lights on and siren off, rolled quietly down the driveway and out the gate.

"Can we leave?" Alice asked Files.

He nodded. He shifted his gaze to Silla. "You okay?"

"More or less." She looked at Alice, face grim. "That man—that dear man. I'm on this. See you tomorrow." Silla headed for her truck.

Files frowned. Watch out, world, Alice thought.

"Alice, I don't need Silla messing with this case."

She was constructing a sensible answer ("Silla will do what Silla will do") when a small black Honda hatchback drove down the driveway and stopped next to Alice and Files. The young male driver leaned out, his face a mask of fear and anxiety.

"Johnny?" she called. She turned to Files. "It's the judge's grandson, Johnny. Student at Texas State."

The boy climbed out of his car. "What's wrong? Where's Granddad? Was that—who was that in the ambulance?" His voice trembled. Alice shivered at a sudden gust of chilly wind.

Files took charge. "Son, I need you to park your car and show me some ID." He turned to Alice. "Okay, you can leave now. Just come sign your statement at my office."

Alice frowned, wanting to comfort Johnny. He was panicking now, starting to shake. "Can somebody please tell me—" he stuttered. She moved toward him.

"Alice, not now," Files said.

Silla had driven up next to them. She stopped, seeing Johnny. "Silla, you can go now," said Files. He waved her forward. She frowned, then slowly drove back to the gate.

"George, I should talk to him," Alice said, her voice low. "Let me have just a moment."

He shook his head, pointed to her car. "You know I need to deal with him first. Let me do this. We know where to find you."

Reluctantly, she left Johnny, his eyes riveted on Files.

"I brought my econ paper to show him! He wanted to see it!" she heard Johnny's hoarse cry. Then Files's deep voice took over, measured, calm.

Files was still interviewing Johnny, taking notes, when Alice got her car turned around. She parked for a moment, knowing she owed David Frohbel a call: he'd need to file the judge's will and alert the executor. She ended her message saying, "I am so sorry. Let me know who's executor and if we can help with security for his home. The investigating detective is George Files. He'll likely want a copy of the will and codicil. And the judge told me to check the codicil."

As she turned out of Judge Mahan's driveway, she found herself wishing again that she and Silla had found the judge's folder earlier, decided to deliver his copies sooner, and that Silla had arrived when he could still be saved. Maybe even in time to keep him from being shot. Or at least before the vultures noticed the body. Was it the smell of blood that brought them? Or the smell of death?

Judge Mahan would've known.

C h a p t e r   F o u r

I Like The Way

Kinsear called as Alice negotiated Dead Man's Curve, returning to her office.

"You're back?" she said. Kinsear's New York hedge fund still asked him to advise on certain transactions.

"Caught an earlier flight. I'm still in the car—hoped I could catch you at the office. But I've got to go back in a couple of days. Alice, did you hear about Judge Mahan? KUT radio just reported that he's dead."

"It's true. Silla found him."

"Oh, no, Alice! Then she called you? Is that where you are?"

"Mm-hmm. We're just leaving his place." Winter sunset already: the sun dropping below the horizon, a blaze of molten gold; the sky above an iridescent rose, fast vanishing. The beauty felt like a blow to her heart.

"What happened?"

Alice realized she was gripping the steering wheel too tightly, then took a breath and described the appalling afternoon—Silla's call, her own frantic race to the judge's home, the bloody bullseye on the driveway around his body.

Silence from Kinsear. "I just can't believe—" She was thankful he stopped before adding "that you've found another body" or, worse, "that your clients keep dying." Finally he asked, "Who did it?"

"No idea."

"I'm sorry. He was a great man. Tough, fair—and lord, could he run a courtroom." He paused. "Are you on your way home?"

"After I go by and check to be sure I locked the office."

"Excellent. Listen, I snagged a table for two at Tillie's. What do you think? Does the *ceviche aguachile* sound good?"

She scolded herself. How could she even think about dinner, about a table for two, about Kinsear, after this dreadful death?

But she felt her shoulders relax, felt a smile begin, found herself taking a deep consoling breath. "I am available. I am so available. How soon will I see you?"

"I'm sitting outside your office even as we speak."

*****

"The thing about Tillie's," he said, "is, we can hear ourselves talk." The hostess had put Alice and Kinsear in a quiet corner with a view of the pasture outside, the dainty alpacas grazing in the moonlight. Inside Tillie's, the ancient town hall building—imported from Vietnam, with original ironwood columns marching its entire length—was lit by a spectacular chandelier.

Kinsear leaned back in his chair. "I like the way the chandelier lights your face, Alice." He and Alice were admiring their glasses of a rosé prosecco.

"I like the way the moon's so bright it's casting shadows," Alice said.

"And you like the way the candles illuminate what's left of your *ceviche?*"

She stared down at her empty bowl. "Nothing's left."

The waiter hustled up with Alice's tilefish with gumbo and Kinsear's shrimp and grits.

Kinsear's brown eyes stared into Alice's brown eyes. "Any suspects yet?"

She shook her head no. "Only vague possibilities, as far as I know. The judge wasn't taking cases any more. One of his old convictions got out of prison a couple of days ago. Also, the judge was writing a history of the county, said it's got tales that some locals won't like. And of course, family issues. He's trying to get Johnny—his grandson—back in order. After freshman year he was on scholastic probation. But now he's a junior. The judge claimed Johnny's working hard, trying to make his grades."

She took a bite of her tilefish, remembering the driveway scene. She blinked, trying to erase the memory. "Files may find something interesting on the judge's phone. I saw the police bag it." She shook her head to dispel the memory, then took another bite. "Umm. This gumbo is just the right hotness."

"Well, that's good to learn. Personally I'm deeply in favor of this shrimp and grits." Silence for an interval. Then Kinsear again: "Let's get serious. Are you sure about your dessert choice?"

"Yes. Chocolate mousse, with et cetera."

"Are you going to share?"

"You're having, what, cinnamon *zeppole* with whiskey caramel? I'm not sure about that."

"All I ask is one bite of your mousse."

She lifted an eyebrow. "A small, modest bite. Right?"

He nodded.

I do love this man, she said to herself, watching his mouth, watching the eye-crinkles, watching his eyebrows as he prepared to raise another topic. But—where are we going to live? How can we merge our lives?

Alice also loved her view of the creek in the valley below, loved her treehouse, loved the three donkeys that provided reliable therapy, soothing her breath, slowing her heartbeat, lowering her blood pressure.

And surely Kinsear loved his Fredericksburg ranch just as much—with his horses, cattle, and many more acres. And the old barn with the upstairs bedroom where he had first persuaded her to stay the night.

Still...

They'd meant to marry on New Year's Day when the kids were still home from school, but Alice's favorite pastor, Laura, was out of town.

"May I have a bite of your chocolate mousse?" Kinsear asked. "Also, a penny for your thoughts. About actually getting married, maybe?"

Alice pushed the little pot of exquisite chocolate toward him, watched him scoop up a spoonful, lick the spoon. "Laura's back," she said.

Kinsear lifted an eyebrow and nodded approval. "She'd be great."

Alice admired Laura McDowell, pastor at the Coffee Creek Presbyterian Church, for her openhearted welcome, her apparent ability to get along with virtually anyone, and her riveting sermons, to which Alice found herself actually paying attention. Huh.

But though in principle she was in favor of marrying Kinsear, for some reason the prospect of a second wedding unnerved Alice. Her relationship with Kinsear felt so private; weddings felt so public.

Kinsear read her mind. "We could just elope?"

But there were kids to be thought of...and friends...people who would feel wounded if they weren't present to applaud and support.

She smiled. "Let's not elope. Won't we want the kids?"

"Yes, and another glass of this prosecco." He waved at their waiter.

Maybe Valentine's Day? Not enough time—Valentine's was just weeks away. Maybe spring break when the kids come home?

However, one key factor, Alice thought, watching Kinsear, was her current recognition that sleeping alone no longer had much appeal. She now wanted to spend every night with Kinsear. As she hoped to do tonight.

Though she couldn't get the sight of the judge's body, helpless on the gravel, out of her mind.

Chapter Five

All The Dirty Laundry

On Tuesday morning Alice reached her desk at seven, just as Silla arrived with a paper bag emitting the toasty whiff of fresh biscuits. Alice dropped her bag on the desk and followed Silla to the office kitchen.

"Camellia Diner?" asked Alice. She found the butter and jam in the fridge and joined Silla at the table.

"Mmm," Silla said, crumbs on her chin. "Also present: Coffee County Detective Alan Joske, eating his breakfast. Likes eggs over easy. Wants us to come sign our statements this morning."

"He say anything else about the shooting?"

"Told me they're curious about some phone calls. But he wouldn't say why."

"You'll get it out of him."

"We're building our relationship." Silla smirked and finished her biscuit. "Done with your edits? Ready to give me that mediation statement?"

"As soon as I finish this biscuit. And lick the butter off my fingers." Alice carried her final draft to Silla's worktable. "Send our client the mark-up and tell him we'll get it to everyone by ten."

Back in her office she stared at the tea table by the window, where just yesterday morning the judge had sat, glasses perched on his nose, carefully reviewing his project agreement. She sighed, then turned to the always-dreaded morning task: plowing through emails. Determinedly punching "delete" over and over, she stopped short when she spotted a message from Judge Mahan, sent the afternoon before at two-thirty, when she was toiling away at the mediation statement. His email included a large attachment labeled "Mahan-drft-cchist."

The judge's voice echoed in her mind as she read his message, which made her eyes sting with tears: "Alice, you're a glutton for punishment. First you wrangled with the university on my behalf, very effectively; then you offered to read this draft. I'm sending you the same one I provided to Tim Johansen. I am grateful for your wisdom and insight—on both matters. I'd appreciate any comments. You'll see in the footnotes the 'to-do's' I still need to finish; I may need your help there. And to top it off, now I dare dream of publication."

Then it hit her. The judge was still alive yesterday afternoon at two-thirty...so who showed up?

She called Files. "Either the judge was still alive yesterday at two-thirty or someone else hit 'send' on his email to me."

"Can you forward the email?"

"Yes, but I'd like to send it without its attachment. It looks like the draft history he wanted me to review, wanted me to comment on. Hence a confidential communication to his attorney." A draft was just that—a draft. She didn't want the judge's attachment unleashed yet.

Silence.

After a few seconds, Files spoke. "For the moment, okay. Can you get here by ten?"

"I can."

"And why did you only now see that email?"

She remembered her dogged editing of the hard copy of her mediation draft, then Silla's call from the judge's driveway and the ensuing horror. Then what? She felt a flush of warmth, remembering Tillie's and her night with Kinsear. "I didn't see it until a minute before I called you this morning."

"See you at ten."

*****

Silla stuck her head around Alice's door. "Just sent you the finalized mediation statement. Looks good. Client called, said it looks fine. I've drafted your transmittal to the mediator."

Alice reread the document and signed the transmittal letter. "Ready to go."

Then she told Silla about the judge's email.

"Whoa! Two-thirty?"

Alice imagined Judge Mahan at his desk, staring at his computer, taking one last look at his draft, then hitting "send." Not much later, he was bleeding out on his driveway.

What happened after he hit "send"?

Alice sent the judge's attachment to print—about 120 pages, double-spaced.

Clutching pages still hot from the printer, Alice scanned the preface, titled "First Settlers." No, not immigrants from the American South, or Europe. Not Mexicans, not Native Americans. Instead, Judge Mahan began with prehistoric immigrants who'd crossed the Bering Strait and enjoyed the springs of the Hill Country at least 20,000 years ago, according to archeologists, in what the Texas Legislature in 1846 would name "Coffee County." Judge Mahan had omitted any identification of the specific archeology site he described. Probably wise, given the temptation of fossils and artifacts.

She flipped through the history. After the preface came a rough table of contents. A few chapter headings included in brackets the names of families apparently mentioned in the chapter. Chapter 1? "Coffee Creek Grist Mill, 1846 [Birnbach.]"

Alice called the Beer Barn office.

"Bill Birnbach."

"Bill! I just learned of the Birnbach grist mill! I didn't know the Birnbach family was here in 1846!"

"Yep." The Beer Barn co-owner was his usual low-key, laconic self.

"Your what, great-great-great grandfather?"

"And great-great-great grandmother. Apparently, she was a pistol. They came from Germany to New Braunfels in 1845, then moved up here to start a grist mill."

"You don't brag about this?"

"Oh, the state erected one of those hysterical markers at the site. But brag? Good lord, Alice, what if we each had to tell the truth about *all* our ancestors? Heroes and villains?"

"I see your point." As she hung up she remembered Ted Johansen's comment at Rotary—that the Historical Commission had "some issues" with the manuscript. "Do we want to air all the dirty laundry?" Johansen had asked.

How had the judge chosen his stories? Heroes only? Heroes and villains? Surely Birnbach would enjoy reading about his family grist mill.

On to Chapter 2. Settlers arriving in Coffee County after the Birnbachs built their grist mill included German immigrants opposed to slavery, Mexican-American families, and farmers from the American South, some with slaves. Alice flipped forward, curious about the impact of slavery. Chapter 3: Judge Mahan wrote, "In 1861 Coffee County, with other Hill Country counties, voted against secession. In 1862, after the Confederacy issued draft orders, Coffee County escaped the violence that occurred farther north and farther west (see Battle of the Nueces)." He'd inserted a footnote number, but the footnote was empty. Battle of Nueces? Alice remembered nothing about that in her high school Texas history class.

She glanced at the clock, an interior twinge reminding her that she was due shortly at George Files's office. But she wanted to get a grip on the contents of this manuscript. She tapped her foot while the printer spat out a second copy, then carried the copy to Silla. "Here's the judge's draft history of Coffee County." She turned to the table of contents. "Look, Silla. See Chapter 1? I've already touched base with Birnbach. You know so many people in town. Do you recognize any of these other names?"

Silla ran her forefinger down the list. "Yes. Several."

"I have to meet Files at ten. We need to spot potential hot spots in this draft. Can you start with the stories where you know the family?"

Silla's eyes were glued to the table of contents. "Tell you one I won't skip." She pointed to Chapter 13, "Last Breakfast" (with "Riley's Horse" in brackets).

"Why?"

"Hoo boy! Wondering about Richard Riley, of course!"

He Added A Twist

Promptly at ten Alice stood in the institutional gray hallway at the Sheriff's Annex, waiting for Detective George Files. She paced back and forth, checking email on her phone, wondering what she'd learn—or be asked. Her phone pinged: text from Frohbel: "Horrified about judge. Can't believe he's gone. I'm the independent executor; Madrone Bank's got his financial accounts. Attaching copy of will and codicil for you and appropriate investigator. Will call you." Alice had scanned through the codicil and had begun on the beneficiaries provision of the will—Johnny would inherit the Blue Creek land, with other assets going to the judge's son and sister—when she heard Files's voice.

"Alice. C'mon down." Files waved at her from halfway down the hall to his office. She followed him, noting his tired shoulders, his thinning brown hair. She settled herself in the miserably uncomfortable chair he kept for visitors. "Coffee?"

She shook her head no. The coffee was worse than the chair.

Files sank into his chair and stared briefly at the stack of documents on his desk. "Here." He handed Alice a typed version of the brief statement she'd given him the day before, in the driveway at Judge Mahan's house: the timeline that included the judge's visit to her office; the agreement that Silla would deliver his folder and documents; Silla's frantic call about finding the judge's body; Alice's race to his property; the EMTs' arrival; her statement that she stayed by the driveway and did not enter the judge's house or touch his body or belongings. Files had added her receipt today of the judge's email. Alice read, nodded, signed it, and handed it back.

"Okay. Now let's talk about the judge's family," Files said, brown eyes focused on her face. "Tell me about Johnny."

"All I know is that he got in trouble his first year at Texas State, bad grades, maybe too much partying. Before college he lived with his dad in California; his dad's a tech guy. I understand Johnny's mother died of cancer. After Johnny got put on scholastic probation, the judge took him in hand. Now he's a junior, making decent grades and working part time." She thought for a second. "Judge Mahan taught as a visitor a couple of years at law school. When you signed up you knew you'd work your tail off, read every case, be ready if called on. The judge was tough. But somehow he made you want his approval. I expect Johnny also wanted to please him."

Files was taking notes.

"Silla gets credit too," Alice said. "She got Johnny a second job, a temporary gig at the stable where she rides, out on Old Hays Highway. She'll have him mucking out stalls, grooming horses, hauling hay. She'll read him the riot act if he's sloppy, or late. Or doesn't stand up straight and say 'yes ma'am' and hop to it when told what to do."

Files grinned in appreciation. "Silla could run the country, couldn't she?"

"No question."

"Okay." Files leaned forward, face serious. "The judge had his phone in his pocket."

Alice nodded.

"A couple of messages raised issues." He peered down at the stack of papers and pulled out what looked like a transcript.

What now? She watched his face.

"One call from Johnny, Saturday morning about eight-thirty." Alice squinted, trying to decipher the transcript. No luck: tiny print, and upside down.

Files read aloud, "Granddad, it's Johnny. You know my econ paper's due Monday at two-thirty. I'm working two shifts today at the Last Corral, nine to four, and five to midnight, then Sunday again nine to four. I've got most of the paper written. I feel lucky to have moved in with some roomies you'd like—dean's list, et cetera—when one of their renters moved out. We're supposed to pay next month's rent Monday. I've already given them my share of the rent, but I need to give them $200 for my part of the deposit they already paid, and the Last Corral won't pay me again until Friday. I can pay you back next weekend. Can I talk to you more about it Monday morning when we take both our cars to Coffee Creek? Love you."

So Johnny might have come by Monday afternoon, after he turned in his paper, due at two-thirty? Killed his grandfather? Alice refused to believe it.

"He could've turned in the paper, driven to the judge's place by say three, had a fight with the judge, and left," Files said. "Then he could've returned at four-thirty to look innocent."

"You don't believe that."

Files lifted his eyes, gave her a long look. "We'll see. But wait, there's more."

He shuffled the papers on his desk and pulled out another sheet. "You know the judge's son? Eric Charles Mahan, is that right?"

Alice shook her head no. "I've never met him. He lives somewhere in the Bay Area."

"You have any discussion with him about his dad's bird project? The gift to the university?"

"No," Alice said.

"Did the judge tell you what his son thought about it?"

"No." Alice was irritated. "If the judge wanted me to know what his son thought, much less wanted me to do something about it, he'd have told me. He knew his own mind as well as anyone I've ever met. He certainly never suggested any concern about whatever his son's opinion was on what he had in mind to do." So what was going on? She asked, "You did call Eric Mahan yesterday to let him know about his dad's death?"

"Yes, from the judge's place. Guess where he was?"

She frowned. Trick question. "No idea."

Files gave a lopsided smile. "Right here. Flew into Austin on the red-eye Sunday night for meetings on Monday. But he'd already left this message late on Sunday." Files lifted the sheet of paper, read aloud: "'Dad, I'm really bummed about this draft agreement you sent me. Nice idea, but nearly $750,000 for the birds? Here I am, trying to get a second round of venture funds for the start-up, and I could sure use a cash infusion of a million. That would really help my credibility with the VC guys. Early inheritance, or even a loan, if that makes you feel better. But I need some cash right away. I've got meetings all Monday; let's talk later. Honestly, Dad, surely you care more about me than this—this birdbrained idea of yours!'"

Alice was appalled by Eric Mahan's reaction. Calling his dad's endowment "bird-brained"? How dared he?

"Did Eric Mahan call his dad again after he got to Austin?" Alice asked.

"There's no record of a later call on the judge's phone. When I called to tell him about the judge's death, Eric told me he'd been planning to call his father on Monday night, after his meetings."

Alice remembered the judge, just twenty-four hours ago, sitting in the sun at her tea table, quietly reviewing the final document. Despite Eric Mahan's bitter message, the judge had gone right ahead with the university gift. In all their discussions, he'd never mentioned to Alice any issue raised by any family member.

"Odd, isn't it?" Files commented, restacking the papers on his desk. "Both son and grandson hitting up the old man for money, with both in the vicinity. Do you have the judge's will? Are his son and grandson heirs?"

"Under the will, yes, they are. They're on the contacts list I gave your deputy."

"Which I've got."

"There's another heir—the judge's younger sister, Lesley Mahan. She's a retired pastor, apparently in poor health, living in a retirement home in New Mexico." She thought back to the will. "The judge also left several charitable bequests. He also added a codicil to his will recently, using the same Fredericksburg lawyer. I'll forward you copies."

"Who's the executor?" Files asked.

Alice grinned to herself but kept a poker face. Was Files finally beginning to learn his way around wills and trusts? She took some credit for that. "David Frohbel, a Fredericksburg lawyer."

He lifted an eyebrow. "Not a family member, then."

"Nope."

"That means he didn't trust the likely candidate? Wouldn't that be his son?"

Alice shrugged. "Acting as an executor in Texas is at least a minor inconvenience, for someone in California." She paused, thinking about the sanctity of attorney-client confidences. But this was a murder investigation. Didn't Files need to know about the county history, and maybe the archeology project? "The judge did indicate he thought it would be helpful for his bank to manage the gift to the university. The codicil also provides additional funds for two projects which the executor must see are completed: assuring that the judge's county history is published, and that an archeology project on the judge's land is not disturbed and is properly completed under his contract with the archeologists. The judge hired me for both those tasks. I assume I'll be reporting to the executor."

"Contract? What archeology project?"

"Looking for evidence of 'human history' in a gulch, a wet-weather stream, on his property."

She realized Files had held back several pieces of the puzzle. "So where was Eric Mahan on Monday?" she asked.

"In meetings at some high-rise office in Westlake, he says. We're checking his alibi. Apparently he's in the last throes of forming a new tech company. When I got hold of him yesterday afternoon, he'd been planning to fly back to the Bay Area this morning. I told him he'd have to come by here today instead, for an interview."

Something didn't add up. If Johnny knew his dad was coming to Austin, mightn't he have asked his dad, instead of his granddad, for help with the rent deposit? Mightn't he at least have told the judge that his dad—the judge's son—was coming to the Austin area?

Maybe Eric Mahan hadn't bothered to tell either son or his dad he was coming to Austin. "Did you ask Eric Mahan if Johnny knew his dad was flying in?"

"Mm-hmm. He says he hadn't called his son. 'Yet,' he said."

Alice was sure Johnny wanted the judge's approval as much as she did, as much as every lawyer in his courtroom did. She couldn't imagine Johnny pulling the trigger on his granddad.

Missing pieces. "Did you confirm what Johnny said? His Monday schedule, with the due date for his paper, and when he actually turned it in?" she asked.

"Working on it." Files straightened his papers, leaned back, and looked at her, raising both eyebrows—his usual signal that a meeting was over. His message light was flashing.

"No signs anyone had been in the judge's house?" Alice asked. "Messed with his desk, or his computer?" She was wondering about the county history.

"Crime scene team hasn't mentioned that."

"Silla said some guy he sentenced to prison got out recently?"

"Yeah, Bo Dupree. We've got people looking for him." Files looked again at the blinking phone.

Alice knew what that meant. Time to go. She stood up.

"Thanks, Alice. I'll walk you out. Let me know if you think of anything I should know."

In the entry hall a civilian stood in front of the duty sergeant's desk. As Alice pushed open the double doors and started outside, she heard the man say, "Eric Mahan, here to see Detective Files."

Well. Files had not exactly tried to introduce her to her client's son, had he?

Puzzled, and slightly miffed—she'd have liked to take Eric Mahan's measure—Alice walked back to her office, shivering in the unexpected chilly breeze. "You've just got time to get to the library board meeting," Silla said.

Alice grabbed her brown bag lunch from the office kitchen and headed for her car. Part of a small-town lawyer's life—serve on local boards, show up for Rotary.

Two hours later when she walked back into the office, Silla, standing by her work table, handed her a stack of clipped papers. "Here are your client billing summaries. Let me know any changes, and I'll get the bills out this afternoon."

Alice's cell phone interrupted. David Frohbel.

"Alice. Your message says you represented Judge Mahan on his gift to the university."

"Right. He told me you'd handled his will and the codicil. Also, he asked me to oversee publication of his county history and monitor the archeology project."

"Also right," said Frohbel. "Just keep me up to speed. Something else I think you should know. He added a twist to his will. In particular, the inurnment provisions."

"Inurnment provisions?" Alice asked. She hadn't gotten to that in the will Frohbel had sent. She still had some trouble getting her tongue around "inurnment"—meaning the placement of a decedent's ashes in a columbarium niche.

"Yep. The judge owns a niche at the Coffee Creek Presbyterian Church's columbarium. You probably know his wife, Muriel, died several years ago. He's already placed her ashes there. He wanted his ashes there too."

"I see."

"His body's at Travis County Medical Examiner's office, right?" Frohbel asked.

"Right. No word yet on when it will be released."

"Well, let me know when that happens. His letter to me as executor asks that the executor request two beneficiaries—his son and grandson—to be present, if possible, for the inurnment. His instruction letter to me says there's a message for each in the niche—not sure when he managed that. I'm to inform them about this before the inurnment, before his ashes join Muriel's and the church seals the columbarium for eternity. Or till Gabriel blows his horn, whichever."

Alice frowned. "Why?"

"Hey, it's what he wanted." He sighed. "I'm going to miss that old man so much."

"David, wait," she said, before he could hang up. "Do the beneficiaries have any notion about the—the messages?"

"No. He told me they were to learn of them just before the inurnment. I'm assuming that was so they can decide to show up for the actual ceremony." A moment's pause. "He didn't explain why."

"You're kidding."

"No."

Alice's imagination raced. Did the judge want his ashes mixed with Muriel's? Did he want special words spoken? Had he left additional instructions? Or information, like a crypto password? Had he placed something of value in the niche, maybe a treasure he feared could be stolen from his home? What might he have placed in the niche that he didn't want disturbed—or known—until after his death?

She thought for a moment. "He doesn't want anyone else to have access to the niche until his own inurnment? Is that the deal?"

Frohbel paused. "Right. I'll keep you posted."

"Same," said Alice.

He hung up.

Alice knew that a common procedure was to seal the niche at least semi-permanently—maybe when the stone facing was screwed on—

after both husband and wife's ashes were placed inside. Since he left instructions that Frohbel was not to reveal the will's provision until just before the inurnment, perhaps the judge wanted to be sure that his beneficiaries, and perhaps no one else, would discover something, or see something, when the niche was opened prior to the placement of his ashes.

What was on his mind? Alice shook her head, perplexed. In addition to micromanaging his beneficiaries' emotions, or obligations, what was he after?

But the niche was Frohbel's problem, not hers. She had her own duties to Judge Mahan...monitor the archeology dig, publish his history. She'd stick to her knitting. No problem.

First, the dig. Files would need to authorize access to the site—a crime scene—for Bender's team. She called Files.

"Let me confirm that the crime scene team's done," he said.

An hour later he called back. "Your archeologists can access the gulch, or ravine, whatever you call it."

A nagging worry rose to the surface. "I'm also worried about the house standing empty."

"We're through there too."

She thanked him. Next, thinking of the judge's empty house, she called her friend Miranda, manager at Madrone Bank. The judge's bank would likely agree that the house needed protection for some period. She thought of Charley's brown eyes and admirable ears. Charley also needed protection. She left a message, told Miranda to consult with Frohbel on any expenses.

Then she emailed Bender: the archeologists could begin work.

Silla cruised back into the office with a stack of billing letters. "Sign these, Alice. But hurry!"

"Why?"

Eyes wide, Silla picked up Alice's copy of the judge's manuscript and waved it at Alice. "Because you've got to read Chapter 13!" she ordered. "I'm not sure, but we might've landed in the middle of—lord knows what!"

C h a p t e r   S e v e n

An Incident In 1847

Alice sat at the antique tea table by the window. Outside, the sun—setting early, in January—turned the trunk of the pecan tree a glowing orange, while wind shook the last yellow leaves off the branches. Inside, she'd turned on the floor lamp by the tea table. Light fell on the pages of the judge's history, stacked before her. She turned to Chapter 13: "Last Breakfast." Just three pages of typescript.

A short time later she was still sitting, staring queasily at the third page. Chapter 13 described an incident in 1847, after Texas joined the Union. The text noted that in 1847 the highly accurate six-shot Walker Colt revolver became available. Peace discussions were ongoing between the Comanches and the settlers pouring into the Hill Country north of San Antonio, into New Braunfels, San Marcos, Coffee Creek, and as far west as Fredericksburg. Buffalo Hump and his army of braves had left Texas to raid northern Mexico, while a remnant of the tribe—women, children, and elderly, many afoot—slowly made their way back north toward the Oklahoma Territory. The chapter went on as follows, with a series of footnotes at the end plus additional notes in brackets:

On a Saturday night in September 1847, a newcomer named Jasper Riley staked his horse for the night down in a gulch with an intermittent wet-weather stream, south of the sparse new settlement called Coffee Creek. Riley was trespassing on property owned by German immigrants Fritz and Frieda Fischer. Frieda Fischer kept a small dairy herd on their property; Fritz Fischer, a watchmaker, was preparing to open a shop in nearby Coffee Creek. Riley's adjacent fifteen acres, which he'd won in a poker game from Coffee Creek shop owner Willie Craig, didn't reach as far as the gulch, but ended at the rock wall built by the Fischers at the boundary of their property. Riley had once again destroyed part of the Fischers' wall to stake his horse by the rivulet in their gulch. The next morning, Riley apparently spotted smoke rising above the gulch and ran to the edge. Below were an old man with gray braids and a young woman with two small children—Comanches, likely heading back to the Oklahoma Territory but too slow to keep up with the rest of their party. They'd killed Riley's horse and were cooking pieces of it over a small fire.

Alarmed by the smoke, Fritz Fischer came running with a shovel, along with Frieda, carrying a hoe. Rushing to the edge of the gulch, the Fischers saw Riley aim his revolver and shoot the old man, then the young woman who was trying to protect the children. Fischer yelled, "They're starving! You staked your damned horse on our property! You can't murder children on our land!"

Riley lifted his revolver and shot both children.

"Murderer! You'll go straight to hell!" yelled Frieda.

Riley turned and shot Fischer, then his wife. Riley apparently didn't notice the sole witness—the Fischers' eight-year-old son, Emil, who'd followed his parents, contrary to their instructions, and was hiding in cedar scrub near the gulch.

Emil fled three miles, staying low in the scrub despite cuts from sharp branches, until he reached the farm of his aunt and uncle, Jutta and Horst Meyer. Horst Meyer raised an armed posse. Hours later, by the time the posse reached the scene, an epic rainstorm was pelting Coffee County. The posse crossed the gulch looking for Riley and found the cabin on his fifteen acres was empty. Along with his pack pony, he'd vanished. They saw no sign of the Fischers' bodies. The posse members, including Horst Meyer, covered the bodies of the dead Comanches and the remnants of the horse with rocks and dirt from the sides of the gulch, then abandoned the chase because of the storm. They reported the Fischer cabin had been ransacked, and, per Horst Meyer, robbed of some valuable items. The thief didn't take the Fischers' broken-down old plow horse.

Emil Fischer went to live with the Meyer family. At the time, his Aunt Jutta wrote down in her journal what Emil and her husband Horst told her they had witnessed, pages of which are preserved in the records of the Coffee Creek Lutheran Church. With no bodies to bury, and Riley gone, no trial could take place. Emil apparently could not speak of his parents' deaths for a number of years. Then the Lutheran pastor in Coffee Creek persuaded him to tell again what he remembered and recorded what he said [see above re: records of Coffee Creek Lutheran Church].

FOOTNOTE 1: County court records show Fritz Fischer filed a handwritten complaint against Jasper Riley in August 1847 for repeated trespass and destruction of the Fischers' rock walls and fencing. No further record.

FOOTNOTE 2: In late summer 1847 Comanche chief Buffalo Hump and his warriors were raiding in Mexico. [cite]

FOOTNOTE 3: Riley apparently had the new six-shot Walker Colt issued in 1847 to Texas Rangers. [cite]

FOOTNOTE 4: Records of initial appointments of Rangers in the 1840's during the war with Mexico include a J. Jasper Riley, but he was dismissed in 1847 for fatally assaulting a fellow Ranger. [cite]

FOOTNOTE 5: In 1860 Jasper Riley apparently told a Bastrop newspaper he acquired wealth from the gold rush and in St. Louis, then returned to Texas. [N.B. Cite Bastrop newspaper] [N.B. To date have located no evidence of Riley in California.] In 1860 J. Jasper Riley married "Edith." [Cite Caldwell County registry; no maiden name provided] [N.B. Will check ancestry records for maiden name/descendants.]

FOOTNOTE 6: Confederate records from early months of the Civil War list "J. Jasper Riley" as briefly part of a militia group assigned to Texas coast but show he left his unit by the end of 1862. [N.B. Riley was not reported present for Galveston or San Jacinto battles. Cite records.]

FOOTNOTE 7: J. J. Riley died in 1910. [Cite death records] [N.B. Need photos of headstone?]

Alice stared into space. How like Judge Mahan to include these footnotes! Dry facts, supported by citation, and his N.B. or "nota bene" notes to self, suggesting further inquiry—indeed, *tempting* further inquiry. Inquiry that could be pursued by any motivated reader.

Silla stuck her head in the office door, coat in hand. She raised her eyebrows at Alice's stricken face.

"Just finished Chapter 13, about Jasper Riley," Alice said.

"Mm-hmm."

"That footnote telling who married whom."

"Interesting, no? Listen, Miranda called you. She can't get security out to the judge's tonight, so she's agreed I can run by and get a key from her to be sure that Charley gets watered and fed tonight. Then I might do a little looking on the ancestry database for Jasper Riley," Silla said.

"Good. One more thing you might look at," Alice said. "When and how did the judge acquire his property? What's its history?" She'd noted the judge didn't include a footnote indicating precisely *where* in the draw the last breakfast incident took place. Did he know, or not?

"I'll check," said Silla, on her way out the front door.

Chapter Eight

He Wanted Facts

On Wednesday morning Silla shot into Alice's office even faster than usual, waving a printout.

"Here's the response to your mediation statement. Whoo-ee! The other side's getting testy! But I don't see anything new in the response to you." She dropped a copy on Alice's desk. "Mediation's still set for Friday. However, on another front—"

"Yes?"

"My new best friend, Alan Joske, is trying to poke holes in Johnny's alibi for the judge's murder."

"Is this the latest from the Camellia Diner?" Alice frowned, sure Johnny would never have killed his granddad. "Ridiculous. But what's wrong with Johnny's alibi? What's the problem?"

"First, Johnny claims that after he and the judge left our office, he picked up his car and went straight to the library in San Marcos to work on his econ paper."

"What's wrong with that?"

"Joske's still trying to find a witness who saw him working on the third floor in a carrel. It would help if the librarians at least cased the joint, at least walked the floors occasionally!" Silla flounced her red ponytail. "When I was toiling away in a carrel, I'm sure somebody heard me cussing my computer and slamming my books shut. But that's not all. Johnny also claims he went to the prof's office before the deadline and dropped his paper through the slot in the door, but no one's been able to reach the prof yet. The prof had told the class the papers had to be submitted by the deadline— at two-thirty sharp. He was going to pick them all up then. After that, abandon all hope, ye econ students. And Johnny says after that he bought gas before he drove to the judge's. But he can't find the receipt."

"Johnny had a copy of his paper with him when he got to the judge's," Alice said. "Have you seen it yet?"

Silla nodded. "Yep. I've seen it and I've read it. I'd asked him to email it to me. Not bad work for a college kid."

"Does his computer show when he polished off the final version?"

"I told him to look. Told him how to look."

"Shouldn't that be enough alibi for Alan Joske? What time Johnny finished the paper, when he turned it in, when he showed up at the judge's house?"

"Joske's got that stubborn Czech thing going," Silla said. "I don't think he much likes Johnny. Maybe he's jealous. Johnny's got some… some appeal." She waggled her eyebrows, smirking. "Brings out my protective instincts." She flounced out.

Alice's cell phone rang—Bender's number on the screen. "Bender! How are you?"

"Alice. Long time."

"Too long." She'd met Bender a few years earlier when he'd reported astonishing cave art on the ranch of one of her first serious clients in Coffee Creek. He'd won his archeology spurs by his exquisite management and accurate documentation of historic excavations—precisely why the judge had chosen him.

"I'm still reeling from what happened to Judge Mahan," Bender said. "Don't suppose you know who killed him?"

"Not yet."

"Okay, I'll cut to the chase. The team's ready to start. We're already out there, getting ready to start setting up. Come visit." He paused, then: "You can bring that antique trowel, but you can't use it." He hung up.

Bender meant Alice's dad's ancient trowel, with its delicate sharp point, lying quietly, along with her flare gun, in a bag in Alice's car, under the front seat. Her father had used it on a dig in Jordan. On the rare occasions when she opened that bag she realized she was hoping to feel vibrations, a message, from him. So far the trowel had been silent. Maybe this time…

She looked at her calendar. Tomorrow night she'd be at a groundwater conservation district meeting where her client's well permit was on the agenda. But she was ready for that; she saw no reason to spend today in the office. She remembered, when she asked about his archeology project, how the judge had deftly sidestepped, saying Hill Country water was "a magnet for humans." Was he trying to avoid articulating a more specific intent? Alice wanted to see the dig site for herself. Maybe she *would* take along the trowel, though Bender would never actually let an amateur mess around in one of his digs.

She stopped at Silla's desk. "Let me have the judge's key—I'll handle the pet food tonight."

As Alice climbed into her green Discovery, her cell rang again—Miranda, at Madrone Bank. Like Alice, she was concerned about the judge's empty house. "I thought perhaps we could ask Johnny to stay there," Alice said, reluctantly. "But on mature reflection... maybe not?"

"Maybe not, so long as he's a possible suspect," Miranda answered. "I'm still trying to set up 24-hour security, per Frohbel. Probably can't get anyone in a uniform out there until tomorrow, but now Silla has a key..."

"I'm happy to be sure Charley gets fed," Alice said. "I don't want to put that burden on the archeologists."

"Agreed."

The executor was charged with protecting the judge's estate. Alice was charged with meeting her contractual obligations to the judge—getting his history published and overseeing completion of the archeology project. At the same time, she somehow felt obligated to protect—what? The judge's privacy? His legacy as a person? His county history research? His reputation? His grandson? All of the above?

*****

As she turned off the narrow blacktop road onto the judge's long gravel driveway, Alice felt she'd misjudged distances on her earlier visit, misjudged the landscape. She remembered driving downhill, passing the live oaks on her right, then curving back uphill toward the judge's house, admiring the hilly grove atop the ridge on the west. But she'd ignored the gulch that cut through the land on her left as she drove into the judge's place. The scattered remnants of an old unmortared limestone wall, now mostly collapsed, were still visible. Now she realized how thoroughly the shrubs and tall grass shielded the drop-off from view.

Bender's ancient white truck with its built-in camper sat downhill well off the driveway, near the gulch, by a small green pup tent. Alice parked and climbed out of her car, then shivered and grabbed her wool blazer. The sun, low in the west, was deceptively bright, but the wind was chilly. Two young men, archeology grad students, she assumed, were wrestling against the wind, trying to set up a large square tent. And, yes, a porta-potty had been delivered; it sat, barely disguised, behind a shower curtain hanging from a lone tree. She felt a wave of relief, concluding these luxe accommodations meant the team planned to spend their nights onsite. Maybe that would scare away unauthorized visitors.

Bender waved from near the tents. "Alice! Come see our setup!"

Bender looked the same—light brown hair a bit thinner, but still that determined face, the sharp blue eyes behind wire-rims. He gave her a side hug as she reached the edge of the gulch. "Good to be working with you again," he said.

She hugged him back. "Same. Hey, what's ABFA?"

He stared blankly, then said, "Oh. American Board of Forensic Archeology."

"Ah," she said. "Listen, your contract with the judge is a bit on the vague side. 'Establish facts and history of the ravine' including 'evidence of human history.' What are you looking for?"

"'Evidence of human history.' Whatever that means." But his eyes didn't leave hers.

"Come on. Did he mention anything specific that might have happened here on his property? In this ravine?"

Bender sighed. "He'd told me the bare bones—excuse the pun—of that 'last breakfast' story. I know the name of the original German settlers—the Fischers. But the judge didn't want to prejudice me. He wanted facts. He wanted a full and neutral exploration of the part of the small ravine, or gulch, that runs across this end of his property." He pointed toward the live oak grove on the western slope of the property. "I told him that it wouldn't hurt for us to understand some history. Sounds like maybe the old Fischer cabin sat downhill from that grove, close enough to the creek to fetch water. Makes sense—the cabin would catch the breeze, stay cool, give the Fischers a good view of their property. A good field of fire, know what I mean?"

Yes, Alice thought, but Fritz Fischer didn't get to use a field of fire, did he? Unarmed, she remembered. Just the man with a shovel and his wife with a hoe, facing Riley.

"So the Fischers came running across the field toward the gulch when they saw smoke, if we believe the story," Alice said.

"Right."

Alice turned and stared at the rocky scrub across the gulch. Somewhere over there along their property line, the Fischers had stacked rocks to make another wall—the one Riley kept destroying. Riley's fifteen acres lay beyond that wall.

From where she stood, the gulch looked about fifty or so feet wide. Downstream to her right, it made an S-curve on its way to meet Blue Creek. Occasional flash floods had scooped out the underside of the steep limestone hillsides that flanked the gulch. Right now the scanty stream below looked small, slow, unassuming. But Alice would bet that when it flooded, it carried big payloads of silt and gravel. This winter had been dry; the stream was just a small rivulet, barely moving.

"I didn't realize this drop-off was here, much less how deep it is," Alice said. "You can't tell, from the driveway."

"Stream profile's likely changed after, what, over 180 years," Becker commented.

"So tell me what you plan to do for the judge."

"The bit of history the judge shared may or may not be an accurate guide. So today we're documenting the current state of the gulch for ourselves, zeroing in on potential areas of interest. We'll document everything before we lift a trowel. As a starting point, I'll assume that, as rumor reports, the posse did cover the horse remains and the Comanche bodies with rocks. Again, I'm assuming that was close to where the Fischer boy said he saw smoke. We'll search for any evidence of past fires, like charred rock. But Hill Country floods could have radically disarranged the streambed."

"What about the Fischers' bodies?"

"If they're even here? Who knows? That's just guesswork. Alice, that whole story may be nothing but hearsay, or conflated stories. Remember, our assignment from the judge was to document evidence of human history in the streambed in the gulch that runs through his property." He paused. "We'll follow all required procedures, of course."

Alice stared downstream. Past the archeologists' tents, the walls of the gulch were covered by tangled, impenetrable cedars, clinging with tough roots to the steep walls, punctuated by white limestone outcrops.

The rocky bottom was composed of a mix of caliche dirt and broken limestone. She turned to stare upstream. One small blue-green pool glinted in the winter sun, with another farther upstream.

"The deer love this place," Bender said. "They bed down under the cedars close to the water."

Alice's imagination flared. "If I had shot two people..." she began.

"With your flare gun?" Becker, amused.

"Hey, a flare gun can be quite effective!"

"So I hear."

"Anyway, if I'd shot two people," she retorted, "and they'd been standing at the edge of this draw, and I wanted to get out of Dodge in a hurry, before anyone saw me, I'd take the easy route. I'd push their bodies off the side and hide them behind or under some big rocks."

Becker nodded. "Could be. You wouldn't leave the bodies for the vultures—a posse would take note of vultures. Maybe use that shovel the Fischer boy supposedly remembered his daddy carrying. Use it like a prybar, lever in some big rocks to hide the bodies. But again, that's pure guesswork."

She squinted up at him. "Bender, did the judge give you any other specifics about what he was after?"

"I can guess what he wanted. As usual, as always, the judge wanted facts. Bones are facts. I mean, he did say 'Look for artifacts of human history.'"

Alice smiled to herself. Yep, that was the judge.

The grad students had finally wrestled the larger tent into submission. "That's our dig tent, where we keep paperwork and tools," Bender said. He yelled to the grad students, "Come meet Alice. Our boss."

The two students wandered over and shook hands. Gordon was tall, with bleached blond hair and a quirky grin. Wayland was shorter and built like a wrestler, with tangled brown hair and intense brown eyes. Bender said, "We're going to start our initial layout."

"So, I can't use my dad's trowel yet."

He laughed. "Dream on."

Alice left the dig and stopped at the house to put out feed and water for Charley. The house felt too quiet; the dog's big brown eyes seemed anxious. She spent some time stroking his lovely ears before she left.

As she climbed into the car, she thought of the trowel under her seat and realized how jealous she felt of the students. For them, the site was an empty theater, with the curtain about to go up, and a play about to begin. Maybe.

On the way home she stopped at the feed store and got two bales of coastal hay for the donkeys. On further thought, she bought a padlock for the judge's fire gate.

Chapter Nine

We Need Help

Alice woke Thursday morning at six to the sound of light rain, just pattering to a stop, along with a favorite smell—cedar smoke borne on winter air. Someone, somewhere, was burning brush, now that the county had lifted the burn ban.

Her cell rang. Who, at this hour?

Bender. "Come out. We need help." He hung up.

Alice struggled into her jeans. No time for coffee. She roared down the judge's drive again, using the gate code. Bender waved her over toward his camper, face grim. Wayland, brown hair tousled, stood next to him.

"We had visitors last night. Uninvited." He cocked his head at Wayland. Alice had already noted Wayland's multihued black eye and fat lip.

"Wayland heard something at midnight, found a guy with a flashlight pawing through our dig tent. Where we keep maps and plans."

Wayland nodded—a one-sided grin. "You should see the other guy! On the skinny side. I bit his ear pretty good."

"How'd he get in?" Alice demanded.

"Through the fire gate, I guess," Wayland answered. "Gordon and I chased him back to the gate, and he squeezed through it. Like I said, skinny. Someone was waiting for him on the other side, in a pickup. Couldn't see the color—looked dark."

"Plates?"

"It was dark, Alice."

"Did he take anything?"

"Naw," Wayland said. "I sneaked up to the tent and saw him trying to take pictures with his phone."

Bender intervened. "We've had our snoops before—you know, rival diggers. Wayland wanted to see who it was, first."

Wayland nodded in agreement, still with his one-sided smile. "We like to see who's dogging us. Who's trying to snitch our data, trying to outflank us."

Bender wasn't smiling. "Get us some guards, Alice. We can't have people messing with the dig. Or with us. This work's too important. Some bigfoot comes stomping in, moving rocks, sliding down the wall of the ravine—we lose control of our site, of the accuracy of our description of the pre- and post-dig conditions."

"Guards..." Alice said. "I think they're on order." She reached for her cellphone, moved away from Bender, called Miranda, and reported.

"I've already hired a company, supposed to start by five this afternoon," Miranda said. "I made sure they understand they need to protect both the house and the archeology project the judge contracted for."

Alice reported what Miranda had said. "You'll have security guards by five. They'll have the gate code." Then, "Oh. Here." She dug the padlock and one of the two keys out of her pocket. She kept one for her file. "Lock that fire gate."

"Good," Bender responded. "Now, want to see our plans?"

'Yes."

He hauled an extension ladder to the ravine, delicately lowered it over. "Don't want to disturb the walls."

Alice climbed down after him. They walked carefully upstream to an area past the first small pool and then fifty feet farther, to an area crisscrossed by wooden stakes and string. A second pool, barely a yard across, lay farther upstream.

"We'll map the whole gulch, the extent of the judge's property. But our best guess—the original bones would've been near here, between the pools. So right now I'm planning to start here."

Down on the floor of the gulch, with clouds above and no view of the landscape, she was stunned by the quiet. Alice no longer heard the sound of cars on the road, of air conditioners or televisions, of radios, or sirens...just heavy quiet. A disquieting quiet. She felt in suspense, felt as if she were hiding, waiting to be discovered, waiting for a pistol shot from above. Like the long-ago breakfast party.

Behind her, Bender took her shoulders in his hands and turned her to face downstream.

"See on the right, Alice? Where the water's carved the S-curve in the walls of the gulch?"

She nodded.

"See the boulder at the end of that curve?"

A massive limestone boulder blocked the right side of the stream-bed.

"Yep."

"It attracts me mightily," Bender muttered. "I'm thinking we may luck out, somewhere around that boulder."

He glanced back at the waiting grad students, watching from the top of the gulch. "Time to get these people working. I'll let you know our progress."

"You think your intruders might come back?"

"That guy didn't get much before Wayland grabbed him. But he'd found our sketches. Wayland thinks he got a picture of only the first page, though." After a moment he said, "Before the security people get here, let me know names and contact info for the company."

Good idea, Alice thought. "Trust, but verify. Okay. Keep me posted."

She climbed back up the ladder and walked to her car. Before leaving she called Miranda and gave her Bender's cell phone number. "He's afraid his visitors might be back and wants to be sure the security folks are the real deal."

"Yikes," Miranda said. "Never thought of that. I'm on it. I'll let him know. And update Frohbel."

After she hung up, Alice realized that—because Bender had said, "We've had our snoops before," she hadn't asked the obvious question: "Who knew you'd be out here?"

She called Bender back, left a message. He must be down in the gulch, trowel in hand. "Who knew your team was onsite?"

*****

Silla looked up from her worktable as Alice, showered and wearing pants and a blazer, entered the office. "Kinsear called, he's out picking up some cows, he'll call back later. Your groundwater client called, said he'd see you at the meeting tonight. Library board chair wants you to call," she reported. Then, lifting her chin—"Ta da! I've finished the judge's manuscript!"

"Any more shockers? Besides the last breakfast?" Alice inquired.

Silla blew out her lips. "Whoo-ee. Plenty to read on farming, growth of Coffee Creek, the Civil War. An interesting chapter on German immigrants resisting the Confederate draft. Then Reconstruction. Then a chapter on farmers and the railroads and on cattle drives from Coffee County to Kansas. Then World War I, the wheat bust, the Depression, World War II, et cetera. Economics. Politics. Not too wordy—he's good at explaining this stuff," Silla concluded. "But for some reason he hasn't filled in some of the footnotes. He's left a bunch of notes to self in the brackets. Okay, Alice, you've got to get ready for that mediation tomorrow morning. After the mediation, you can read Chapters 20 and 21. Chapter 21's sad but...cinematic, I'd call it. Chapter 20 is eye-opening and hilarious. Well, hilarious in some ways..."

Alice had wondered about those incomplete footnotes. What had the judge left out? What had he planned to add? The judge's manuscript sat on a desk corner, tempting her. But Silla appeared, a file under each arm. "Here's the groundwater permit file," she said. "I've added the posted agenda for the meeting tonight. Remember, it starts at six. And here's the mediation file for tomorrow morning." She laid both on Alice's desk.

Alice left for the groundwater meeting. Her client's permit was granted as requested, with no drama. Then she drove home in the dark and sat by the fire, reviewing the mediation file. In contrast, plenty of drama here: the question was how to turn it to her client's advantage tomorrow.

Chapter Ten

I Was Her Favorite!

By seven-thirty on Friday morning, Silla had brewed coffee and arranged the conference table for the mediation. Alice arrived with a large tray of breakfast tacos from Flores with a variety of fillings—*migas*, potato-egg-bacon, and *al pastor* with grilled pork and mango salsa. She left them in the kitchen with Silla and hurried back to her computer.

The mediation involved the will of Minnie Clarke Mason, a ninety-seven-year-old woman who'd left a large estate including Clarke Ranch outside Coffee Creek. Alice represented Minnie's executor, Gavin Mason, a young Austin lawyer, who was one of Minnie's five grandsons. The irate claimant—Minnie's seventy-year-old niece, Lola—claimed her aunt had promised her an antique diamond brooch and matching earrings, which had been in the family for generations. Minnie's will, however, bequeathed the jewels to Sara, Minnie's only granddaughter—a cousin of Gavin Mason. Lola had hired a lawyer, Wilfred Reed, from Blanco. He'd filed a complaint alleging Sara exerted undue influence over Minnie.

After seeing Lola's skimpy discovery responses, Alice proposed early mediation, thinking the case should never go to trial. She remembered Minnie as an extremely capable woman. She hoped the combination of Claude Harris, an experienced mediator, plus the fragrant presence of breakfast tacos and the strategies she had in mind would move the opponents to "yes" by lunchtime.

She reviewed her notes one more time.

"Come right in. And here's Claude, right behind you." That was Silla at the front door, greeting Alice's client—Gavin, the beleaguered executor of his grandmother's will—and the mediator, following him up the sidewalk.

"Alice! Here's Gavin!" Her client marched into her office, anxiety on his face. Alice patted his shoulder and took him to the tea table by the window for last-minute thoughts.

"Hi, Alice!" called Claude Harris, in the front hall. "I'm heading for your conference room."

Once again, Silla at the front door: "Good morning, folks. Straight back to the conference room. Breakfast tacos on the credenza."

Alice heard feet shuffling past—Lola and her lawyer.

"Let's get this show on the road," Alice said to Gavin, gathering up her notes.

Claude Harris delivered the usual mediation preliminaries, then asked Wilfred Reed, Lola's lawyer, to explain why Lola was entitled to jewels based on her aunt's promises—which Reed admitted were not in writing and were not overheard by other witnesses. Indeed, Lola could not name a single witness who'd been present when her aunt supposedly promised Lola the diamonds. Lola now claimed that during Minnie's last illness, Sara, Minnie's only granddaughter, must have exerted undue influence on Minnie before Minnie made her will.

Then it was Alice's turn: Minnie had met with her lawyer to execute her will a year before her death, when she was still healthy, still entertaining guests, still attending church, still running her ranch. In her will she'd made her wishes precise and clear. In choosing her grandson Gavin as her executor, she'd picked a competent lawyer sworn to obey the law. Indeed, she'd later added a codicil to provide funds to care for her horses after her death. She could've changed her disposition of the jewelry then, but she didn't. Lola had no claim to the jewels.

When Alice finished, Claude separated the parties and took ten minutes to work over each side, pointing out the risks each side faced if the case went to trial—first with Lola and her lawyer, in the conference room, then with Gavin and Alice, in Alice's office. Then he reconvened the parties in the conference room.

To her satisfaction Alice noticed a little salsa on the front of Lola's jacket and a faintly greasy look to her mouth. All the potato-egg-bacon breakfast tacos had disappeared. Good sign. You wanted the other side not to feel...hungry.

Claude gave the floor to Alice.

"Lola, I'd like to go over some of the questions I asked at your deposition. You said you admired your grandmother, right?"

Lola nodded.

"How many years did she run her own ranch?"

"Over sixty."

"Did she handle all the cattle sales until the end?"

"Yes, she did."

"I understand she was elected to the vestry at her church and also served on the board at Madrone Bank. In your view did people value her opinions and her judgment?"

"Well, yes."

"Did you consider her a good businesswoman?"

"Oh, yes." Lola furrowed her brow, not sure where Alice was going.

"Do you remember how many years she served on the vestry at Holy Spirit?"

"At least twenty. She was on the vestry until the year before she died."

Now Lola's lawyer was frowning. "This has nothing to do with whether Minnie promised those jewels to my client!"

Alice turned back to Lola. "But in your opinion people respected her decisions?"

"Yes, but..."

"Did you love the ranch?"

"Yes, of course. I went there all the time."

"To the best of your knowledge, was the ranch Minnie's to sell or keep?"

"Well, yes."

"I believe you told us that Minnie had three sons, five grandsons, and one granddaughter?"

"Yes."

"At your deposition we discussed that in her will Minnie designated particular gifts for each grandchild. Is it still your recollection that she left her first-edition books to one grandson; her Corvette to another; her horses to her third and fourth grandsons; her art collection to grandson Gavin; and her diamond brooch and earrings to her granddaughter, Sara?"

"Yes."

"We also discussed, did we not, that Minnie also had three nieces and two nephews?"

"Yes."

"Is it accurate to say that under the will Minnie left all her property, except her charitable gifts, to her own direct descendants, i.e., her children and grandchildren, and that she left none to her nieces or nephews?"

"I guess so."

"Can you tell us any reason you believe you alone should have been treated differently from Minnie's other nieces and nephews?"

"I was her favorite!"

"Meaning her favorite niece?"

"Yes!"

"Switching gears now. Is it your understanding that Minnie's grandfather bought the diamond jewelry for his wife, Flora, Minnie's grandmother, after going on a cattle drive up to Dodge City and selling his herd?"

"That's what Minnie said."

"And when Minnie's mother, Jennie, died young, did Minnie's grandmother leave the diamonds to Minnie?"

"Yes. I mean, Minnie had hold of them then." Lola shifted in her seat; her lawyer was frowning.

"So when Minnie left the diamonds to her granddaughter, Sara, wasn't she continuing the tradition her grandmother started when she gave them to Minnie, who now has left them to her own grand-daughter?"

Lola didn't answer.

"Is it possible that Minnie left the diamonds to Sara because she wanted them to stay in her direct line?"

Lola muttered, "I still think she meant for me to have those dia-monds."

"In your discovery responses, you've not provided us with any writ-ten promise from Minnie or identified a single person who recalls hear-ing her promise you those jewels, so why do you think Minnie meant you to have the diamonds?"

"It was our private discussion!"

"What precisely do you claim Minnie said?"

"Well, I know I told her how much I loved them. And she smiled and hugged me. That's how I know. I could tell she wanted me to have them!"

"But not from anything she said, correct?"

"Well..." Then Lola sat silent.

"Let's turn to your claim against Sara. Can you describe even one occasion when her granddaughter, Sara, allegedly pressured Minnie to leave the diamonds to her?"

"Sara could've been on the phone with her any time!"

"Do you know of any instance when that actually happened?"

Lola's face grew mulish, but she didn't answer. Lola's lawyer, Wilfred Reed, sat staring at his fingernails, his expression resigned.

"As Mr. Reed no doubt told you, it's your duty to provide all evidence of your claims. So far you've provided nothing. No witnesses. Nothing written, nothing recorded, nothing heard." Alice felt her temper rising. "Instead, you're slandering Minnie's granddaughter. With zero evidence."

For the first time, Lola looked taken aback. Her eyes flickered sideways to her lawyer and back. Her jaw slacked, slightly.

"Remember when I asked at your deposition how your family members feel about your lawsuit? You said they told you to drop it. Wouldn't Minnie agree with them?"

No response.

"Frankly, wouldn't Minnie be horrified by this lawsuit?"

No response. Claude intervened. "Time for a break. Lola, Wilfred, you stay here."

Claude had perfectly timed that break, Alice thought. Because she had an idea...

She and Gavin reached her office. "Gavin, let's talk."

*****

"You want *me* to do it?"

"Yep. Lots easier for her to say 'no' to me than to you."

Gavin nodded. "Here goes." He and Alice walked back down the hall to the conference room. Alice knocked on the door.

"Come on in." Claude waved them back to their seats. Across the conference room table, Lola looked both angry and anxious.

She blinked in surprise as Gavin, not Alice, led off.

"Lola, you may not know that Minnie didn't have a chance to give away many of her personal belongings before she died. But you remember her death was rather sudden."

Lola nodded. "I didn't even get a chance to say goodbye."

Without missing a beat Gavin continued. "Of course she'd already designated items for Sara, but she also left behind quite a significant amount of what I believe you'd call costume jewelry—not necessarily gold, or gems, but of good quality—you know what I mean. She'd given the boys all of her husband's jewelry, the cuff links, tie pins, tuxedo studs. But the women's costume jewelry remains, including those spectacular hat pins and earrings and her favorite holiday jewelry. You told us just now that you thought from her smile, and her hug, that you were Minnie's favorite niece. How would you feel about taking charge of all of that costume jewelry? It'll be an undertaking—there are several boxes full. You may want to choose some favorites for yourself, but if you'd like you could also pass along some of the items to Minnie's other nieces and nephews. You might have a better feel than I for who should get particular pieces."

Lola's face changed. Her eyes widened, her eyebrows lifted, her mouth opened slightly. She glanced at her lawyer. "Well, I...I guess I could do that." She sat up straighter. "Of course I know all those girls. I could probably decide who'd look best in which piece." Pause. "You'd—you'd what, just deliver all those boxes to me?"

Gavin nodded. "I would gladly delegate to you the job of taking care of all the costume jewelry. Remember, it's quite a job. I've counted up at least twenty hatpins, forty sets of earrings, seventeen bracelets, nineteen necklaces."

"Hatpins," Lola said. "What about the hats?"

Gavin glanced at Alice, then smiled at Lola. "I've got ten hatboxes. Indeed, one of them holds Minnie's Stetson. Do you mean you'd be willing to take care of the hats too?"

"What's a hatpin without a hat?" Lola asked.

"And if you agree to undertake this, Lola, we'll agree, the two of us, that this dispute is over? You'll provide this very needed help, you'll select some favorite pieces for yourself, I hope, and you'll drop the lawsuit?" Gavin pressed.

Again she glanced at her lawyer.

"It'll be a lot of work," Gavin added. "I do appreciate your taking this on for—for Minnie."

Lola nodded. "I agree. I'll do it."

Claude looked at Alice and at Lola's lawyer. "You two draft me up a mediation agreement right now, in Alice's office. I want it signed before anyone leaves."

Just as Alice and Wilfred Reed stood up, Silla opened the conference room door. "Hope you all don't mind, but in about five minutes Flores is bringing over some chicken enchiladas with verde sauce and sides. And beers for those who may wish."

"Excellent," Claude said. "Thank you. Not a bite for the lawyers, though, until they finalize the agreement and get it signed."

Walking back to her office Alice whispered to Silla, "Were you listening at the door?"

Silla tossed her ponytail. "Nope. Just my sense of timing. I've already emailed you our draft mediation agreement so you and Lola's lawyer what's-his-name can fix it up fast. But as soon as you're done and we get these folks out of here, I need to show you what I found out at the courthouse."

Chapter Eleven

Learned Some Good Stuff!

All parties signed the mediation agreement. Lola and her lawyer left, followed by Claude.

Gavin thanked Alice, thanked Silla, rolled his eyes, said "Thank you, Lord!" and sailed out the front door.

"That was a ridiculous lawsuit in the first place," Alice grumbled. "But all's well that ends well."

"Johnny Mahan called during the mediation," Silla said. "Sounded upset. Said please call when you get a chance."

Back at her desk, Alice called Johnny's cell.

"Oh, Alice, thanks."

"Can you talk?"

"Yes. Just finished class, on my way to work. The Last Corral, you know." His voice sounded flat, dispirited.

"So what's up?"

He snorted. "I can't even begin to tell you what it feels like, that that man could think I would shoot my grandfather."

"You mean Detective Files?"

"No, Alan Joske. The red-headed twerp. He kept asking about the $200 check I needed that Granddad gave me on Monday morning! And I still can't believe Granddad isn't there! Won't be there!"

Alice sighed, trying to think of comfort. "Joske's just doing his job. It's not pleasant sometimes." Silence from Johnny. "He doesn't understand how you loved your granddad. But Silla and I do. We loved him too."

"I know."

"So, Johnny, help me out on a couple of questions. First, did the judge ever mention any plan for an archeology project out at his place?"

"Archeology? No. I would have remembered, because it sounds interesting."

"One more question. Before he died the judge hired me to see that his county history gets published. Did he show it to you?"

"Oh, sure! At least the economic history chapters. Wanted them to be accurate, but not boring. The big droughts, the Depression, people trying to make a living growing peaches or raising angora goats for mohair. I haven't studied economies on such a small scale—you know, county-sized, especially as far back as a century-and-a-half ago, when the county was barely settled. So I read them, but there was nothing much I could add about accuracy. He was all over the facts already."

"All over the facts—how? How did he keep track of data for each chapter? On his computer?"

"He kept all his printouts, all his materials, in separate manila folders, numbered the same as his chapters. Said that was so he could go back and re-read and highlight the material."

"Where'd he keep those folders?"

"In the wooden file cabinets under his desk. Why?"

"His executor's David Frohbel, in Fredericksburg. The executor has to protect the decedent's estate. The judge's bank's now paying for a security guard out there at night, but I'm worried someone—someone who doesn't like the judge's county history—might try to grab the research materials."

Silence. "Seriously?"

"If someone didn't like a particular chapter, say. Anyway, Johnny, I'm sorry about the police. They're doing everything by the book, trying to find his killer. That means checking on all of us."

"I know, I know. Alice, thanks for listening. It's just—I miss him so much." And he was gone.

She'd meant to ask him about his father. Had they connected at all? And what about the empty footnotes?

But now, time to plunge into the judge's manuscript. Silla had called Chapter 20 "somewhat hilarious" and Chapter 21 "sad." Alice turned first to the "sad" chapter, even though it was dated later, in 1929, because, in the midst of tears and anger over the judge, she was hoping to wind up with a bit of hilarity from Chapter 20. She picked up the judge's manuscript.

*****

The judge wrote:

> In 1929, at the end of a prosperous decade, Rupert Baxter's Coffee County Farmer's Bank was thriving. After a plentiful wheat harvest, Coffee County farmers sold their crops to the Missouri-Pacific Railroad and began streaming into town the first week of Septem-

ber, anxious to deposit their cash. They lined up on Travis Street in front of Baxter's bank, a limestone building with stout front doors, high ceilings, and an imposing steel vault behind the counter. All week Rupert Baxter, sixty-five and rotund, greeted the farmers and waved them to the teller's window, where young Edgar Trivet waited to count their deposits. "Edgar's my new right hand," Baxter informed the depositors. "We're growing here in Coffee County!"

On Friday afternoon, Baxter stood alone at the teller's window. Edgar Trivet had not shown up that day; he'd sent a message—"intestinal issues." Just before closing time at four o'clock, as Baxter prepared to lock up, three armed robbers masked in black bandanas burst through the front door. They locked the door behind them and forced Baxter at gunpoint to empty the vault. Then they tied him to a chair, raced out the back door, and escaped in a gray 1929 Ford Model A.

Edgar Trivet had vanished. The robbers were never caught. At first Baxter refused to believe Trivet had betrayed him. Then the bank failed, leaving a bitter legacy for Baxter and his depositors. Within weeks 1929's "Black Tuesday" hit the New York Stock Exchange. The Depression had arrived.

Alice shuddered. No FDIC deposit insurance in those days. She read on:

An excerpt from the journal of a local pastor mentions that Baxter's daughter, Patience, an unmarried schoolteacher, told him no one at church spoke to her anymore. Baxter died within a year, reportedly of a broken heart. Patience Baxter had two Biblical references engraved on his tombstone: I Timothy 6:10 and Psalm 146:3. After his death she moved to Austin and taught third grade at Wooldridge Elementary until her death. She left her small savings to her local philanthropic sisterhood chapter.

Alice pulled her grandfather's heavy old King James Bible off the bookshelf and turned to I Tim. 6:10: "For the love of money is the root of all evil...." Then Psalm 146:3: "Do not put your trust in princes, nor in the son of man, in whom there is no help." Alice concluded Rupert Baxter's daughter, Patience, had determined there was no help in Trivet. And how lonely Patience must have been that last miserable year, caring for her father after he became a pariah in Coffee Creek.

Hadn't Silla promised Chapter 20 was more fun? Alice turned backward a few pages and read as follows:

> *The Coffee Creek Ruskin Club was already active by 1901 when the Texas Federation of Women's Clubs held its first annual meeting in Waco. As the name suggests, women across the state were forming clubs, pressing for more culture and better education. In 1925, at the November meeting of the Coffee Creek Ruskin Club, members heard a presentation by a nurse who had worked with birth control advocate Margaret Sanger. One member, already a mother of five, showed special interest in the discussion and the equipment presented. However, years later that member's daughter, referring to the unexpected arrival of her mother's sixth child, reported that her mother had ruefully confided (with a wink): "I must have gotten my 'hat' on crooked that night!"*
>
> *Fn: This Coffee Creek Ruskin Club meeting took place ten years before the Dallas birth control clinic (first in Texas) was founded and eleven years before the U.S. Supreme Court made distribution of contraceptive devices legal under certain conditions. See also Coffee Creek Bicentennial Reminiscences (anon. entry).*

Alice did a double take, then whispered, "I get it." She shook her head, laughing. "Silla!" she called. "She got her hat on crooked! Maybe a diaphragm?"

Silla appeared at the office door. "Don't you just wish you'd been at that Ruskin Club meeting? And don't you just wish you'd heard what those ladies hinted at to each other? And what they told their husbands that night? 'So, honey, how was the ladies' lunch meeting today? Y'all have tea and cookies? And gossip?' 'Mm-hmm, sugar. Learned some good stuff!' Maybe not mentioning it was about birth control...''

Alice and Silla burst into giggles. Then Alice wrinkled her nose. "That was just short of a century ago. Not sure we've made much progress."

Silla snorted. "No kidding."

Alice thought for a minute. "This reminds me. I owe Files a copy of the judge's history. But on the cover let's put our big red stamp: 'Attorney-client communication, privileged and confidential.'"

"Got it."

"Okay. What'd you find out at the courthouse?"

"I'll show you." Alice followed Silla to her desk. Silla picked up a clipped bundle of paper. "History of the judge's property." She placed it in front of Alice.

One of Alice's early assignments as a first-year law firm associate was drafting a mineral title opinion. She spent terrified hours learning to run titles. The responsibility felt crushing—stating an opinion as to who owned what, based on blurry signatures and smudged dates. But she knew she was dealing with valuable information—a property's history. Now she'd taught Silla how to run titles at the courthouse—far easier since the probate clerk put most title documents online.

"You wanted me to find out when Judge Mahan got his land," Silla said. "He and Muriel had owned property there for forty years. When they first bought, they took out a construction mortgage, presumably to build the house. Records show it's been paid off. Now here's the interesting- part. I checked title back to 1846—the deed to Fritz and Frieda Fischer for the hundred-and-fifteen acres that family originally owned, including the gulch and some acreage on the other side. If you match the legal description in the old deeds to the plat maps in the tax records, you can pretty much tell."

"What happened after the Fischers were killed?"

"Looks like Emil's uncle, Horst Meyer, rented it out in Emil's name. Apparently Emil had started one year of med school at Tulane but left to serve as a medic in the Confederate army. Then I found a deed from 1867, where Emil Fischer deeded his family's land to Horst and Jutta Meyer, in exchange for the Meyers' undertaking to fund Emil's medical school education. The Meyers later sold it to Willie Craig's family, in 1870, where it stayed until the Craigs sold it to the judge and Muriel forty-some years ago."

"Wow," Alice said. So Emil had survived. She'd worried he'd been just the age to die in the Civil War. She wondered where he'd studied medicine, where he'd practiced.

Silla smoothed her bangs away from her eyes. "But wait, Alice, there's more. About four years ago, the judge bought another fifteen acres—the poker game property along the road that Willie Craig once owned and then deeded to Jasper Riley."

Alice's eyes widened. "So that fifteen acres really belonged to Jasper Riley?"

"Yep. I followed the deeds all the way back. Looks like in 1849 that fifteen acres was sold for taxes. I'm thinking Jasper lit out for somewhere after he shot those poor people— and never dared come back."

Alice's mind raced. Maybe the judge, like a wise landowner, simply wanted to buffer himself when adjacent property became available. But if the judge bought that property four years ago...wasn't he was already working on the county history?

"Did the judge go looking for the owner? Who sold it to him?"

"Of course I checked," Silla said smugly. She pulled the deed from her stack of papers.

Alice read, "White Resources, Inc., Grantor, hereby..."

"Who's that?"

"Local land speculator, apparently. Company's dissolved."

Alice stared at the deed. Surely four years ago the judge had already heard of the "last breakfast." But why buy those fifteen acres? Maybe to protect the rest of his property?

She looked at Silla. "You know what we need? We need to get into the judge's house. We need those manila folders."

Silla raised interrogative eyebrows.

"Well, we need to protect the judge's footnote material, don't we? According to Johnny, there's no computer backup of all the paper he accumulated."

"Let's go," Silla said, glancing out the window. "It's a sunny afternoon. The security guard will let us in. On the way, couldn't we drop off Files's copy of the county history at the Sheriff's Department?"

Alice nodded. Time for a road trip. While they were at the judge's, she thought she might look for something else...

Chapter Twelve

The Famous Silla

Alice punched in the judge's gate code. Downhill she saw Bender, in ball cap and chambray shirt, sleeves rolled up, waving as the Discovery sped past him down the driveway and then up to the house.

"After we get those folders, can we visit the archeologists?" Silla asked, turning and gazing back at Bender.

"Yes indeed."

The bank's security guard, opening the front door, frowned when he saw two women parking in the driveway and carrying two empty banker's boxes up the steps. While he scrutinized Alice's driver's license, she called Miranda at the bank. "I'm going to take those folders to my safe, because there are no back-up copies. Can you explain?" She handed her phone to the guard. Alice heard Miranda's voice instructing him. He listened, nodded, and stood aside to let them in. Charley trotted forward; Alice knelt down to greet him, feeling she might be falling in love with this dog.

"He's about to have lunch," said the guard. He and Charley returned to the kitchen.

The house was quiet as a library and smelled a bit like one as well—books everywhere, in shelves by the fireplace, on the coffee table, in the window seat, stacked beside what looked like the judge's favorite reading chair.

Alice led Silla down a short passage to the judge's office. His oak desk was covered with notebooks, yellow legal pads, and a laptop. Alice tugged open one of the two wooden file cabinets that supported the judge's desk. "Aha." The entire drawer contained manila folders, some thin, some fat with paper, each labeled with a chapter title and number. "Let's take a look."

She pulled out the first folder, labeled Chapter 1. Sure enough, backup information—printouts of internet information on the Birnbach Grist Mill, copies of photos from the Texas History Center, family tree info on the Birnbachs. Silla began loading folders into the first banker's box, then the second.

Alice, one ear listening for the guard, opened the second drawer. Personal folders: insurance. Long-term care. Pension. Medical records. Federal tax returns. Coffee County property tax. Wildlife management backup data. At the back, a folder labeled Deeds. Alice pulled it out and was about to open it.

"You ladies got what you came for?" The guard, bulky, unsmiling, stood at the office door.

Alice slipped the Deeds folder into the second box and slapped on the cardboard lid. "All done. Thanks." She stood, smiled at the guard, and squeezed past him as he reluctantly moved out of the doorway.

She and Silla loaded the boxes into the car and drove back along the driveway, slowing to a stop near the archeology tents. Bender walked over to greet them.

"Silla, meet Bobby Bender." Bender extended his hand, staring at Silla. "And Bender, this is—"

"I know. The famous Silla."

Silla, strangely, was speechless.

Alice looked back and forth at the two silent people staring at each other. Finally, Silla released Bender's hand.

"Um...would you like me to show you around?" Bender asked, eyes on Silla.

"Sure!"

Well, well. Alice grinned to herself.

"We've got everything ready to go," Bender said, nearing the edge of the gulch. "Up there"—waving toward the area far upstream, past the first small green pool—"and then along the big curve downstream, past that boulder, you remember, Alice."

"No more visitors last night?"

"No. But..." Bender squinted across the gulch. "We did see a flashlight over there, around midnight. Wayland went to investigate—didn't find anyone. Heard a motor. Whoever it was must've left." He turned, signaled to Gordon and Wayland, who walked over to join them. "Alice, you left a message, asking us who knew we were out here for this dig. I can't think of anyone except my secretary, at the conservancy. Guys, what about you?"

Gordon shook his head. "I told my parents I'd gotten a chance to do a dig. But I sure didn't tell them where, or for whom."

"Same," said Wayland.

Alice frowned. She'd have to ask Johnny, too. But who else might have known? "Okay, next question. What's the worst thing someone could do, to mess with your work here?" She needed to figure out what else should be done to protect the site.

"We've been talking about that. Drive a bulldozer up the creek?" Bender said. "Or—we'd be screwed if a huge rain-bomb hit this area and flooded the gulch. But that would require a spate of rainy weather, and we're having the driest January on record. Or what if someone backed a dump-truck full of rocks up to the edge of the gulch and dumped them on our excavation area? Or stole our equipment?" Bender smiled. "Never had anyone do that. So far. But that flashlight last night...it did feel like someone spying on us. Could be kids. Wayland, you went over there this morning, right?"

Wayland nodded. "I'd seen another driveway leading off the road into the acreage on the other side of the gulch. If you're driving to the judge's house from town, it's just before the turnoff to his driveway. There used to be a chain across it. It's been cut. I walked up this second driveway—it was a struggle, it's overgrown, looks unused for years—until I could see our tents, a couple of hundred yards away, across the gulch."

"Ah." Maybe she and Silla would take a look. Because that second driveway, she was sure, led to the judge's after-acquired fifteen acres.

"Wish us luck," Bender said. "We're starting work up past the first little pool this afternoon."

Silla smiled her trademark smile. No, not the trademark smile. This smile had even more oomph. "Bye." But Alice noted that as they turned to leave, Silla gazed up and down the gulch, looking puzzled, then—Alice recognized the look—dubious.

*****

Alice exited the judge's driveway and slowed to make the turn onto the narrow gravel drive Wayland had mentioned. She and Silla hopped out of the car. On the ground between two concrete gate posts lay a cut chain. Alice picked up the cut end. The chain itself left rust in Alice's hand. But the cut end?—no rust. "Looks recent," she muttered.

Past the cut chain, the gravel drive disappeared into tall grass and a tangle of cedar scrub. "Someone's been parking here." Silla pointed at the tire tracks.

Had someone found a back door to the gulch? Who?

*****

Driving back to town with Silla, Alice hit Files's number—now in her cellphone "favorites" list, along with numbers for Kinsear, Silla, and Alice's children.

Files answered, sounding grumpy.

"Just one thing," she said. "Johnny Mahan's upset, not knowing whether he's still a suspect. He loved his granddad. Did you finish checking his alibi? Did you look at his computer to see when he finished his paper? Or ask his professor when he turned it in? And satisfy yourselves about the $200 the judge gave him?"

Files sighed. "Joske was supposed to call him and tell him—looks like his alibi checks out, at least preliminarily. But come on, Alice, we're swamped." His voice changed. "If you had the feds breathing down your neck, second-guessing every move you make..."

"What about Eric Mahan? Johnny's dad?" Alice interjected.

"Why do you care about him? Or his alibi?"

"Because he's Johnny's father. Even if he's a jerk—not calling his son when he's just a few miles away—it's too awful to contemplate that he'd shoot his own dad."

"I'll get back to you later on that. Meanwhile, this county history you dropped off? This is what the judge attached to the email he sent you the afternoon he was killed, right? You marked it confidential. Is this something I have to read now? Can it wait?"

"It's still a draft, so please treat it as attorney-client confidential until Silla and I finish some fact-checking. The judge already showed it to the Coffee County Historical Commission. Its treasurer, Tim Johansen, said he's concerned that it includes some unpleasant stories. It's my job to be sure the judge's history gets published in some form, with or without Historical Commission participation. That's something the judge hired me to do. But first we need to fact-check and finish his footnotes. He obviously meant to do that himself. He didn't get a chance."

Silence. "So?"

"Maybe you could read Chapter 13, about an old murder. It's short."

She heard Files snort. "In my spare time?" he said. "No, Alice, of course I'll read it. I just hope it helps move us forward." He hung up.

Alice turned on Sun Radio. Oh, good—Emily Gimble singing "Mess Around" with Floyd Domino and the All-Stars. Soon, with Alice beating time on the steering wheel, Silla and Alice were singing along, while Emily belted out "Ever'body do the mess-around!"

When the song ended, Silla said, "That felt good. When was the last time you went dancing?"

"Can't remember. Before Christmas, at the Beer Barn Holiday Bazaar?"

"Well, the Beer Barn calls."

"Yup."

Long pause. Silla asked casually, "Does that Bender guy like music, at all?"

"He helped us find Blanton Geddes. Remember?" Years earlier Alice had represented the executor of the fabled but missing singer-songwriter.

Silla nodded. "Lord, what a loss. Blanton Geddes—a true cowboy poet."

"So Bender probably likes music." Alice glanced at Silla. "Are you planning to give him some guidance, musically speaking?"

"Not tonight. Got a date."

"Ah?"

"Alan Joske's taking me to hear The Georges, down at Gruene Hall. Oldest dance hall in Texas, right? We'll see if Joske can dance."

When they got to the office, Silla helped Alice load the judge's folders into the massive safe that squatted heavily in the conference room closet. Alice had bought it from Cowman's Bank when she first opened her Coffee Creek office and had it bolted to the joists beneath the office floor.

"Maybe you'll winkle some info out of Joske about the murder investigation?"

Silla handed another batch of folders to Alice, then tossed her red ponytail and grinned. "I won't do anything too unscrupulous."

Alice rolled her eyes heavenward. "The poor man. He won't stand a chance."

Silla just smiled. But she looked preoccupied. Not Silla's usual face... Alice left, puzzled.

Chapter Thirteen

Kept Them Stashed

Saturday morning, dark but clear. Alice woke before dawn, went out on the deck to see the stars, the planets. Was that Jupiter? And Saturn a bit lower? She checked her sky app. Yes, planets in view. The air was quiet: no birds yet. Back inside she made her espresso, foamed some hot milk, toyed with the *New York Times* crossword. Saturday's was always tough.

No Kinsear today—he'd had to take the early flight back to New York. Going to the office held no appeal. Too early to call her daughter, Ann, in New England, finishing senior year; too early to call her son John, six hours ahead of her in Edinburgh—he was doubtless in the midst of team practice for his rugby game.

Alice sighed, wondering if a second pot of espresso would help.

Her cell phone rang. Silla.

"Alice, I need to see the judge's property again. If those boys are looking for horse bones, they may be starting in the wrong place. What are you doing?"

"Pulling on my jeans. Meet you at the office?"

"Yes. Listen, it's windy, so bring a jacket. And wear sturdy shoes." Silla hung up.

Did Silla really think the archeologists were starting in the wrong place, or did she just want to see Bender?

*****

Alice buttoned her jeans jacket over a wool sweater and tied a bandana around her neck against the wind. She hummed on her way down the creek road to her office, happy to have a mysterious project with Silla and hoping her hiking boots were sturdy enough for the gulch. She wondered how Silla's date with Joske had gone—obviously it hadn't taken her mind off the archeologists.

Silla had already parked in the office driveway. She stood by her truck, decked out in Saturday riding regalia: jeans, her roughout cowgirl boots, and puffer vest over a denim jacket.

Alice rolled down her window. "Straight to the judge's?" she asked. "Hope those archeologists are early risers." It was only seven-thirty.

"What we need to do, Alice, is park at that little driveway with the broken chain. I want to hike from there to the creek. Across the fifteen acres the judge bought—the old Jasper Riley part."

"Ah." Alice's mind raced. "Let's grab some breakfast tacos for the troops, shall we?"

"Definitely. Enough for all."

"So, can Joske dance?"

"Sorta. Has about two moves. The Georges have a good drummer, thank heavens. Listen, I may stay out there to see what a dig's like. I'll take my truck and follow you," Silla said. She climbed into her truck.

Right, Alice thought, smiling to herself. Just to see what a dig's like.

Armed with two bags of breakfast tacos, Alice and Silla sped south, then turned onto the blacktop road to Willie's Store, then west on Geisberg Lane, slowing for Dead Man's Curve. They turned into the overgrown drive with the cut chain and parked. They grabbed the Flores bags and locked Silla's truck and Alice's car.

"Follow me," said Silla.

The two women pushed their way through vicious cedar scrub. Alice tried to dodge the agarita bushes, with spiny leaves that could pierce blue jeans, and repeatedly batted cedar branches out of her face. For a short distance she could feel gravel underfoot, along the disused driveway. Then Silla stopped. "Now we need to bear right."

"Looking for this side of the gulch?" Alice said.

"Yep." They pushed their way through another hundred yards of scrub.

"Looks like, even after he bought it, the judge didn't build anything over here," Alice said.

"Also didn't cut the cedar," Silla noted.

"Or prune the live oaks," Alice added. She was wondering if the judge bought the fifteen adjacent acres four years ago, when he was beginning to think about a county history, because he knew of the "last breakfast" and felt a need to protect the gulch from any incursions by trespassers. Was he already planning to preserve any evidence?

"We've seen plenty of deer poop out here. The judge didn't hunt, did he?" Silla pointed to some antlers, whitened with age, by a tree trunk. "Just a bird guy?"

"Think so. There's the gulch."

They crossed a field broken by limestone rock, dotted with rust-colored clumps of tall bluestem grass, waist-high, and passed the remnants of an old unmortared stone boundary wall—more gaps than wall. Alice imagined Riley leading his horse toward the gulch and discovering he'd screwed up when he accepted acres of dirt with no water, then repeatedly kicking down parts of the Fischers' wall on this side of the gulch.

She and Silla followed a narrow deer trail through a wide gap in the old stone wall to the edge of the gulch, where the trail plunged downward through spiky cedar branches toward the bottom. Okay for deer, but too steep for me, Alice thought. I wouldn't risk an ankle going down that.

Bender stood directly across the gulch on the other side, staring across the streambed at them, a quizzical expression on his face. "What's up? We're all dressed, so feel free to come on over."

Alice looked down at the steep drop-off below her feet, then upstream, where Bender had already begun to stake out his first dig area. Silla was right to wonder, Alice realized.

Silla, still carrying the bags of tacos, stood on the edge of the drop-off, gazing back at Bender.

"You don't ride horses, do you?" she said.

He frowned. "No. Why?"

"How do you think Riley would get a horse down this side of this gulch, given where you're planning to dig? Carry the horse down? Lower it with ropes? A man who obviously was too damn lazy to dig a well on his own property, so just trespassed on someone else's water?"

Bender stared at Silla. His eyes widened. One eyebrow went up. He looked upstream, at the proposed initial dig site, then back at Silla. "I assumed the Comanches might've cleaned the meat and cooked it above the last little pool before Blue Creek," he said.

"But look how steep the sides of the creek are," Silla said. "Let me show you something." She walked downstream along the edge of the gulch to a point where the Fischers' old rock wall had virtually disappeared and the walls of the gulch looked equally steep and gravelly. Alice followed cautiously, clutching her bag of tacos. Silla, facing downstream, began gingerly picking her way slantwise partway down the steep side of the gulch. She turned and descended slantwise in the opposite direction, back toward Bender, until she reached the bottom. She was now a good hundred feet downstream from Bender. "Switchbacks," she called. "He'd have used switchbacks to get the horse down. Down the deer trail."

"What deer trail?" Bender called.

"The one that the deer made nearly two centuries ago that's been washed out for the last 180 years," Silla yelled back. Bender grinned, then turned his head, staring upstream at the area he'd already staked.

"And if you think that's where the horse bones are," she said, following his glance, "you'd probably be…"

"Digging in the wrong place," he finished for her. "Well, we flew the gulch with a drone and showed the films to a geologist colleague, hoping to learn the gulch's configuration over the last two centuries. He looked at the film and said, 'Bones? Floods? Hard to tell. Maybe just upstream of an obstruction. Or possibly on the far side, maybe buried under the bank. And with flash floods, who knows? Again, hard to tell after all this time. Good luck.'" Bender shook his head. "But from what you're showing me, the horse was probably butchered where it was staked, maybe farther downstream than I'd assumed. And cooked upstream of where it was butchered, but close by." He pointed back at the currently staked area. "So I guess we may be, um, pullin' up stakes if we don't find anything back there, looking farther downstream as well. Okay, let me get the ladder."

Alice followed Silla upstream along the streambed. Then she and Silla, each clutching a Flores bag, climbed up the extension ladder Bender was holding for them on the other side of the gulch, near the archeologists' tents.

"We brought breakfast," Alice announced.

"Excellent!" exclaimed Gordon. "Beats dry cereal with canned milk."

In morning sun, next to a small campfire, Alice, Bender, Silla, Wayland, and Gordon arranged themselves in camp chairs, polishing off the breakfast tacos.

Bender wiped salsa off his lips. "The judge hired us to look for 'evidence of human history' along the entire length of the streambed where it crosses his land," he said, finally. "But we don't have to start at one end or the other. We can start in the middle."

"Yes," Alice said. The sooner the better, she thought, because if indeed deadly events occurred here long ago, those events may tell us why the judge is now dead.

*****

Bender took them back to their two vehicles in his pickup. "I've got an appointment this morning, but I'll drop by later this afternoon," Silla told Bender. Alice took off, leaving Silla and Bender standing by Silla's truck, still deep in conversation.

They'd make an interesting pair, Alice thought, driving back to Coffee Creek. She'd known Bender for years but knew nothing of his private life.

She unlocked her office—quiet on Saturday morning, except for the faint hum of the refrigerator. Alice opened the conference room closet, entered the combination on the office safe, retrieved the "Deeds" folder and took it back to her desk. If Silla were here, she'd insist on making a copy before she entrusted any original to Alice...but Silla was away, so the mouse would play.

Alice leafed through the papers. The oldest was at the back of the folder. She started there, with a deed dated four years ago, conveying to the judge and his wife the fifteen acres Riley had once owned beyond the streambed. Next came the survey, then a letter to the judge dated three years ago from White Realty, LLC, claiming to represent a willing buyer for the fifteen acres. The judge had scribbled on the letter: "Called, said not interested, no more calls pls." Next came another letter a year later from Rusty James, a local realtor: "Judge, we have a highly motivated buyer for the fifteen acres you own on the undeveloped acreage on the far side of the wet-weather creek. We can offer an additional $5,000 per acre above current county valuation."

Again, the judge's crabbed handwriting: "Called Rusty, asked who's interested? Rusty said client's confidential—would only say local buyer. Told him no."

The last letter in the file was dated just months ago, in November, again from Rusty: "Our firm has a highly motivated buyer for your entire property, including your house, at county valuation plus bonus of $2,000 per acre." The "entire property" amounted to a hundred-and-thirty acres. Over a quarter of a million in bonus? Alice frowned. Who was so "highly motivated"?

The judge had stuck a yellow sticky note on Rusty's letter, noting, in the judge's cramped handwriting: "Rusty called re: letter. Oddly insistent. Got pretty shirty with me. I said no deal if I don't know buyer identity; if he couldn't tell, quit calling. And straighten up or I'll call his mom."

Alice smiled. Her parents always used that phrase—straighten up! It meant—exactly that. Also, quit what(ever) you're doing.

But who was Rusty's client? Why wouldn't Rusty level with the judge? The judge had strong reasons to ask the identity of anyone buying the fifteen acres he'd just bought a few years earlier. Any landowner would want to know the identity of the new neighbor, and what threats of noise, lights, animals, etc., might be involved. Any landowner would consider what zoning or building restrictions might apply: the judge would never sell if he ran the risk of his buyer putting up new structures close enough or tall enough to invade his privacy. Oh lord, Alice thought, and what about the trees? The judge wouldn't want a buyer lopping down trees, diminishing options for his birds. She personally cringed at the thought of soil erosion that careless logging could cause, with dirt clogging the creek.

Alice, who loved her own piece of dirt, believed strongly in hanging on to real property. She couldn't think of a single reason why the judge should sell those adjacent fifteen acres.

She'd met Rusty James at Rotary. Maybe she'd call him, ask about the mystery buyer. If he wouldn't tell her, maybe he'd tell Files...

She called Rusty's real estate firm. She'd just finished leaving her message when the office doorbell rang—unusual on Saturday morning. She looked out the window: Gavin's car. She hoped the settlement with Lola hadn't unraveled.

"Come in!"

"Alice! I was over at Minnie's place. Lola came by and brought me something I want you to see." He patted his briefcase.

When she got him seated at the tea table, he said, "Remember I took Lola all of Minnie's hat boxes? To go with the hat pins?"

Alice nodded.

"Well, Lola found this in the Stetson hatbox, which Minnie kept on the highest shelf in her closet." He opened his briefcase, pulled out a bundle of letters, tied in a faded blue ribbon. "Thank goodness for the mediation settlement. Lola opened the hat box, but when she saw these inside, she brought them straight to me. She promises she didn't read them, though I could tell she was curious."

He set the bundle on the tea table. Alice detected a faint, faded scent of *Joy*, which reminded her instantly of Minnie. She gently picked up the ribboned stack of one-page folded forms, then looked inquiringly at Gavin.

"Love letters," he said. "Love letters to Minnie, from World War II. V-Mail. I had to look that up. Starting in 1942 letters to and from military personnel were sent on special forms, a single sheet microfilmed to save weight and space."

"Holy cow." Alice loosened the ribbon and gently picked up the V-mail form on top, addressed in careful block letters to Miss Minnie Clarke, Clarke Ranch, Coffee Creek, Texas. The sender, "S1 Timothy Cave, c/o Fleet Post Ofc.," had scrawled "September 15, 1944" below his name.

"S1 meant Seaman First Class," said Gavin.

Alice looked back at the earliest envelope in the stack, which Seaman 1st Class Cave had dated June 18, 1942.

"I've read that first one, and some of the others," Gavin said. "Apparently, Timothy joined the Navy in June 1942, right after his freshman year at UT. Minnie was only—what, sixteen or so? The Cave ranch sat right next to Clarke Ranch, I know that. Anyway, over those two years, she got at least fifty or so letters from Timothy."

"But what happened?" Alice asked, afraid of the worst.

"He was killed when the *U.S.S. Johnston* went down, in the Battle of Leyte Gulf," Gavin said. "October 1944."

Alice squeezed her eyes shut, imagining the boy, the sinking ship. "Did you know about him?"

Gavin shook his head no. "There was a family rumor that Minnie had a true love who died in World War II. But she never said a word to any of us about it. After the war she married Granddad Mason and was devoted to him."

"But she never gave away these letters," Alice said.

"Never showed them to anyone, apparently. Kept them stashed in her Stetson hatbox. And of course none of us were allowed to touch any of her hatboxes, especially not that one. Your Stetson's sacred, right?"

Alice nodded. She owned only one Stetson—a small straw fedora, with a modest but becoming leather band. But she allowed no one else to touch it. Or the hatbox.

"So those letters were safe in the hatbox, as long as Minnie was alive."

"Right," Gavin said. "Not sure what I should do with these, actually."

"That's why she appointed an executor, Gavin. You get to make the tough decisions."

Small chuckle from Gavin. "No one warned me how tough this executor crap would be."

"Heavens, no!" Alice said. "Why would we do that?"

Gavin shook his head, smiling, and left.

Now, alone in the Saturday quiet, Alice considered her next step. She spent a few minutes with Coffee County Bicentennial documents on Google, then returned to the judge's Chapter 13, with its unfinished footnotes. What had he intended to include?

And what about Tim Johansen? What additions did the Historical Commission need?

Then she picked up the phone, waited for him to answer, made a proposal.

"Sure! Meet you at the Beer Barn at twelve-thirty."

Chapter Fourteen

We Have No Proof!

Alice grabbed her favorite table at the Beer Barn. The town's iconic roadhouse served excellent Tex-Mex from eleven a.m. on, with music and dancing from happy hour till midnight. Already the air was heady with the tempting smell of cumin and chiles from the kitchen and the hoppy aroma of the artisanal brews at the long antique wooden bar.

The table Alice considered her own sat at the far end of the bar. Recalling Wild Bill Hickok's advice, she always chose the chair on the back wall, where she could observe the entire beer hall, from the double front doors by the bar to the dance floor and music stage. As she was well aware, Hickok hadn't taken his own advice the afternoon he joined a poker game in the Deadwood saloon where, holding aces and eights, he was shot in the back of the head by Jack McCall.

Alice disliked being surprised. Indeed, avoiding being surprised was one of her main goals as a lawyer. While she enjoyed startling her opponents, she clung to the belief that if she dug deep enough into a case, she'd avoid the horror of being surprised by the other side.

Tim Johansen pushed open the double doors at the Beer Barn entrance, spotted Alice and made his way to her table.

"Great idea, Alice. You're improving my Saturday."

The barkeep hustled over with menus. Alice ordered one of the Beer Barn's artisanal drafts, Blue Hole Ale. Tim asked for a Fireman's Four. "Fresh redfish, today," the barkeep said. "Cook's making fish tacos, on the spicy side."

"Great," said Alice.

"Same here," said Tim.

"Thanks for coming, Tim," Alice began.

He held up a hand. "I want you to know I'm sick about the judge's death. Sick."

She nodded. "He left me a job to do. Making sure his county history gets published. Either by the Historical Commission—I know he hoped for that—or otherwise. You mentioned at Rotary you had concerns."

The beers arrived. Tim took a sip. "I'm a CPA," Tim said. "Tracking down missing details—that's my job. I'm sure you feel the same."

"Yes. The judge was also a stickler for details," she said.

"He gave the board copies of his draft, like I told you at Rotary. He told us he was aiming for his little book—that's what he called it— to be comprehensive enough to give vignettes that really made county history come alive, but obviously not to be encyclopedic."

"And you'll remember his preface underscores that the book partly includes oral history, reporting the stories that people told."

He nodded, reluctantly. "He did say that."

"You were worried about the chapter on the Fischers?"

"Yes."

"Why?"

"Well, the judge used real names. The Fischers and Jasper Riley. Riley disappeared. But there was no trial. No Fischer bodies were found."

"Does that make the story less true?" Alice felt indignation rising.

"I'm chairman of the Historical Commission board. Imagine if I get us sued for defamation. How could I defend and claim that chapter's true? You're not defaming someone if what you say is true, right? But for the judge's Chapter 13? We have no proof!"

"Did you say this to the judge?"

"I did. I told him one of our donors was concerned enough to mention that to me. He said, 'I haven't finished the footnotes. Don't worry, I plan to do a little more digging around.'"

Alice suppressed her laugh. The judge had indeed planned a little more digging. But did Tim know what sort?

The barkeep arrived with platters of fish tacos, crema and salsa on top, plus guacamole with the Beer Barn's own tortilla chips. Tim lifted his eyebrows in approval. Alice took a bite of the crema and salsa. "Mmm." After a few happy moments of silence, with both concentrating on the flavors the kitchen had achieved, Alice set down her fork. "So you knew he'd be adding details, right?"

"Yes. That was a relief to the board and one of the donors who'd seen his manuscript."

"Donors? I'm surprised anyone but the board sees the drafts people submit."

"We have a couple of significant givers," Tim said. "Serious history nuts. If they ask, we give them a chance to read the manuscripts we plan to publish. Anyway, one donor expressed strong concern about the judge's manuscript. I told her I'd spoken to the judge and that he promised he was going to fill in the details, including the references. And said he was going to do a little more digging around!" He laughed.

"Which donor was that?"

"Winifred Hutton. She expressed real concern about the lack of proof. Said she didn't want us to get sued."

"When did she get involved with the Historical Commission? She's not from Coffee County, is she?"

"No," Tim said. "She grew up in Dallas, but now she owns a ranch west of town. She started making big donations over a year ago. It's been a huge help. In fact, she's the one who presented us with that early framed map of Coffee County. You may have seen it hanging in the reading room at the library. It's really quite valuable. We thought it would be safe there until we get a room of our own somewhere."

Alice had seen the map, with its large silver frame, because the library board on which she served met in the reading room. The head librarian had complained that the donor insisted it be screwed to the wood-paneled wall so no one would waltz off with it. "But Tim, seriously: would someone really sue the Historical Commission? Have you ever been sued?"

Tim heaved a sigh, shook his head. "No. But what if the judge doesn't offer solid proof of what happened to the Fischers? What about relatives of Jasper Riley?"

"Did you raise this with the judge?"

"Yes, I mentioned concerns. Like I said, he told me not to worry. I believe the words he used were that he'd be sure the references were 'unimpeachable.'" Tim finished his fish taco, then attacked the last of the guacamole.

Alice sipped her ale, watched him for a moment. Finally, he leaned back in his chair. "Thanks for lunch, Alice. Listen, until we know what details he planned to add, I can't recommend that we move forward."

We'll see about that, Alice thought. Tim seemed a little too impressed by—maybe a little too cozy with—Winifred Hutton. "My assistant and I will take a look at the research the judge put together. We'll keep you posted." Deliberately vague. She signaled the barkeep for the check. "Thanks for meeting me on short notice, Tim."

As she signed the bill, Tim hovered, apparently intending to walk her to her car. But Jorgé Benavides, one of the three Beer Barn partners, materialized at their table. He greeted Tim, then turned to Alice: "Do you have time to stop by the office for a minute?"

Thankfully, she did.

*****

After she finished strategizing with the Beer Barn partners about plans for the upcoming South by Southwest festival, Alice walked to her car, making a mental list of information she wanted but which George Files hadn't yet provided. Maybe he'd be in his office? Yes, it was Saturday, but in the middle of an ongoing investigation of a judge's shooting death, with the higher-ups breathing down Files's neck? He'd be there.

She parked at the courthouse by the Sheriff's Annex. The duty sergeant notified Files he had a visitor. She stood waiting at the end of the hall, its gray linoleum adding no cheer to the gray walls—or to the gray tone of Files's face.

"C'mon back." He turned; she followed him, noting the sagging shoulders, the weary pace.

In the office she stared at the unwelcoming metal chair in front of his desk. "If I bring a pillow, would you let me keep it on that chair?" she asked, lowering herself onto the cold steel.

He just sighed. "What's up?"

"Remember I told you the judge had asked some archeologists to do some investigation on his property? You said they could start work."

"I vaguely remember. 'Evidence of human history' or some such thing."

"Well, a couple of days ago an intruder broke into the archeologists' research tent at the judge's place. They caught him taking pictures of maps or drawings and chased him back to the gate, but he got away in a truck."

"Interesting, Alice. How come I'm only just now hearing about it? Somebody doesn't want the police snooping around?"

"Bender says the archeology team's been invaded by snoopers on other digs—trying to see what they're up to. This time it was too dark to see the color of the truck or the license plate. It was parked on the other side of the gate, so the invaders didn't have a gate code. Wayland—he's one of the grad students—says he did get a good bite on the guy's ear before he got away. Anyway, we've now padlocked the fire gate. So, did you get a chance to read Chapter 13?"

"Yeah, scanned it. What does that have to do with anything?"

"Yesterday Silla went to the courthouse and examined the judge's property history. The judge's place includes all of the original Fischer property. About four years ago he also bought the original fifteen acres that Jasper Riley won in a poker game. Unfortunately for Riley, those acres border Geisberg Lane but didn't include any frontage either on Blue Creek or on the wet-weather creek in the gulch on the Fischer property. Which is probably why Riley kept trespassing with his horse. After the judge acquired the fifteen acres, someone got a broker to call the judge, asking to buy those acres, but because the broker wouldn't identify the buyer, the judge repeatedly refused. Most recently, in November."

Files lifted both eyebrows. "So maybe this isn't random archeology. Or maybe whoever wanted that fifteen acres is worried about the archeologists. But we don't know who?"

"Right. Now it's your turn to share. Did the crime scene team ever find a shell casing near the judge's body?"

"Nope."

"So either a calm, savvy shooter...?"

"Or a revolver," Files said. "Probably an oldish .38 caliber, we think. Don't have a ballistics match yet for the bullet that hit the judge."

"Heavy revolver," Alice muttered.

Files nodded. "One bullet in the back. From maybe eight feet away."

"So he was marching back to his house, with the camera and telephoto in his right hand...?"

"Sounds possible."

Alice felt baffled. "Why did he have his back to—whoever shot him?"

"Doubt he was expecting to be shot."

She felt a sudden stab of fear. "Johnny doesn't have a gun like that?"

"No. Nor his dad, apparently."

She tried to repress her sigh of relief.

"No other leads?"

Files shook his head. "Why do you think the feds are breathing down my back?"

Alice drove back to her office and parked in the driveway, thinking of footnotes. Already three on Saturday afternoon; Live Oak Street was quiet; Kinsear was busy in New York. She didn't like Johansen's comments about possible defamation. Maybe she'd grab the judge's footnote folders and start getting a grip on the data, figuring out the gaps that needed to be filled.

Chapter Fifteen

A Significant Donor

Alice extracted the judge's footnote folders from the massive safe, made a pot of coffee, and settled down at her desk. With time alone, digging through paper—it felt like being back in law school, reading cases. Okay, Jasper Riley, what are the facts? What's your story?

The folder for Chapter 13 was thicker than most of the others. The judge had stapled together printouts of local contributions to Coffee County's 1976 Bicentennial History. The then owner of Willie Craig's Country Store, eighty-year-old Willie Craig IV, recounted how his ancestors had built a store in Coffee Creek in 1846 to serve newly arriving German settlers:

"My great-grandparents, Willie and Virginia Craig, opened their small store in 1846 in Coffee Creek, close to the current City Hall. They also bought some land south of town, stretching from Blue Creek up to what's now Geisberg Lane, where one son planted corn and raised some cows. Our neighbors were the Fischers. Our family is grateful we still own most of our original property because of its frontage on Blue Creek. Willie Craig learned a hard lesson after one poker game in 1847 at the Coffee Creek Saloon when, penniless, he had to cover his debts to a man named Jasper Riley, who'd reportedly been turned out of the Texas Rangers for killing a fellow Ranger. Willie deeded Riley fifteen acres on the north side of his Blue Creek land, bordering what's now Geisberg Lane. When Riley discovered his new acreage had no water, he rode up to the store and threatened Willie with a Colt pistol. Willie never played another hand of poker. He promised a silver dollar to each grandchild who agreed not to gamble."

Interesting, Alice thought. This confirms Riley had a Colt pistol and confirms his anger that his poker win didn't include water access. But Willie Craig's tale didn't mention the Fischers or the dead Comanches. Surely that could have been part of the story?

The importance of water... The image of Wayland's black eye popped into her head. Alice picked up her cell and called Bender.

"Want to come visit?" he said. "We should talk."

"What if I bring supper?"

"Excellent. Some big appetites out here in the chilly weather. The team's grown to five. See you about five-thirty? Also,"— his voice changed—"Silla left right after you did. Do you think she might come too?"

"On Saturday night? I'll check." Alice smiled to herself and called Silla.

"Bender asked, huh? Okay. I'll bring cookies," Silla said.

Alice called in a supper order to Flores, then put away the footnote file, resolving to finish it later. Out the front window of her office, she watched a large black pickup slow down in front, then move slowly forward, pausing momentarily at her driveway until a red Mercedes convertible pulled in and parked at her curb. Out climbed Winifred Hutton: red pantsuit, blue scarf over her hair, hand-tooled leather handbag swinging from her shoulder. She stared at Alice's office, then strode up the walk and rapped on the door.

Alice picked up her phone, put it on voice memo. Then she stood, straightened her shoulders and opened the front door.

"I saw you were here. This is a convenient time for me," said Hutton. She took a few steps into the entry, looked around—bookshelves, coatrack, Silla's work table. Hutton lifted a disdainful eyebrow. Alice assumed Hutton's legal teams occupied the top floor of a prominent high rise, with an elegant lobby and enormous conference rooms.

Alice looked at her watch. "I'm leaving in fifteen minutes. Come this way." She walked Hutton back to the conference room, pointed at a chair, said, "Have a seat," sat down at the head of the table and gazed at Hutton.

Hutton unwound the blue scarf and leaned back, face confident. "I'm here on behalf of the Historical Commission, concerning Judge Mahan's so-called county history."

"You're not on the board, correct?" Alice asked, knowing the answer.

"No. But I'm a significant donor, as I'm sure Tim Johansen will confirm."

"So when you say you're here on the board's behalf, what do you mean?"

"I mean that no one with any sense can want the Historical Commission sued for defamation, that's what I mean! Which means the Historical Commission will not be publishing Mahan's document!"

"Defamation's a serious charge, Ms. Hutton. Have you read the entire manuscript? If so, what precisely do you claim constitutes defamation?"

Hutton leaned forward, eyes flashing. "As you already certainly know, I strongly support Richard Riley in his bid to represent our district. Chapter 13 of this scurrilous text is defamatory. It defames Jasper Riley. It could—it could harm Richard Riley."

"So Jasper Riley is Richard Riley's ancestor?"

"I didn't say that! Just having the Riley name defamed is unfair to the candidate with the same name!"

Alice tilted her head. "Do you have any proof that the current written record is untrue? Do you have proof that Jasper Riley did not shoot Mr. and Mrs. Fischer? Or that Riley did not shoot two Comanche children, a woman, and an elderly man? If so, please share it."

"You've got it backwards! There's no *proof* that there was any such shooting!" Hutton burst out. "Where are the Fischers' bodies? They likely just ran off!"

"You don't credit the account their own son told to his aunt and uncle and later to his pastor?"

"Of course not! A mere child?"

"A frontier child, though. And the posse's report of finding the Comanche bodies?"

"Just rumor! And who cares! They'd killed his horse!"

Alice sneaked a calming breath. "How could Richard Riley possibly be defamed by an oral account made by the Fischers' son, 180 years ago, which was recorded by his aunt and later his pastor? No one claims *Richard Riley* killed anyone." Yet. She saw again the judge's body, dead on the gravel... "Surely you don't claim everyone in Jasper Riley's family tree in the past 180 years could claim defamation?"

Hutton lifted her chin, glaring at Alice. "If the Historical Commission publishes this chapter or anything scurrilous about Jasper Riley, it's highly likely the board will face a defamation suit." She leaned back. "The Historical Commission has no money for lawsuits. So the board won't let that happen."

"Let me be sure I understand. You offer no proof that Judge Mahan's account is untrue or erroneous. Yet you suggest someone will sue the board for defamation if the board publishes this chapter. And it sounds as if you—though a 'significant donor' to the Historical Commission—would be the person funding such a lawsuit. Am I right?"

Hutton didn't answer that question.

"I'll confirm with Tim when, and if, the board makes any decision to publish, or not to publish," Alice said, trying to keep her heart rate down. She could feel her cheeks turning pink. "Of course, such a decision by the board won't prevent publication of the judge's history of Coffee County."

"What do you mean?" Hutton snapped.

"Just what I said."

She watched Hutton's face change, watched the realization flood her face. "You mean his family might still publish it? His executors, whoever they are?"

Alice didn't intend to share client information. She merely shrugged.

"Even if the Historical Commission has the good sense not to publish?" snapped Hutton. "Well, you'd better tell his executors and his heirs they can be sued for defamation in a New York minute!"

"What makes you believe such a suit could succeed?"

Hutton stood, grabbed the leather handbag, and hissed at Alice, "You will regret this—this utter lack of respect!"

"Lack of respect for whom?"

"For—for the Riley family!" Hutton held the back of the chair and leaned forward, her face furious. "That draft of the judge's is full of error! It's defamatory! And you? You're a nothing, a newcomer to Coffee County, a two-bit lawyer! You'd better watch yourself! Have you any idea who I am? Have you never heard of HFH, LLC? Or Hutton Family Jewelry?"

Alice shook her head no, watching Hutton's face redden.

Hutton stood, breathing hard, "You're finished here. Finished! I'll see you never get another client!"

"How do you plan to do that, Ms. Hutton?" asked Alice, interested. She glanced at her watch. "I've got a few more minutes."

"You just watch. Just watch! I'll teach you that you can't mess with me!"

"The same way you did your Hockaday classmate?" Alice snapped.

"You...you worthless piece of nothing! Bitch! You haven't seen the last of me! You will regret this!" Her voice changed, lower, grim: "To your dying day!" Winifred Hutton spun on her heels and marched out.

Chapter Sixteen

Where Exactly Will You Be Looking?

Alice turned off the voice memo app on her phone. She closed her eyes, took a deep breath. Back in her office, she watched through the window as Hutton tied on her blue scarf and roared down Live Oak Street in her red Mercedes. Red and blue—her patriot outfit.

Defamation. Not my area, Alice realized. She rehearsed the standard: truth is a defense to a defamation claim, but the judge didn't have actual *proof* of any shooting by Jasper Riley, just the statement of little Emil Fischer, recorded at the time by Mrs. Meyer—the boy's recollection of what he'd seen. She knew a mere statement of opinion didn't provide a solid basis for a defamation claim. But the boy's statement didn't constitute an *opinion*, did it? Furthermore, did Richard Riley—or any descendant of Jasper Riley—have standing to sue at this late date?

She thought of the recent Virginia lawsuit—dismissed by the trial court on the first round, she recalled—where a local man claimed he'd been defamed by an article describing his Civil War ancestor's extensive slaveholdings. Plenty of families doubtless had similar histories...

But didn't she have some obligation to protect the judge's reputation? A defamation suit wouldn't help.

And her own reputation? With Winifred Hutton threatening to kill her career?

Alice sighed. Maybe, just maybe, the archeologists would find evidence. Even proof. But 180 years later? Her heart sank. Too much to ask.

Five-thirty. She picked up her keys. Then she dodged back to the kitchen and grabbed a six-pack of Negro Modelo Especial and another of Fireman's Four. That could enhance a campfire dinner. At the H-E-B grocery she picked out apples and oranges from the produce aisle. As she waited in the checkout line, her pocket vibrated. "Hello?"

A tentative voice: "Alice Greer?"

"Yes?"

"We didn't actually meet at Rotary. This is Dedra Riley." A pause. "Umm, Richard Riley's my husband?"

A little upspeak, Alice noted—made a woman sound tentative. "Yes, I know."

"I hate to bother you on the weekend. I wonder if we could meet sometime soon? Tomorrow or Monday?"

Very interesting. First the candidate's sponsor; now his wife.

"Can you tell me what this is about?"

"It's—it won't take long. Just—about the campaign."

"What about first thing Monday?"

"Thank you. I can drop off the kids at school and be at your office by, say, nine?"

"That works."

"I really appreciate this. Thanks."

The candidate's wife sounded harried. Uncertain. Was it mere co-incidence that Dedra Riley called just after Winifred Hutton's visit?

What a day, Alice thought, starting with Silla's early call demand-ing to return to the dig. Files. Tim Johansen. Winifred Hutton. The call from Dedra Riley.

She wanted a cold beer and a warm fire.

The western sky blazed pink and orange. Last stop, Flores, where her order was ready. The cashier helped Alice load two heavy pans of enchiladas, with all the sides, plus two bags of chips and a heavy bag of fresh hot tortillas. As the sunset faded, she turned south toward the judge's property, inhaling the essence of chiles all the way.

Kinsear called.

"Where are you?" she asked. "Getting on the plane to Austin?"

A sigh. "Not yet. Interminable meetings all day, but we've worked out most remaining issues. One final meeting tomorrow morning, then I'm on the 1 p.m. flight from JFK. I skipped the team dinner tonight. Too tired to try to speak another word of any language but Texian."

Alice laughed. "Hey, you're bi-dialectal, right? New York finance lingo and ranch boy."

"May I buy your dinner tomorrow night? And stay with you?"

She shut her eyes. "Yes, yes, yes."

He hung up. Alice hummed all the way to the judge's driveway.

*****

Parked downhill to the left of the judge's driveway near the gulch she spotted Silla's green truck, Bender's white camper, and several dusty vehicles. The tent village had grown: five small tents plus the big green planning tent. Sparks flew up from a large bonfire surrounded by camp chairs. Silla and Bender sat next to each other, heads together, engaged in deep conversation. Alice smiled to herself, thinking of Silla, thinking of Bender, thinking of the mysteries of attraction between—well, people who didn't know each other yet but still felt the magnetism of the new person.

That was the feeling that swamped her about Kinsear, their first year of law school…and then when they finally met again, some twenty years later, the afternoon he opened the wrought iron gate into the tree-shaded Altburg beer garden in Fredericksburg and walked up to her table.

She felt that same thrill, watching Bender and Silla.

They caught sight of her at the same time. Bender hurried over to take charge of the big pans of enchiladas. Silla, cheeks flushed, grabbed the two six-packs of beer. Alice got a quick grin from her. "I just got here," Silla said. "Had to see what was going on."

Feeling a bit like a caterer, Alice poured fresh tortilla chips into a big wooden bowl, poured the Flores salsa roja into a pitcher, and placed the stack of still-hot tortillas, wrapped in foil, on the folding table.

"Okay, folks! Come meet Alice!" Bender called.

Alice waved at Wayland and Gordon. Bender introduced the new arrivals: "Alice, meet Jock Dickinson—known as Dr. GPR. Also, his assistant, Katie Buenz. She's got her anthropology degree and is now training on GPR. We'll hear more from them once we get some results."

"GPR?"

"Ground Penetrating Radar. It's used to locate utilities. Archeologists use it to try to locate artifacts, and sometimes bodies. It may be our best chance of finding whatever it is you're looking for."

She looked again into their faces. Jock Dickinson: forty-something, intent, non-smiling, dark-haired. Katie Buenz: big smile, dimples, sharp eyes. Both looked like they spent most of their time outdoors.

Alice shook their hands. "I can't wait to hear about GPR. Thank you so much for being here."

"Thanks to Alice, it's time to eat," Bender announced. Suddenly the table was mobbed with hungry scholars ladling Flores enchiladas onto plates, adding tortillas, adding salsa. Silla's molasses sugar cookies were disappearing faster than snow in sunshine. Alice waited until the line dwindled to Silla and Bender, then filled her plate and sat down next to them.

Beyond the firelight she saw two odd orange-painted pieces of equipment—like lawnmowers, with double long handles but with a central insert that looked like a computer. "What are those?" she asked.

"GPR systems," Bender said. "We're starting tomorrow morning."

"How does it work, GPR?"

"Radio waves. The radio signal goes down through soil, water, whatever, and bounces back in a way that can identify a difference in reflectivity between the subsurface and a target. For example, if we see something large and metal, it will send back a distinctive wave. Subsurface reflectivity depends on whether it's clay—that's bad—or rocks, or sand. And whether the subsurface is wet or dry. A pile of rocks reflects differently than a layer of clay. I don't think we'll see clay in the draw. And I hope this weather holds. There's a bit of water still, but we sure don't want flooding."

"Can you really spot bodies? A skeleton?" Alice asked.

Bender exhaled. "Well, with bones, it depends. If they're dry bones—maybe. But bones that have been in water may not reflect too differently from water. That makes bones exposed to water harder to spot. And if they've been soaked for nearly two centuries? But now, if we saw something metal—that would be highly reflective."

"You mean—like a belt buckle?"

"Right, but that would also be pretty small. I'm worried about using the GPR equipment in the bottom of the draw. We need to draw a workable grid with our equipment, with pretty narrow lines. It would be easy to miss something small. Anyway—GPR is a slow, tedious process. We've laid out a couple of grids. We'll run the equipment in perpendicular directions. We don't want to miss anything. But Alice,

I've got to warn you."

"What?"

"GPR is often used in nice flat grassy cemeteries. It can identify, say, a wooden coffin, or a body inside a coffin, where the chest is still full of air. But I'm not sure we'll succeed, trying to run these machines along the bottom of a rocky creek full of boulders."

Her heart sank.

"If we could just find the Fischers' bodies..." she muttered.

"It's been 180 years."

"I know."

"Reportedly nobody found them back in 1847."

"But who knew where they were left? And what about the Comanche victims? Where exactly will you be looking?"

"Upstream, for the Comanches. That's assuming they killed the horse and washed its meat downstream of where they were cooking. Meaning they cooked it upstream of where Silla points out Riley would have led his horse down a couple of switchbacks to reach the bottom of the gulch where he staked the horse." Bender sighed. "If the Comanches had any metal on them—that would be much more reflective, for GPR purposes."

"Maybe a knife? To cut the meat?"

He nodded. "Maybe. Of course, a knife could have rusted away, given the time frame."

Damn, Alice thought. She wanted proof sufficient to deter Winifred Hutton from bollixing up the judge's history.

"But I'm warning you now, Alice, if we do detect any Native American remains, I'm not turning a trowel. First thing we do is be sure to comply with NAGPRA."

"With what?"

"Native American Graves Protection and Repatriation Act. My understanding is the judge's property isn't within tribal lands under NAGPRA, but we'll double-check. In any event, I'd recommend we get in touch with the Comanche Nation up in Oklahoma."

The judge would do whatever the law required, and more. He'd bend over backwards, Alice thought.

Bender continued. "As to the Fischers? We've hypothesized that since he was in an all-fired hurry, Jasper Riley climbed down to the bottom of the gulch, climbed up the other side to where the Fischers lay, then threw their bodies down into the gulch and dumped dirt and rocks on them. *Maybe* their bodies are still somewhere in the draw, what with boulders and tree roots, but we all know how ferociously it floods when a rain bomb hits. Frankly, their bodies and the Comanche bodies may have been washed into Blue Creek over a century ago."

Damn again, Alice thought.

But something bothered her now about the image of Riley shoving the Fischers' bodies down into the draw. She wasn't sure why.

"Alice!" Silla exclaimed. "Check out the moonrise!"

In the east, across the draw, an enormous golden moon floated silently above the horizon.

A great horned owl boomed its low call off in the trees. Another owl answered.

Wayland put more logs on the bonfire. Sparks flew.

Alice peeked at Silla, talking to Bender, her face alight. Alice smiled to herself. Wonder if Silla will stay out here tonight...?

She herself shivered and stood, surveying the tents, the faces around the bonfire, the deep darkness in the woods across the draw. She hoped nothing would disturb these active scholars, these investigators of the past, as they lay in their sleeping bags tonight, alone...or otherwise.

"I'll come by tomorrow. Thanks, everyone!" She waved at the archeologists and Silla and walked back to her car, still shivering in the chilly night air. She drove home feeling very alone. She punched in the gate code, watched the gate swing open, and drove down the driveway to her dark silent house. So quiet, out here. She unlocked the door, flicked on some lights. Sleeping alone on this winter night held no appeal. She kept thinking of the bodies in the draw, of Jasper Riley's fury, of little Emil Fischer watching as shots rang out.

But after this day—after the confrontation with Winifred Hutton—Alice was bone-weary. She fell asleep with the bedside lamp still on, reminding herself that, thank God, Kinsear would be back tomorrow.

Chapter Seventeen

Ask Forgiveness Of Corpses?

Sunday morning. Son John called from Edinburgh, where he was finishing a master's in economics. "Freezing cold, Mom," he announced. "Why did I pick the northern edge of the planet?"

"Good weather for thesis writing?"

He groaned. "Yeah. I worked on it all morning. But we've got a football game this afternoon." He meant rugby. She hoped he'd protect his brain case.

Daughter Ann called from Boston—last semester of her senior year. "Everything's covered in ice. Yesterday I crunched all the way to the library!" But she conceded that later she and her roomies had filched serving trays from the kitchen and gone sledding down the hill behind the dorm. Along with their dates. "I'll send pix, Mom. Gotta go!"

Alice checked the weather. Still fair, chilly—highs near 60, though—and no rain. She gritted her teeth, remembering Winifred Hutton's visit. Maybe today the orange GPR machines would succeed in finding proof of Chapter 13.

Meanwhile, a little house tidying, then church. Laura McDowell, Alice's favorite, was preaching. She warned the congregation that her sermon might set everyone's teeth on edge. "You know, just because some characters made it into the Old Testament—or the New—doesn't mean they acted like saints. Moses's siblings, Aaron and Miriam, fought. Peter denied Jesus. Jacob robbed Esau of his rightful inheritance. Jonah refused to accept his preaching assignment. Moses didn't even get to cross over into Canaan. But ultimately—they were faithful. We can't be perfect. We try, we fail. And indeed, perhaps our text includes stories about these non-saints because—despite their flaws—they ultimately kept the faith. Perhaps all of us have kept a secret; something we did that we don't want to confess. But my guess is that everyone in this sanctuary is still trying to be faithful. Otherwise—would we be here?" She laughed.

Interesting, Alice thought. She had sins she didn't plan to confess, pretended didn't exist. She didn't believe in absolution. But she did believe in—what? Persisting, maybe.

Suddenly Jasper Riley came to mind. Had he ever regretted what he did?

Hmm. What if he had? What if he'd sought forgiveness? Would that change her scornful assessment of the man?

How do you ask forgiveness of corpses?

The choir rose for an anthem Alice had never heard, based on Acts 17:26, with a solo from Alice's favorite soprano. Up soared her voice, on "the bounds of their habitation."

Departing, Alice got a hug from Laura, who asked, "How's Kinsear?"

"Fine. He'll get back from New York this afternoon."

"Well, I'm ready whenever you are!" She'd promised to officiate at the wedding.

Alice smiled. "To be announced!"

She headed for the office. Surely the judge had some footnotes to support Chapter 13? She checked her phone for the umpteenth time. Nothing yet from the archeologists.

Alice spent the next few hours at her desk, reviewing every word on every page of the remaining material in the judge's footnote folder, hoping for definitive evidence supporting Emil Fischer's tale of the murder of Fritz and Frieda Fischer at the hands of Jasper Riley. The judge had pulled together a copy of Fritz Fischer's earlier handwritten complaint filed in the old county court, alleging Jasper Riley's repeated trespasses and destruction of the Fischers' rock walls. The judge's notes indicated he'd consulted Coffee County historical records but found nothing more on Fritz Fischer's complaint. As to newspapers, the first edition of the *Neu Braunfelser Zeitung* came out in nearby New Braunfels only in 1852, five years after the murders, and the first edition of the *Coffee Creek Caller* wasn't published until 1853. The Texas Historical Commission, with its 600-plus historical markers on Texas highways, contained no record of Jasper Riley or the murders in Coffee County. Judge Mahan had consulted the Bullock State History Museum: "Struck out again," said his handwritten note. He'd also scanned the digitized newspapers at the Dolph Briscoe Center for American History: "Nothing."

Alice rubbed her eyes, thinking. If the judge—retired, with all the contacts and resources available to a federal judge—hadn't found historical evidence, should she even try? But what about genealogy re-cords?

He'd labeled the last group of papers in the footnote folder "Fischer Family Docs." First came a photocopy of a page from a family Bible—the first entry, in German, in 1837, documented the wedding of Fritz Fischer and Frieda Meyer; the second, in 1839, recorded baby Emil Fischer's birth. Then came a photocopy of pages from the journal of Emil's aunt, Jutta Meyer. She'd later signed and dated the pages in May 1857, ten years after the murders. Clipped to the journal pages was a copy of Emil's description of the deaths as told to the Lutheran pastor in Coffee Creek. The judge's sticky note said both photocopies came from the records of Coffee Creek Lutheran Church. The next set of photocopies bore a sticky note in the judge's handwriting stating they came "from Mrs. Lizzie Bond, Taylor, Texas, Jutta Meyer's great-granddaughter." He'd scribbled down a street address. The first page contained Lizzie Bond's recollections, handwritten and dated in January 2022. She wrote that family lore claimed that Jutta Meyer's memory never changed and that Jutta Meyer remained on the lookout lest Jasper Riley or any of his relatives ever returned to Coffee County. Lizzie Bond also reported that, according to family history, Emil Fischer's medical studies at Tulane in 1859 were interrupted by the Civil War, in which Emil served as a medic; after the war ended, with the Tulane medical school in disarray, Emil traveled to Baltimore to finish his medical training.

Lizzie's note ended, "I have asked my neighbor Cindy to help me locate any descendants of Emil Fischer." But the judge's sticky note reported Lizzie Bond died in March 2022.

Lizzie Bond provided two additional documents: a photocopy of the 1867 deed from Emil to his Aunt Jutta and Uncle Horst Meyer, reciting that he was giving them his family's tract as recompense for their support for him and payment for his medical school tuition. She also attached a photocopy of a brief letter from Emil to his Aunt Jutta. The cramped writing read: "I carry Papa's pocket watch with me always, the one that you found in his waistcoat at the cabin. It's all I have of him or of my beloved mother. I shall never sell or give it away but shall wear it forever."

Alice felt her eyes sting. That young man, so alone.

The judge attached one more document: a photocopy of a hand-written complaint filed in October 1847 in Coffee Creek court by Horst Meyer on behalf of the Fischer family, alleging theft of property from the Fischers' cabin, including "a small leather bag of ten German gold coins bearing dates from 1838 to 1846" and "a black leather case containing four pocket watches of value, being one gold key-winding pocket watch made in London by John Hyde, one gold pocket watch made in England by M. J. Tobias, one Swiss quarter-hour repeater pocket watch, and one gold key-wound pocket watch made in Paris by LeRoy & Cie., each marked by the initials FF on the back." The judge's sticky note: "Nothing more in the court archive."

Alice closed the folder in frustration and dropped it on her desk. Horst Meyer's handwritten complaint—though interesting—led no-where. The judge's last "to-do's" were still undone, and even if more family memories could be found—were they *evidence*? Evidence she could rely on in getting the judge's history published? Evidence worth jeopardizing Riley's campaign, per Hutton's accusation? Evidence worth running the risk of a defamation lawsuit against the Historical Commission—or the judge's estate?

She vowed to run the defamation issue past Kinsear when he got back. Maybe he'd call soon.

*****

Her cell rang—but it was Silla, not Kinsear.

"How's the dig going?" Alice asked.

"Long day so far, and I didn't get here until early afternoon." Silla's voice lacked its usual bounce. "Don't know how these guys can stand this GPR grid work. Back and forth! Stay in your lane! Not easy, down on that rocky gulch bottom. We were looking for the Comanche bod-ies on the half of the gulch closest to where Riley supposedly climbed down. Nothing so far."

"Rats," Alice said. "No knife? No bullets?"

"Couple of fishhooks. Modern."

"What's next?

"Set up a new grid on the other side of the gulch and start there tomorrow."

"How come they couldn't do the whole width of the bottom of the gulch today?"

"Your grid has to have narrow lanes or you might miss a key target. And Lord, Alice, the gulch is nothing but rocks."

"Nothing yet on the Fischers' bodies?"

"Nope. Maybe they'll have better luck tomorrow. See you then."

Alice hung up. She stared out her office window at empty Live Oak Street and felt her shoulders sag. She'd hoped for results, for a find, for facts.

As she watched, Kinsear's elderly Land Cruiser pulled up at the curb.

She opened the office door and met him on the sidewalk. Kisses. More kisses.

Kinsear looked at her inquiringly. "You look a little down. Even with me making my usual impressive appearance. Gonna tell me what's up?"

Alice recapped the week, including the grand finale—Winifred Hutton's visit. "To top that off, Silla called and said the dig hasn't found anything yet. And I need for those archeologists to find some proof!"

"It's only five," Kinsear said. "What if we pick up some barbecue for them? I'd like to see Bender again."

He and Bender had met on a steep hillside in Coffee County when Bender helped excavate the body of a long-lost singer.

Alice glanced at him, loving the touch of gray in his curls, the light in his brown eyes. "Brilliant. Although they're getting spoiled—we took them breakfast and dinner yesterday." She called Silla back. "You still there? Kinsear's offering barbecue for all."

"What a man. Resounding thank you. I was just about to go pick up burgers or something. Okay, hurry up! I'm starting to drool!"

*****

Kinsear phoned Pig Pen BBQ in Dripping Springs and placed a large order.

"Heavens. They'll have enough for breakfast too," Alice laughed.

"Nothing wrong with brisket for breakfast when you're outside digging in the cold," he retorted.

Armed with a load of brisket sandwiches, pulled pork sandwiches, ribs, coleslaw, and beans, they turned off Highway 290 and headed south toward Blue Creek, then turned onto the road toward Willie Craig's store. Twilight had fallen. As they passed the store, an enormous dark pickup truck roared toward them, halfway over the center line. Alice veered onto the shoulder, furious. "Talk about taking your half out of the middle!" she gasped. "I hate those big trucks with huge brush guards! What do they think they're doing, fighting a war?"

"Dangerous," Kinsear muttered. "Who were those guys?"

"Were there two?"

"Yep."

As they neared the 90-degree left turn onto Geisberg Lane, Alice slowed sharply for the unbanked curve with its flashing yellow warning light. "Local name, Dead Man's Curve," she said, straightening the car. "Always a thrill. Okay, now it's barely a mile to the judge's driveway."

"Stop! What's that?!"

Startled, Alice jammed the brakes and pulled onto the right shoulder, wary of the drop-off.

"See those lights down there?" He was out of the car in a flash.

Fifty feet away, downhill, headlights lit up the trees, headlights at an odd angle.

Alice turned on her flashers and hurried to the side of the road. She spotted the stylized "H" on the rear of the small black car. A Honda...

"Call 911!" yelled Kinsear. He was putting his cellphone on flashlight. "One driver."

Johnny. Johnny's car. Alice fumbled for her own phone, got EMS, gave them the location. "On the road you'll see my green Discovery! The wreck's downhill below the road."

"Keep your phone on, ma'am. We're on the way."

Clutching her phone, Alice hurried down the rough slope, grabbing saplings to slow herself, thinking the nearest EMS team was at the intersection with Highway 290. How many minutes?

She reached Kinsear, who stood by the driver's-side window, the safety glass starred with impact.

"That's Johnny," she said, staring through the cracked glass, her stomach in a knot. "Judge Mahan's grandson. Is he alive? What do we do?"

"I think the doors are locked, or jammed. But his head's still bleeding, so he's still alive." The shaggy blond hair, leaning against the window, had red patches. A trickle of blood crept down the glass. "We could break out the other window and get in, but I'm afraid to move him, with a head injury. And maybe neck."

Alice hurried around to the passenger door, frantic to help Johnny. Yes, locked.

"The right rear took a big hit," Kinsear said.

"So did this side," Alice said. "The window's cracked, and the door's all scraped, like it hit a tree."

Lights, noise, the piercing wail of a siren. Alice clambered back uphill as the ambulance slid to a stop behind her car. One EMT hurried downhill toward Kinsear; two others began pulling out a stretcher.

"It's Johnny Mahan, Judge Mahan's grandson," she told them. "We were heading to Judge Mahan's place when we saw the headlights down there."

She heard another siren. Police.

Her phone rang—Silla. "Alice? You okay? We're starving, is all."

"Listen, Johnny's car went off the road. EMTs are here. Can you come get the barbecue? We're just down Geisberg, not far from the judge's driveway."

"Oh no! Johnny just left! I'll be right there."

A Coffee County police cruiser pulled over and parked. Alice recognized Deputy Everett Berry as he walked across the road to her. She also recognized the other deputy from the judge's murder scene—Gerald Olson—as he jumped out of the cruiser and hurried downhill toward the EMTs.

"We meet again," Deputy Berry said, pulling his notebook from his pocket. He looked down the road as Silla's headlights approached. She slowed, parked her truck on the other side of the road, and ran across to Alice and Berry. Kinsear had left the EMTs to their work. He climbed back up to the road and joined the group.

"Ms. Greer, do you know who's in the car down there?" asked Berry.

"It's Judge Mahan's grandson, Johnny," Alice said. "He'd just left the judge's place."

Silla nodded. "He'd stopped by before his bartender gig in San Marcos. Said he needed to be there by six."

Berry: "When did he leave you?"

"About five-fifteen."

Berry again: "Would he have gotten there on time?"

Checking if Johnny was speeding, Alice thought.

"Yes," Silla said. "He had a good forty-five minutes. The bar's only thirty minutes away."

Olson climbed back up and motioned to Berry. The two conferred, then returned, facing Silla. Berry asked: "Did you see his car when he got to the judge's today?"

"Yes."

"Was it dented?"

"No."

"How do you know?"

She glared. "I went to meet him when he got to the judge's place. We talked. I introduced him to the archeologists."

"There's a big hit on the right rear, looks new. Rear taillight's smashed. Did you see any of that when he left you?"

"No."

"What about the passenger door?

"No. I'd have seen that side and the rear of the car when he left."

Deputy Berry turned to Alice, notebook ready. "Tell me what you saw, why you're here."

"Ben Kinsear and I picked up barbecue at Pig Pen's, for the archeology team at the judge's," Alice said. "We'd passed Willie's store when a huge black pickup, big brush guard, nearly blew us off the road. Partly in our lane. When we got around Dead Man's Curve, Ben saw the headlights downhill, off the road. They were tilted that weird way. We stopped. He went down to see the car, and I called EMS."

Berry turned to Kinsear. "You didn't touch anything?"

"No. The boy's head was against the window," he said. "I could see the blood. I was afraid to move him, worried about his neck."

"What about the black pickup? Any identification? License? Decals?"

Alice and Kinsear glanced at each other, then shook their heads. "It was coming at us so fast, I almost had to run off the road," she said. "I think it was a Dodge Ram. That ram's head on the front grille."

"Crew cab," Kinsear said. "Black brush guard. Two men in the front. That's all I got."

Alice watched Olson, flashlight aloft, walking slowly down the road in the lane Johnny would have been driving from the judge's place. He bent, shining his flashlight at the pavement. Alice saw a few red sparkles. Johnny's taillight? That should convince the cops that he'd been hit.

Olson waved to Berry, then called, "Traffic cones and tape. And lights."

The EMTs had extracted Johnny from his car and were inching their way back uphill, carrying the gurney. They slid the gurney into the back of the ambulance. An EMT began attaching an IV.

The ambulance pulled away, lights flashing. Another cruiser arrived; deputies set up crime scene tape and floodlights around an area of pavement. A crime scene team surrounded Johnny's car.

Silla and Alice stowed the barbecue in Silla's truck. Silla handed brisket sandwiches to Berry and Olson before carefully turning her truck, avoiding Olson's traffic cones and tape, on her way back to the judge's place.

"You know where to find me," Alice told Berry. "Kinsear and I need to follow Johnny to the hospital."

Kinsear handed Berry his card.

Alice looked at Berry's face. "First his grandfather, now this. Will Johnny be safe in the hospital? If he lives?"

Chapter Eighteen

Wasn't An Accident

Alice held Kinsear's comforting hand as they stood at the ER window at St. David's South. "Can we see Johnny Mahan? Can you tell us how he is?"

The clerk looked at his computer screen. "Auto accident out near Geisberg Lane?"

"Yes," Alice whispered. She didn't think it was an accident.

The clerk frowned, staring at the screen. "He's not allowed any visitors. Um, there are police with him."

"Is it by chance Detective Files? Can you tell him or whoever's there that Alice Greer is here? I'm—I represent his grandfather."

The clerk nodded. "I'll let someone know."

Alice and Kinsear found two chairs together. Alice looked around at the faces—anxious mothers, fathers, girlfriends, boyfriends, maybe elderly spouses. People were quiet. She saw a few empty seats on this Sunday night; she expected it had been a zoo the night before.

Kinsear put his arm around her shoulders, gave her a firm squeeze.

"This isn't how I planned our evening," she whispered.

The door to the treatment rooms opened. Detective George Files scanned the room, spotted Alice, tilted his head, motioned her toward the hallway behind him. Kinsear joined her. Bright lights, scurrying RNs and MDs and techs in scrubs; gurneys along the walls.

"He's alive. Badly concussed. But he can move hands and feet. At the moment they hope he won't need surgery."

Alice let out her breath, closed her eyes, opened them again. "Will you have someone watching his room?"

"You think that accident wasn't an accident?"

"I'm very worried that it wasn't," she said.

"Why would someone try to harm Johnny Mahan?" Files asked.

"Or scare the shit out of him?" Kinsear added.

"Well," Alice began, "he's now the heir to the judge's place. Someone who doesn't want any more digging out there might think getting Johnny out of the way would solve that problem."

"But it wouldn't, right?" Files asked. "Aren't you charged with getting the archeology completed? And publishing the judge's book?"

She nodded.

"Even if that puts Johnny in harm's way?"

Lights, smells of alcohol and cleaning solution, dinging bells. Alice felt nauseous.

It wasn't just the hospital smells and sounds that made her feel sick: it was the choice Files described—failing the judge versus leaving Johnny in harm's way. Surely she needed to avoid both. "He's safe here? You've got someone watching? All night, and after he gets moved to another floor?" she pressed Files.

"At the moment. Okay, I've got to go. The nurses said you can probably see him tomorrow."

"Can someone let him know we came?"

He nodded and opened the door back into the waiting room, where every face looked up hopefully as they entered, then fell.

*****

"I'm starving," said Kinsear.

"We gave away all the barbecue! What were we thinking, not to keep any?" Alice groaned.

"It's just gone eight. Tillie's is still open." He called, pleaded, thanked them.

They retrieved his car at her office, left it at her place, and raced toward Tillie's. In ten minutes they'd navigated the winding road along Onion Creek and were at a favorite table, with a view of the old Vietnamese ironwood piers and the artwork on the walls. Alice lifted her flute of prosecco and touched his glass. "Well, welcome home. Again, not quite how I planned it. But I'm so glad you're back."

She knew he'd stay the night.

And in an hour, Kinsear signaled for the check, met her eyes, and said, "Let's go home."

*****

At four a.m. Alice slipped out of bed, crept out onto the kitchen deck, shivering, and gazed up at the winter stars. The Milky Way lay like a glittering stole across the heavens. In the west the gibbous moon was setting, turning a streak of cloud to silver. She hurried back in, slipped back into bed, keeping her icy feet away from Kinsear's warm legs. She thought of her John and Ann, then of Johnny in the hospital...his mother and grandparents dead, and had anyone called Eric Mahan? She got out of bed again, found her phone, and texted Johnny's dad, apologizing for the late night message. "I'll check on him again tomorrow and can take a message. I assume his phone is with him—will check," she promised.

How fast that black truck had hurtled toward her car! With what force, she thought, it must have slammed into Johnny's fender. Life was so fragile, death so sudden...

Again she slipped back into bed, still tucking her icy feet away from Kinsear. She snuggled up next to him until she felt his hand reach for and enfold hers. And so they lay, until the hour before dawn, when Kinsear proposed intriguing rearrangements, each more and more satisfying to each of them. She held him tight, then tighter, aware every second of the joy of being together. Then the moon was down; the room was dark; they sank back into sleep until sunrise.

*****

Monday morning. Alice made coffee while Kinsear grated longhorn cheddar and chopped up some cream cheese for his famous "extra cheesy" scrambled eggs. While he cooked he got on the phone with Javier, who took care of Kinsear's ranch outside Fredericksburg. "I'll be there in an hour with a new float for the horse tank."

Alice tugged on jeans, her mid-calf cowgirl boots, flannel shirt, and a fleece jacket, and followed Kinsear to his car. He kissed Alice in the driveway. "Here's hoping your archeologists have better luck today." And he was gone.

Alice stood a moment in the morning chill, looking across her pasture. After all those hours schlepping bags of winter rye seed up and down the gravel drive, seeding the bare spots, seeding the roadside, she was gratified to see new green swaths of rye. A nice change from winter's dry tawny grass.

Across the pasture, on the edge of the ravine that crossed her property and ran down to the creek, early sun lit the silvery limestone rocks that some settler decades ago had stacked into an unmortared wall. In the Hill Country, rain slowly ate away at the layers of limestone, old seabed, that lay below the thin soil, leaving fields full of rocks, many at least a foot in diameter. Early settlers, arriving well before the advent of barbed wire, slowly stacked the rocks into stone fences for their livestock.

Back when the prior owner ran cows on this land, building that rock wall was a labor-intensive but cheap way to keep cows out of the ravine. Now she noted a couple of gaps in the wall. Were they created when kids unstacked the rocks, looking for a quick way to scramble down to the occasional pools below?

Alice walked toward a gap in the rock wall at the edge of the ravine, enjoying the way the sun lit up the gold and orange lichen on the rocks. The gap opened to a narrow flat stretch of ground, then plunged down through a tangle of cedar and oak to the bottom of the ravine, which usually held a little wet-weather creek. Deer bedded down by the creek, but the ravine was so steep her burros chose not to try to reach water that way. Indeed, she'd never seen them graze beyond the gap.

Rainwater slowly pried loose the fossils in the rocks—snail shells, oyster shells, clam shells the size of a fist, which Alice's kids collected with gusto. Exposed rocks grew as holey as Swiss cheese but remained impressively heavy. What had settlers thought about those fossils?

She started back toward her house, then stopped. Turning in a slow circle, she looked north, east, south, and finally west, toward the old rock wall. "The bounds of their habitation," she murmured, loving that line. As she walked back, she thought of little Emil Fischer, helping his dad roll rocks to the edge of their pasture to make a wall. She pulled her cellphone from her pocket.

"Bender? I've had a thought."

"Thoughts are welcome. Thoughts are needed. Come on out."

"In a bit." First, she'd agreed to meet Dedra Riley at the office at nine. Then she needed to check on Johnny.

Chapter Nineteen

Armed All The Time

Richard Riley's wife was right on time. She drove a mom-mo-bile—a bulky silver SUV with three rows of seats and a "Coffee Creek Schools" decal on the rear window. Alice watched from her office window as Dedra Riley sat, staring at her lap—at her phone, probably—then out the windshield. Finally she climbed out and walked slowly to the office. Mom clothes too: nice jeans, chic shirt, down vest.

Since Silla wasn't in yet—picking up mail—Alice met Dedra Riley at the door. "Come on back to the conference room." Her office was private space...clients only. Dedra Riley wasn't a client. Or even a friend.

They sat. Alice waited, lifting an eyebrow. She didn't intend to start the conversation.

"Thanks for agreeing to meet with me," Dedra Riley said, after an awkward moment. She didn't seem to know where to begin.

The conference room door opened—Silla, back from the post office. "Coffee?" she asked.

Dedra nodded gratefully.

Alice said nothing. She hadn't called this meeting. What did this woman want?

When they'd stirred and sipped their coffee, Dedra took a breath and said, "You're wondering why I'm here."

"Right."

"I wanted to ask you about—about one chapter in Judge Mahan's county history."

"Yes?" No reason to make this easy for this candidate; any reason to go easy on his wife?

"Is it true that you—that you're in charge of the judge's history?"

"I can't discuss client matters, Mrs. Riley."

"Please call me Dedra!" Her face was turning pink, the brown eyes anxious. "I heard about part of the book from Winifred Hutton. She's—she's helping fund my husband's campaign."

Alice waited.

Dedra shifted in her chair, eyes on Alice, her anxiety almost palpable. "The part about a man shooting—shooting Indians who were stealing his horse. Cooking his horse."

"And shooting two small children. And also shooting his neighbors," Alice added. Might as well fend off *ab initio* any claim that horse stealing (and worse, horse cooking) was a capital crime and that Riley had simply and justifiably taken the law into his own hands. "What about the Fischers?"

"But no one ever found the neighbors! They probably just ran off!"

Alice waited some more.

"I mean, there's no *proof* he killed the neighbors!"

"The Fischers' son told his aunt and later his pastor the story of what happened. Documents show this."

"But maybe he just made it up because he wanted to excuse his parents for running away!"

"There's no evidence they ran away. Why would they run away from their only son?"

"Parents get tired!" Dedra cried. "Parenthood's hard."

Now Alice had a crying wife in the conference room. She got the box of tissues from the credenza and handed it to Dedra.

"I've got three children," Dedra sniffed. "At Coffee Creek Elementary." She looked up, face pleading. "Nancy's five, Anna's seven, and Shawn is ten. I don't want their classmates hearing that a guy named Riley shot Indian children!" So those children mattered, after all?

Alice cocked her head. "But what if it's true? Your husband Richard is related to Jasper Riley, then?"

Dedra hunched her shoulders. "I've never done the research. But..."

"But Winifred Hutton?"

"I think she's checked into it, and she thinks Richard's—Richard's related."

"Did you know she came to see me Saturday?"

Dedra shifted in her chair. "She—she mentioned she might speak to you."

"That's one way you could describe it." Alice leaned forward, scanning Dedra's face. "You want Richard to win this state rep seat?"

Dedra furrowed her brow, staring at Alice. "Yes. He—he needs this career. It'll be good for him." She paused momentarily. "I mean, he'll be good at it."

Alice thought of the string of law firms where Richard Riley had briefly been employed. "Not really cut out for law practice?" That was the kindest way to put it.

"That's true," Dedra sniffed. "He's—he's more interested in policy issues, I think. I've gone back to work part time as a nurse. But I'm hoping—I'm hoping—"

All too clearly his wife just hoped he'd finally make some money. But would he be a mere puppet for Winifred Hutton?

"Does Richard have his own ideas about good government policies? You're not afraid he'll be forever tied to Winifred Hutton?"

Dedra stiffened, let out a long breath. "That woman. She—she just takes over everything. She's always coming by to talk to Richard. I can't get a word in edgewise. I don't really like her being around the children, either. She's armed all the time! Even in my house!"

"Armed?"

"You know that hand-tooled leather purse?"

Alice nodded.

"She takes it everywhere. She carries her dad's gun in that bag. She adored her dad, apparently."

"What kind of gun?"

"I don't know. She told us but—I try to block gun stuff out. My— my brother was shot when he was thirteen."

Alice was horrified. "Shot—how?"

"His friend was 'showing him dad's gun.' And it went off. And my brother died. Gut-shot."

"I am so sorry," Alice said. Maybe that was another reason Dedra didn't want to hear any of the Jasper Riley story.

Dedra looked down at her hands, clenched in her lap. After a moment, she lifted her head. "She's kind of a gun nut. I mean, upstairs she has some old pistol—I think it's a pretty famous Colt—framed on her wall, with a plaque, like it's—oh, a shrine or something!"

"A—a Colt pistol?" Alice asked. "Walker Colt?"

Silence.

"Never mind. That's not why I came," Dedra said. "I just hope you'll keep that story— about—about Jasper Riley shooting the Comanches who killed his horse—out of the county history. There's no evidence! It would be so damaging to Richard's candidacy."

"What about Riley shooting the neighbors, the Fischers?" Alice asked again. "The written record's part of the evidence." Maybe—she mentally crossed her fingers—maybe GPR would reveal *something*...

"But there was no trial, no nothing! Please think about my children," Dedra pleaded.

"And if it turns out to be true? If more evidence is found? Then what?" Alice demanded.

Dedra's face went blank. "If more evidence is found? I hadn't thought of that. Surely that won't happen, at this late date."

"If it does, what will you tell your children? Point out they're not genetic copies of Jasper Riley? They're the sum of all their relatives!"

Dedra gazed at Alice for a minute. "If you were a kid, what would you think?" She gave Alice a pleading look, then picked up her purse. "Thanks for letting me come by. I hope you'll—you'll think about my kids."

Alice wanted to respond—"But not about those Comanche kids? Or the Fischers' kid?" But she contented herself with, "You understand my job is to meet my own legal obligations."

Dedra looked puzzled. She frowned, started to speak, then slowly stood and turned toward the conference room door.

Alice opened it for her, followed her down the hall, and closed the front door behind her.

Now Alice felt wrong-footed, uncharitable, unsure. Had she messed up this meeting? Would the judge's history screw up Dedra's children? If so, what responsibility would Alice bear, if she left Chapter 13 as it was?

How would she feel if Ann and John were told the story of one of Alice's own relatively wicked ancestors? Because, indeed, one ancestor had fled to Mexico after at least allegedly shooting a man during Reconstruction. Would Ann and John feel tainted by the mark of Cain? Or would they feel like Alice did—untouched by a story of uncertain provenance and wobbly facts? Yes, she knew of other family tales on her side as well and suspected there were plenty she didn't know about. And that didn't count legends of Jordie's fierce Scottish forebears, brandishing their claymore swords.

Alice's working assumption was that families generally ascribe virtue to their own ancestors—hard work, good behavior, frugality, good taste. Maybe they give all that credit without taking into account other factors. What about luck? About being in the right place at the right time? About their ship of immigrants not being the one that sank in the Atlantic? About the sheriff who was a friend of your ancestor coming by one night to warn a wild young son, "Better leave town tonight, and don't come back for at least a year"? Alice thought her family, probably every family, had some problematic ancestors who got in trouble and conveniently disappeared for a time, like that wild young son. But the stories about disgraced or criminal ancestors generally were only oral, were somehow omitted from the written family history. So weren't our family histories inaccurate by omission?

Time to visit Johnny. But she still worried about Dedra's question: "If you were a kid, what would you think?"

She told Silla where she was going and stewed all the way to St. David's South.

Chapter Twenty

The Bounds Of Their Habitation

A large uniformed man stood up abruptly from the chair outside Johnny's room. He checked a notepad. "Okay. Alice Greer, you're on my list. Five minutes, the nurse says."

Johnny was propped up in bed, two black eyes, bruising all down the left side of his head. His green hospital gown was tied loosely around his neck. Alice could see marks, maybe from the seatbelt, on the right side of his neck and the top of his left shoulder.

"Beep!" The automatic blood pressure machine sent its message to the nurse's station.

Johnny still had the shocked, puzzled look of someone who'd been minding his own business, driving down his own side of the road, when inexplicable violence exploded. But he apparently needed to make some sense of the event and slowly told Alice what happened.

"I'd been at the dig. I really enjoyed hearing the archeologists talk about the project." He managed a smile. "I've never known exactly what they do—it's really interesting. But I wanted to be on time for my shift at the Last Corral. I remember leaving Granddad's place. I turned onto the road and thought how dark it was. Then suddenly there were big headlights in my rearview, coming up fast. I thought they wanted to pass me—but then, WHAM! I tried to keep control but—no way. I just remember gripping the wheel, with trees banging the car on the right side."

Alice had been wondering about something. "Did you remember seeing that truck before? Black Ram Charger, crew cab. Big brush-guard in front."

"I don't know—oh." He looked at the ceiling, thinking. "Maybe in the parking lot, at the Last Corral. I can't swear to that."

"You get a young crowd there, mostly?"

He nodded.

"Remember seeing two guys, one 50-ish, beer gut, the other skinnier, younger, possibly in jeans and cowboy shirts?"

Johnny leaned his head back on the pillow, closed his eyes. "Maybe."

The nurse stuck her head in. "We got your phone charged."

"Oh good!" he said. "Thanks."

Alice shook her head, smiling. A twenty-something without a

phone? Unimaginable. But she had a new question. "Johnny, you said it was dark when you turned onto the road. Then, suddenly, lights behind you. Where do you think they came from so fast?"

"Oh," he said, looking up at her. "Yes, I see. I'll bet the truck turned out of that overgrown driveway, the one that had the cut chain on it." He frowned. "But who?"

He glanced back down at his phone, then looked up at her, eyes wide. "My dad's coming!" He stared back down at the message, then up at Alice. "He says you texted him!"

"Of course I did. He'd want to know."

"Well—but he's apparently on a flight to Austin right now!"

"That's okay, isn't it?"

Johnny settled back on the pillow again, staring at the ceiling. "We don't always get along. But I'm glad he's coming."

The nurse stuck her head back in. "Five minutes are up."

Alice found herself leaning over, reflexively planning to kiss Johnny's head—but no. Bruises everywhere. And she wasn't even related. Maybe he'd get a kiss from his dad? But she felt very proud of Johnny, so she told him so, promising she'd report later if the archeologists had found anything today.

*****

Next stop, the judge's place. Crime scene tape still flapped at Dead Man's Curve. Alice drove cautiously down the judge's driveway and waved at Bender, standing by the tents, holding a coffee mug.

"The bounds of their habitation..." she thought, wishing she could sing like that soprano.

Bender met her as she parked by the drive. "We're having a heck of a time with the GPR in this rocky gulch," he said. "Archeologists love dirt. Rock, maybe not so much. But still, we have hope. We're moving the GPR grid to this side, up just above the little pool. Maybe we'll get lucky."

"Come with me," Alice said. She led Bender, skirting the remnants of the old gray rock wall that paralleled the gulch, several feet away. She reached the point where the wall petered out, creating a gap, maybe six feet wide. Wider, Alice thought, than Emil would need to climb down to get water. Beyond the gap Alice saw the flat shelf that ran along the back of the rock wall before reaching the steep slope slanting down to the bottom of the gulch, covered with a tangle of spiky-branched cedar. Because you wouldn't build your rock wall right on the edge of the gulch, would you? That would waste your work, if you built too close to the gulch and the rock wall collapsed or needed repair.

The shelf was heaped with massive chunks of heavily eroded limestone, bearing the dark oxidation stains of long exposure. Undisturbed for a long time, Alice thought. She pointed at the heap, then waited.

The sun broke through the clouds—welcome warmth on Alice's shoulders. Bender stood next to her. "Did someone break the wall here?" he asked. "'Something there is that doesn't love a wall.' Frost, right?"

"You mean frost heaves?" Alice punned. "Like in New England, where a frost heave spills 'the upper boulders in the sun, And makes gaps even two can pass abreast.' Then he goes on about hunters, and neighbors." She paused. "Or murderers?"

She looked at him, one eyebrow lifted.

"Oh," he said. "Oh..."

"If the wall was to keep the cows in the Fischers' pasture, you might not leave a big enough gap to tempt a cow down a really steep slope," Alice murmured.

"I can see it," he said, staring at the shelf. "If you're trying to hide bodies, don't throw them in the gulch, where heavy rain could send them downstream. Maybe move them to a shelf on the other side of the wall then...borrow rocks from the wall. Heap them up to hide the bodies. Hey, didn't it rain really hard that day?"

"Supposedly poured so hard the posse quit."

"So the ground would've been a mess anyway." Bender stepped closer to the rock wall. "If you moved some of the rocks off the wall onto the adjacent shelf...maybe making or expanding a small gap in the wall... it would just look like the farmer wanted a gate there. He could always put the rocks back. Besides, the posse must have seen the Comanche bodies left in the gulch—why would they assume the Fischers' bodies had been hidden? Then the posse was pelted with rain and had families to get home to before the roof leaked..." His face hardened. "I dunno, Alice. Seems like a risky play for that Riley guy. But definitely worth a look." He stared at the shelf, with the heaped rocks blackened and dissolved by the years. "Even though the rains have carved this steep gulch, you know, something could conceivably stay put on this shelf for a good long time. Maybe. But who knows. You gonna stay and watch?"

"No," she said. "There's something else I need to get done today."

"Chicken!" he said. "We who stay get to roll the dice and try to scan the rocks. Spend all our energy and then—jackpot? Bones? Or...nada?" He stared at the rocks on the shelf. "How in the world will the GPR work on that?"

"That's why they pay you the big bucks," she said. "Let me know!"

And she left, thinking about the risks and rewards of archeology. Dig, dig, dig...and nothing? Or...something amazing? Like the chipped rocks at the Gault site, north of Coffee Creek—showing human presence some 20,000 years ago?

Those newcomers to Texas, at the Gault site...what were their rules about murder?

*****

Alice called the office to touch base with Silla. "Detective Files heard about Johnny and wants to talk to you," Silla announced.

Maybe if she showed up in his office, he'd spill some information? Alice parked at the Coffee Creek Courthouse and made her way to the info desk in the Sheriff's Annex. The sergeant called Files. She waited at the end of the hall until he appeared at his office door and waved her down. She noted the tired lines around the eyes, the sag in the usually erect shoulders.

"Have a seat, Alice. The deputy says you were at the hospital. Johnny say anything about who hit him?"

She squirmed her way into the least uncomfortable arrangement on the metal chair. "Johnny said he might have seen the black truck or one like it at the Lost Corral, where he works part time. But he's not sure." She paused. "You're wondering who maybe lay in wait for him?"

"Yeah. Oh, one piece of news. A state trooper tracked down Bo Dupree."

"The guy who just got out of prison? The one Judge Mahan sentenced?"

"Yep. Unfortunately for him, or fortunately, he wound up in the hospital in Waco the day he got out—acute appendicitis. Solid alibi for the judge's murder."

"Johnny says his dad is flying in."

"Good," Files said. "I'd like to figure out his deal. Weird family dynamic, as our social service people would say."

"I've got a question," Alice began. "You know the judge's telephoto lens and camera?"

"Yeah?"

"Did you see any helpful pictures on it?"

George Files frowned. "Like what?"

Alice had a vision of the judge, carrying his telephoto lens and camera up the ridge west of his house. "You asked what I thought, remember? My guess was he'd either been about to go birdwatching, or was coming back. And since he'd sent me that email with his draft history, around two-thirty, I suspect he was ready to get out of the house for a while. He'd told me earlier he was desperate to get a picture of this American kestrel that had been hanging around the trees on the ridge near his house."

"Huh. Joske said there were a bunch of bird pictures on there. I mean, maybe a hundred. You know how you hold down the button and get a zillion? The judge did."

Typical birder, Alice thought. "But nothing more?"

"No, the picture series is nothing but branches, twigs, sky, with bits of bird thrown in. They're pretty fast, right?"

"Very fast." She paused. "But nothing else?"

"Nope, last picture's that bird, landing on a utility wire. About 3:10 p.m., based on the camera readout."

"Nothing later?"

"Nothing. You mean like, did he take a picture of whoever shot him?"

Alice cocked her head. "What about *before* he started filming the bird?"

Files frowned. "Why would he do that? You mean he'd see someone in his driveway and then be filming birds for five minutes? Sounds crazy."

She raised an eyebrow.

He looked at her steadily for a couple of seconds, then picked up the phone. "Joske? Can someone bring me the judge's camera? The one with the big lens?" Files turned to his computer screen. Alice sat silent, checking email on her phone.

Then Joske appeared at the door.

"Okay, Alice, come here." The three gathered behind Files's desk. "Alan, go backward through those bird pictures."

"Backward?" But Joske did. Files was right, the judge had tried and tried to get the kestrel in flight. "It just goes on and on with this bird," Joske said.

"Keep on," said Alice.

Suddenly the camera screen changed, to a side view of a tan Toyota pickup, parked on the gravel driveway circle, sun reflecting off rolled-up windows. No way to see the driver. "What time?" Files demanded.

"Three-oh-five." Joske looked horrified by this discovery. He hit the reverse button—more kestrel attempts. He went back to the pickup.

"Blow it up," Files said. "We can't see the plate, but isn't that a ding below the left taillight?"

The three studied the picture. "Looks a bit rusty, that ding. Taillight's intact," Alice offered.

"Maybe a 2006 Toyota?" Files guessed.

"I'll ask Deputy Olson, he's encyclopedic on vehicles," said Joske.

Files looked at Alice. "Any ideas?"

She shook her head. "Someone in that truck shot Judge Mahan."

"Check registrations," Files ordered Joske. Joske hurried out of the room.

Files looked up at her. "How'm I gonna tell the feds?"

She shook her head. "You'll find this truck. I know you will."

Alice left, then sat in her car for a moment, putting off her return to the office. She was chewing on an idea when the phone rang. Kinsear. She was relieved to have him home again, not somewhere in a tall building in New York, but back at his ranch where she could find him.

"Alice? Remember Muddy Mackin?"

"Of course I remember Muddy. Is he okay?"

Muddy Mackin, a West Texas rancher, had hired Alice to help protect music written by a missing singer-songwriter named Blanton Geddes, whose talent raised him to coveted "cowboy-poet" status in Texas music. Muddy lived alone on a spread near Marathon, north of the gloriously isolated mountains of Big Bend. Kinsear had bonded with Muddy over their mutual love of rare books about ranch life in the West.

"Not really. He sounded really down. Lonesome."

"Can't you persuade him to move here? M.A. would love it."

"We'll see."

"Sounds like you're going to go see him?"

"I've left. I'm almost to I-10. Listen, can you stay out of trouble while I'm gone? I'm worried about you, and I'm going to keep worrying until the police track down the judge's killer, and whoever ran Johnny off the road."

"Muddy's got nobody else, Ben. You're probably his best friend."

"I love ol' Muddy. I'll call from the road. Okay, listen. I like to be able to find you. While I'm gone, just don't go anywhere without your phone. Promise?"

"Love you."

But there was something she wanted to do, right now, before she grabbed lunch. Shouldn't take too long...

Chapter Twenty-One

Deep Freeze Action

Middle Creek emerged somewhere west of Coffee Creek and meandered around in the Hill Country, providing dammed-up little reservoirs for a few rich ranchers until it escaped and emptied into the Pedernales.

Alice turned her Discovery off the highway onto a small road that meandered, like the creek, between big pastures with expensive fencing. Spectacularly beautiful horses grazed in the pastures. Who owned all this? She passed a typical ornate ranch sign, arching above a driveway with careful ironwork declaiming a clever name. Ah, the horses belonged to Brandon's Branch. A mile later, the next sign proclaimed The Double Downs. Out in the field she saw a flock of goats guarded by a big white Great Pyrenees.

The road narrowed, curved. She drove cautiously around the bend. On her right, high above supporting stone plinths, rose the usual arch with one word in large wrought iron capitals: HUTTON. There was an ornate iron gate, but it was standing wide open. The driveway was long and well maintained. It ran across the pasture and split. Part of the drive continued uphill toward a grove of stately live oaks surrounding a large white house. The rest of the drive wound to the left, downhill. Curious, Alice drove slowly past the gate and around another bend, her eyes following the driveway as it curved toward what looked like farm buildings. In the pasture she saw no horses but did spot a few prize longhorns—these were white with black spots and horns so wide Alice wondered how the animals kept their balance.

She braked, squinting at the impressive outlay: stables, a big round pen, an impressive white livestock barn, and a long pole barn for vehicles. In the pole barn she could just see a tan fender. A pickup? She couldn't tell for sure, but a bit of fender jutted beyond the other vehicles.

Alice's eyes moved across the field, along the fence.

So far, not a single "no trespassing" sign.

She turned the car and started back toward the big Hutton gate. A FedEx delivery truck in the opposite lane braked, then turned into the drive.

Alice followed. The FedEx truck continued straight up the long hill toward the white mansion standing under the spreading oaks and parked in front. Off to the side Alice saw Winifred's red convertible, a large black pickup, a white Prius. Alice turned left, following the drive downhill and around a rise.

She arrived at the work area. Nice stables: long buildings, with a small fenced area on one end and a second story on the other—maybe rooms upstairs for the help. The livestock barn: limestone foundation, wooden walls with fresh white paint; a cupola on top with a weathervane. A couple of wood-fenced corrals, including a jumping arena. Off behind the barn, another large round corral with tall wooden fencing. Alice snorted and shook her head, thinking of the contrast to her own tumbledown red barn, where she had to wrestle open old wooden doors to drag out bales of hay for her burros. The Hutton operation looked smooth, well-oiled, expensive.

And across the road from the stables stood the long pole barn she'd glimpsed from the road, eight bays, concrete floor, for ranch equipment. They'd built an odd wooden enclosure in the last bay to the right. She spotted two Gators (she'd always wanted to drive one), a horse trailer, a large tractor, an equipment trailer, and a tan Toyota pickup...

She turned down the road in front of the pole barn. There it was, right in front of her: the tan Toyota truck. Vintage. Alice drove closer, peering at its rear. Yes. A ding, just above the left rear taillight.

Her heart pounded. Must call Files, she thought. Must get a picture too. She reached for her phone. Then she heard the rush of heavy footsteps, bass voices on both sides of her car.

"Yeah, it's her, the lawyer. Same car, same license plate." Then, "Yes ma'am, we got her." Alice dropped her phone down her shirt, shoved it farther, inside her panties and behind her jeans zipper, just as a shadow fell. Her car door opened; strong arms dragged her halfway out of the car, smashing her face to someone's big chest. Someone else cursed from the passenger side, fumbling with her seatbelt.

She couldn't talk, couldn't see. Then someone pulled her hair and she glimpsed, for one second, a red plaid shirt, before the second someone tied a bandana around her head, over her eyes—she saw for a brief second that it too was red, before the knot was yanked tight. And now Big Chest turned her around, still clutching her so tightly she could hardly breathe, while Blindfold Guy stepped on her feet and grabbed her hands, crushing them together in front of her, and bound them tightly palm to palm in what felt like handcuffs made of plastic zip ties. Police zip ties, she'd heard them called. She felt him poking another zip tie through the handcuffs, then tugging it through a belt loop on her jeans.

"Nice ring," muttered Blindfold Guy.

"Leave it! Do the boots," grunted Big Chest, flipping Alice back around, mashing her face into his chest. Alice tried to kick, but he stepped on the toes of her boots. She felt Blindfold Guy's hands on her calves, messing with the inside loops on her boot tops. When he quit, Big Chest turned her around, switching hands but still gripping Alice by the elbows, her back to his chest.

"Let me go this minute!" she gasped.

No answer. "Where's her damn phone?" grunted Big Chest.

"Has to be in the car. I'll look."

Big Chest walked backward, dragging Alice toward where she thought she remembered the pole barn. He dragged her up a step onto the concrete slab.

"Let me go! Kidnapping's a felony!"

"Shut it."

She heard a hinge creak, and now she sensed shadows. Big Chest let go of her elbows and shoved her so hard she fell, hitting her head on a wall. Felt splintery, like wood. The floor was cold concrete.

Outside, voices. "Remember, she said leave no marks." That was Blindfold Guy. "Deep freeze action, right?"

"Yeah. You find that phone?" Big Chest's voice.

"No. Not in the purse. Maybe it fell between the seats."

"Well, find it!"

Footsteps coming closer. She rolled to her stomach on the concrete. Big Chest again. He reached down, slapped her jeans pockets in back, poked the front jeans pockets, then felt with both hands down the front of her shirt. Alice flinched in horror. "Shit," he said and stomped back out.

She heard slamming, then metal clinking, then the snap of a padlock.

"I can't find it," said Blindfold Guy, outside.

"Not on her," said Big Chest. "Check the car again."

"Already used a flashlight. Didn't see it."

"Give me the damn flashlight!"

Alice lay still. Small consolation to hear those words, "Remember, she said leave no marks." She assumed "she" was Winifred.

What was a deep freeze action?

How the hell could she get out of here?

Alice heard car doors slamming, muffled curses. She hadn't heard an engine—how had they surprised her at the pole barn? Maybe sneaked up in the Prius?

Now she heard nothing, nothing but an occasional gust of wind. She rolled to her back, pushed with her heels as she scooched backward to the wooden wall, tried to sit. She bent her knees and slid upward, against the wall. How to remember which wall was which? First she tried as hard as possible to get her hands close to her eyes to pull down the blindfold. But she couldn't pull her wrists up more an inch or two above her waist and couldn't bend her neck down far enough. Well, try again later.

Then she turned her face to the wall, trying to bend her wrists slightly outward, and touched the wall with her fingertips. Yes, wooden planks. She edged sideways, turning her boots left, then right, counting six steps, and ran into a corner. More planks, then a panel that wiggled; must be the gate. Jiggled it. Ah: two sides to the gate, padlocked together in the middle. She kept going to another corner—more planks. Here she felt hay under her boots. She turned again—back to the first wall. Looking up, she could just see light through the bandana.

So, no roof over the high walls of the vet stall...it was protected by the metal roof over the pole barn.

All alone. No water, no food.

But she still had her phone. She experimented, trying to see whether zip ties gave her any latitude: she could pop the jeans, but couldn't unzip them. She could, working finger by finger, insert her fingers (but not her thumbs) partway into her jeans, but her wrists were so tightly bound together she wasn't sure her fingers could actually retrieve her phone. And she couldn't see anything. How to dial? Dammit, she'd meant to charge that phone earlier in the car. And now she couldn't and needed to save power. She should also silence the ringer—she couldn't let her captors hear that she still had her phone. Was there even wi-fi here? Internet? Working hard, she got her hands, wrists, and palms mashed together in prayer mode, down into her panties, and managed with the pinkie finger of her left hand to find the volume switch on the side of the phone. Down, right? She pushed it down as far as it would go.

Then again came voices and footsteps. Using both pinkies she shoved the phone farther down into her panties and managed to shove it all the way down to her crotch.

"Likin' it in there?" Big Chest's voice. "Hope so, cause that's all you're gonna get."

"Let me out of here right now!" she yelled.

He just snorted. "Enjoy your time in the vet stall. It'll be your last."

She heard a car start—sounded like hers. Where were they taking it? Then she heard a gate slam some distance away and footsteps departing.

Silence.

Alice shivered. January, in the Hill Country. About time for another snowpocalypse? She recited her new mantra. Vet stall. No water, no food...and no warmth.

Deep freeze.

Oh, wait; there was some hay. She inched her way back to the hay. Sitting on the hard concrete, with her boots zip-tied together, she used both feet to push the hay into a pile. Pretty awkward way to build a bed, and not a core exercise she planned to adopt.

Chapter Twenty-Two

Almost Unthinkable

The air got colder; the light visible through the bandana dimmed. Alice managed to slide her jeans down so she could pee in the corner she'd designated as her toilet. It took gymnastic moves: clutching the jeans, panties, and phone between her knees during the process, then rearranging them.

With no water, that would soon become less of a problem, she figured.

She sidestepped, fingertips to the wall, back to the locked gate. Vulnerable to some strong kicks, maybe? She turned her back to the gate, slid down to the concrete, rolled over, knees up, feet up, and kicked both boots as hard as she could at the wooden gate. Like the worst core exercise ever...

Again. Again. Until her knees gave out. Must save strength.

She groped her way to the opposite corner, which she'd designated as her bed, scooched down the wall, then wriggled under some of the hay. An early bedtime. Hours passed. She felt darkness descend, but no sleep.

What she wanted was water. Then some more water. Later on, maybe a glass of red wine, preferably a light Italian red.

But first, water. Also lunch and supper, since she'd had neither. But what? A grilled cheese sandwich on homemade bread, with plenty of butter, and longhorn cheese. Maybe sharp white cheddar, but the important thing was butter and proper toastedness, and the meltiness of the cheese.

She salivated, swallowed.

In another day, that too might be less of a problem.

Finally she slept, but woke every hour or so. For a while she saw some light through the bandana, the pearly coolness of moonlight.

*****

Morning came. Tuesday. Day two. Dew had fallen on the hay, on her hair. She shivered—it couldn't be warmer than forty degrees. Early on she heard noise from the stables—men's voices. She hallooed: "Hey! Get me out of here!" Then, repeatedly, "HELP! HELP!"

But the voices vanished. Surely someone would come check on her?

She scooched her back to the wall, managed to slide up again and felt her way to the gate. Back down to the concrete floor. She rolled onto her back, lifted both knees, and again began kicking the gate. Bam! Bam! Bam!

Nothing. No splintering sounds. No one came to inquire.

The light grew yellow. Must be past her usual arrival time at the office. Maybe Kinsear had called her, more than once. Or maybe not—she imagined Kinsear and Muddy spending a rollicking evening, telling stories, sipping bourbon. By now, Silla might be at the office, possibly worried, or at least puzzled. Maybe Silla even now was trying to call her. And possibly her kids. But all of them might simply conclude she wasn't in phone mode—maybe at a hearing at the courthouse or at the salon for a haircut. Alice tried to remember if she had any appointments today. She couldn't remember one. Her heart sank a bit more. If Alice had no appointments, Silla wouldn't necessarily worry when Alice didn't show up, would she?

What about John and Ann? Were they feeling a disturbance in their mother's force? An urge to call?

Alice mainly wanted water. What kind of people were these, not to check on her? Not to provide water, food, a blanket? At a minimum, water?

Slowly she faced the almost unthinkable: they didn't plan to come back until she was quietly, finally, dead.

How long would that take? Food wasn't the real issue...but how long did people last without water? Three to five days? Didn't the brain start to shut down after three days? Tomorrow would be day three.

She should keep track of time. But how?

She wriggled her fingers, found a piece of straw, stuck it in her right jeans pocket. Grasping at straws, right? she thought. A straw calendar.

Maybe she should hope for a different worker outside, someone who was neither Big Chest nor Blindfold Guy, some human being with a heart and enough courage to help her.

She heard nothing except an occasional bird. She tried another pee in her designated corner. Her stomach ground, hungrily. Her tongue felt dry.

Okay, get busy. She managed to scoot back to the wall and stand up. On her morning trip around the four corners, her fingertips searching for information, she found a nailhead sticking out of a plank, a nailhead she hadn't felt with her fingertips yesterday. A nice big nailhead, though at an awkward level, about heart-high. Carefully she turned around, back against the wall, bent her knees and wiggled her boots backwards until she felt the nailhead low on the back of her scalp. She bent her knees a little farther, slowly inching down, but not slowly enough—now the nailhead had caught her scalp, at the occipital bone. She rose half an inch, leaned her head forward to escape the nailhead, then leaned back and carefully began lowering her head again, a warm trickle of blood creeping down her neck. The nailhead caught the bandana. Alice leaned her head back while bending her knees again—then inched sideways.

Light! The bandana was still caught on the nailhead. But it was off her head. Blinking, listening for footsteps outside, Alice surveyed her domain. She was in a space about eight feet square, with vertical plank walls ending about eight feet from the floor. Several feet above the walls she saw the pole barn roof. The gate that formed the fourth wall was made of two sections of wood planks, eight feet tall and meeting in the middle. Wide enough to admit a bull.

She could see, she could dial! Now for the phone.

She worked her bound hands down into her panties, into her crotch, with her pinkies pushing the phone back up toward her navel.

With the phone partly sticking up from her jeans, she sank onto her hay bed and eased the phone out. The phone fell onto the hay. Fine. If Big Chest or Blindfold Guy showed up, she had a place to hide it.

She crouched on her knees in the hay, the phone arranged before her. Leaning forward, with one thumb she pushed the round circle on the bottom, waiting for the black screen to blaze to life with its welcoming collection of icons. Still black. She pushed again. Then again. Had she somehow turned her phone off? Holding the phone still with her pinkies, with her right ring finger she pressed the turn-on button, pressed it hard, kept pressing it. You need to hold it down, Alice! Remember how long it takes? She moved it so the phone was perpendicular to the floor, put her left thumb on the button and pushed hard, waiting for the white turn-on slider to appear.

Nothing.

Frantic, she tried again, and again.

Her phone was dead.

She stared at it, stunned.

Then she considered workarounds. Maybe, before it died, someone had taken action? Asked Files to check cell towers? That would work, wouldn't it? She blinked, trying to focus, trying to remember about cell towers.

It might work, but only if someone had asked him...

Her lips were cracked. Her tongue felt as dry as a towel.

Chapter Twenty-Three

Like Jericho

Time passed. She noticed that her one tiny trickle of pee for the day was lurid orange-yellow in the pale cold January light.

If no one knew where she was, Alice concluded, she was on her own. She had to escape.

How? With nothing to stand on, no way to climb over the walls, concrete floors, no way to dig out?

That left—kicking down the walls. Like Jericho, the walls must fall! First she test-kicked each of the three plank walls. Nothing; they didn't crack, or creak. The two-part gate on the fourth wall must be the weak link. She lay on her back, boots on the gate planks. One, two, three—KICK!

Over and over.

Nothing happened.

Damn fine construction here, on this little enclosure, this so-called vet stall.

She lay on her back, staring blankly at the pole barn roof and the bit of blue sky visible at the end of the pole barn, thinking how swollen her tongue felt. Then she heard a buzz. A buzz in the sky. She squinted, looking for the buzz, at the unclouded day, blue as blue. Willie, singing "O the land of an unclouded day..." She wanted to hum. But she couldn't. Only a croak emerged. The buzz returned, then faded.

The gate consisted of two sides made of vertical planks. The two sides of the gate opened in the middle. The hinges were outside, at the top and bottom of each side of the gate. Maybe she could weaken a hinge if she kicked the inside. Then there was the padlock: she'd heard Big Chest locking the padlock that held the two gate sections together. A loose screw would be nice.

Still lying flat on her back on the cold concrete, she wriggled closer and closer to the double gate until her bottom was about a foot away from the gate and her knees were bent. She placed her boot soles on the bottom of the right section, reared backward and then kicked the gate. BAM!

The gate shuddered but bounced back. Nothing splintered. She tried kicking again, over and over. Nothing. The hinges held; the planks held. She moved sideways and attacked the bottom of the left section. No progress there either.

She lay back, eyes closed, too tired to move, too tired to cry. Or maybe too dry; anyway, no tears came.

What about, instead of kicking the bottom of the gate, trying to kick the planks closest to the padlock? The padlock was about waist high, so harder to kick. She wondered if the screws that held the lock plates were smaller, shorter, than those on the gate hinges.

After staring up at the center of the gate for a few minutes, she assumed a variant of what her yoga teacher might call donkey pose, lifting her legs straight up and then back over her head. Then she arched her back, gave a mighty heave and kicked the middle of the gate with both boots.

BAM! Had she heard anything hopeful? A small splintering noise? Was she starting to hallucinate? She tried again, then again.

The light had changed. The sun was setting. In January dusk fell early.

She was too tired to move. Maybe she could manage one more kick, in a bit.

She curled up in the hay and slept.

*****

Morning again. Pale cold light. She lay shivering in the hay. Wednesday? If so, day three. Alice managed to roll up to a sitting position. Then she scooched backward to the wall and willed herself to stand. Shaking with cold, she stared at the gate. She inched her boots across the concrete, put her shoulder to the right section of the gate, then leaned back and crashed her shoulder into the gate again.

A splintering sound. She backed up and hit the gate again, as hard as she could.

The right section gave way. She heard a piece of metal hit the concrete floor outside. Maybe a screw? Disbelieving, Alice pushed open the gate, shuffled outside, then peered at the padlock. It still was locked through the two loops, but the lock plate on the left section had popped loose.

Alice bent down, retrieved a screw, gripped it between thumb and forefinger and cautiously inserted it again, so that the gate once again appeared padlocked.

Outside it was silent. She stared down at the concrete floor of the pole barn, with its sharp edge where the concrete ended. Goal: get her zip-tied boots off her feet. She leaned on a supporting pole, slid down and sat with her boot tops at the edge of the concrete. She inched backward, wriggling her feet.

The boots were off.

Alice picked them up and padded down the pole barn in her socks, hoping for water. If it was like hers at home—yes. At the end she saw the hose bib and hose, handy for washing vehicles. She turned on the hose, leaned over, guzzled the stream of water. Well water, yes, with a faint sulphur smell, but so delicious. She drank until water sloshed in her empty stomach, then picked up her boots and headed for the stables.

The birds were beginning to sing, cardinals and chickadees. But as yet she saw no sign of any humans.

She reconnoitered the stable. No worries about bothering the horses—there weren't any. No fragrant horse smell, no stamping, no snuffling. Hutton's ranch was a charade, Alice realized. A stage set.

She spotted a windowed door that looked like it belonged to an office. Carrying her boots, she slipped through the door. Below the window sat a desk and chair. The interior walls held equipment on hooks— helmets, a chain saw, rakes. She headed straight for the three-foot-long branch loppers hanging on a hook—sturdy loppers used for cutting cedar and pruning small branches. She tiptoed to lift the loppers off the hook with her bound hands, then realized she'd have no control over the loppers until she got rid of the zip tie attaching her bound hands to her belt loop. She laid down the loppers and surveyed the tools again. On one section she recognized farrier tools like those Red kept in her barn for cleaning and trimming a horse's hoof. Picks, rasps, nippers. She spotted some small orange-handled hoof trimmers, like those used for goats and sheep, hanging about five feet from the floor. She dragged over the chair from the desk and clambered up, straining her bound wrists to reach the trimmers.

Clutching the trimmers awkwardly below her breasts, she angled the blades toward the belt loop itself. Surely belt loops would be easier to cut than zip-ties. Wrists aching, she worked the blades back and forth until the denim loop finally frayed, then yielded. The plastic zip tie fell to the floor. Now to free her hands.

She peeked out the door window. No humans, no vehicles in sight. Ears cocked for any noise, she laid the loppers on the floor, handles apart so the blades of the lopper opened. She squatted with a foot on each handle, then moved her right foot an inch closer to the left so the lopper blades began to close. She leaned forward, maneuvering her hands to slip the zip tie binding her left wrist onto the cutting blade. Plan: cut the zip tie without slitting her wrist. Again she inched her right foot closer to the left, enough to tighten the cutting blades, and began rocking back and forth, pulling her hands toward her each time, sweating as the zip tie cuffs burned her wrists.

She leaned back, still squatting with a foot on each handle, the zip tie biting into her wrists, and inched the right handle closer to the left. Were the blades sharp enough? Frustrated, she rocked back and forth, harder and harder.

Her wrists flew apart as the tie on her left wrist popped loose, cut ends waving. The other cuff was still attached to her right wrist, but her hands were free. Alice stood, picked up the loppers, and cut the zip tie on her boots. She stomped her feet into the liberated boots and hung the lopper and the trimmers back on the wall.

She could walk! She could use her hands!

What about food?

A half-eaten family-size bag of Cheetos sat on the desk, rubber-banded shut. The breakfast of champions, no? She grabbed the bag, hurried to the door and opened it a slow inch, just wide enough to peer out at the driveway. No trucks, no noise. Clutching the Cheetos she hightailed it back behind the pole barn and found a hiding place in the nearby cedar scrub. Now for Cheetos. Salt on her tongue, crunch in her mouth. Another handful, another bite. A sudden noise made her jump. She looked up to see a squirrel chittering on a nearby oak.

"Sorry, buddy. I am eating every single one of these."

After her Cheetos breakfast, she had a pee in the cedar scrub, then confirmed the coast was clear before returning to the pole barn hose to wash her Cheeto-orange fingers and drink more water. She slipped back into the cedar scrub to reconnoiter, peering from the stables to the barn and beyond. Where had Big Chest and Blindfold Guy stashed her car?

Fingers crossed that they'd left her fob in the car—made sense if they planned to move it again and assumed she'd never get out of the vet stall.

On the far side of the stables stood a large circular fenced pen, perhaps originally for training horses. She couldn't see over the plank fence, which looked about six feet high. The sun was well up now; it must be at least ten. Why weren't Winifred's lackeys at least checking on the longhorns, seeing to their food and water—demonstrating the better side of humanity, so different from what her prison guards had offered her? Maybe they planned to wait for day three to end before bothering to check the vet stall. What plans had they made for her body? Put her in the Hutton family cemetery? More likely they'd dig an unmarked grave somewhere off the property, never to be found. Where her children, Kinsear, Silla, friends, family could never stand nearby, thinking about her, leaving a flower or two.

She shook her head, staring through the cedar branches. Time to get busy. Find the car, fast. And if not, find a route back to the road. Surely a fire gate must exist somewhere along the Hutton fence line. Climb out, burrow out, survive. Cheetos, water—she felt almost human again. Filthy, of course. Not thinking clearly yet. Get over it, Alice. Time to move. Get as far away as possible from the vet stall.

First stop, the circular pen beyond the stables. She cocked her ears. Still no sound of cars or trucks on the gravel drive. Why not?

She remembered a shovel hanging on the stable office wall. Potentially useful as a weapon, or to pry her way out under a string of barbed wire. Get that first, on the way to the circular pen? But possibly dangerous, if checking the vet stall was the staff's first order of the day.

Alice slipped out of the cedar scrub, took a few steps beyond the branches, listening hard. She heard tires on gravel, back uphill toward Winifred's fancy house. She couldn't let anyone keep her from getting her car. So, maybe no shovel. If she heard road noise she could hide— sort of—in the patch of tall bluestem grass surrounding a persimmon tree partway to the road that led past the stables toward the pole barn. She'd made it nearly to the persimmon when an engine roared, tires spraying gravel. Alice dived into the tall grass. What fresh hell was this?

Where Have You Been?

An old tan Land Cruiser careened around the curve. Peering through the grass, Alice blinked. The driver braked, jumped out, started running for the stables. Kinsear!

She stood, yelled. "Ben!"

Her voice broke. She tried again. "Ben!"

Almost to the stables, he stopped, turned, saw her. "Alice! Stay there! I'm coming!"

He pounded up the hill past the pole barn, grabbed her, hugged her to his chest for what felt like minutes, warm, glorious. She buried her face in his flannel shirt.

"You're freezing cold. Where have you been?"

She lifted her face, pointed. "Inside that. The vet stall."

He stared at the pen.

Then he looked down at the plastic handcuff loop still on her right wrist. She held up her wrists, showing him the red ridges made by the plastic ties. "And there was one on my boots," she said.

"How'd you get loose? Wait, tell me later. Let's get you safe first." His brow furrowed. "What's that orange stuff around your mouth?"

"Cheetos." She pointed at the stables. "Found them in there this morning."

More tires spraying gravel. A Coffee County Sheriff's cruiser sped around the curve and braked behind the Land Cruiser. Alan Joske jumped out and started running past the stables toward the round pen—but was quickly passed by a slim figure with a red ponytail.

Alice gasped. "Silla!"

"She saw your car, Alice. That's how we found you."

George Files climbed out of the cruiser's driver's seat and spotted Kinsear and Alice beyond the pole barn. "Hey there!" he yelled.

"Come on." Kinsear, arm around Alice, walked her down the hill to meet Files.

"Alice, Alice," said Files, shaking his head. "You've led us a merry one this time." He scanned her, head to toe. "Are you okay to talk right now?"

She nodded.

"You were out here, right? On the Hutton property?"

Alice confessed to following the FedEx truck into the property.

"I saw a glimpse of a tan fender in the pole barn. The gate was open. I didn't see any 'no trespassing' signs." Files might as well know...Hutton would probably claim she was trespassing.

Files rolled his eyes. "Who caught you, and where'd they put you?"

She pointed to the vet stall at the far end of the pole barn, thinking of Big Chest and Blindfold Guy. "Two guys locked me in there. The vet stall, they call it. Maybe the two Winifred Hutton calls her 'hands.' They blindfolded me. Zip-tied my wrists and then attached them to my belt loop so I couldn't get the blindfold off. Zip-tied my boots together. There's some hay in the vet stall. Otherwise—no food, no water. And it was really cold..."

"Were they talking to Hutton?"

"I think so, maybe by phone. I heard them say they'd got the lawyer, that it was the same car. I think they saw my car at the office the day she showed up."

"No food? No water?" Kinsear's face was dangerous.

"I went straight for the water this morning when I got out of that pen," Alice hastened to say, pointing to the hose bib at the end of the pole barn. "And Cheetos..."

"Well, just a damn minute," Kinsear said, reaching into the pockets of his barn jacket. "Here. A six-pack of Hershey bars with almonds, and some granola bars, and an orange, and—"

"Hershey bar first, please."

Kinsear unwrapped the first bar.

"Yum," Alice said through a mouthful of chocolate.

Never had chocolate tasted so good. She shut her eyes, let the milk chocolate melt on her tongue, chewed an almond.

"Healing power of chocolate. Can't beat it." Kinsear watched Alice intently, then pulled a water bottle from his other pocket. "Here."

Alice took a long swig, then another. "More chocolate, please." Kinsear unwrapped another bar. After the second bar, Alice held up her hand. "More later."

Files stood watching. "How'd they catch you?"

Alice stared at him, trying to reconstruct her memory. "I'd stopped the car. I was trying to turn on my phone. I didn't hear them coming. The guy I call Big Chest yanked open the driver's door and hauled me out. The other guy opened the passenger door, unlocked my seat belt and shoved me toward Big Chest. Blindfold Guy. "

"Okay," Files said. "That helps me with where to look for prints. How'd you get that bruise on your cheek?"

She remembered that dark moment. "Concrete floor. When they shoved me in the pen. I couldn't put my hands out, couldn't make my feet work."

Kinsear took a long deep breath, fury in his eyes.

Files again. "Are you okay to show me where they put you?"

She did. They walked slowly to the pen, Kinsear's arm around Alice's shoulders. But when she neared the wooden gates, Files stopped her. "Don't touch anything. It's a crime scene."

He pulled on gloves, opened the gates, peered inside, Alice watching next to him. He took pictures of the interior. The red bandana lay on the floor.

"That's the blindfold?"

She nodded. "I finally got it off. I used that sticking-out nailhead." She pointed. "Slid my back down the wall till the bandana stuck on the nailhead. Felt like I nicked my scalp, but I could finally see."

Kinsear lifted the hair on the back of her head. "Still some blood," he said.

"And if you're wondering, I peed in the corner," Alice added. "Till I ran out of pee on day two."

Kinsear's face tightened.

"How'd you get out?" Files asked.

"Lay on the floor. Kicked the gates with the heels of my boots, over and over. This morning the lock broke."

"And then?"

Files pointed to the dangling zip tie on her wrist.

She took a deep breath, remembering. "I sat on the concrete and used the edge to pry my boots off. Then I could walk. First, water. I found the hose at the end of the pole barn. I kept thinking...this is the third day." She closed her eyes, took another deep breath. "Water and more water. Then I found a door to the office in the stables. Found a lopper, laid it on the floor, found some goat clippers, got my wrists free. Cut the tie on my boots."

"Sorry about this, but hold still," Files said, using his phone to take pictures of Alice, including her wrists, another zip tie dangling from her belt loop, another zip tie hanging from one boot, the streak of blood on her scalp and neck.

"And you found the Cheetos," Kinsear added.

Alice remembered the crunch, the taste on her tongue, of that first salty bite. She felt as if her brain was coming back to life. Then she remembered. "George, the truck's here! The truck in the judge's photo! That's what I came to find!"

"*What?*"

"Right there!"

Files stared back past the tractor and the Gators at the tan Toyota truck parked in the pole barn, strode over, walked around it. He examined the ding below the left rear taillight, pulled out his phone, took more pictures.

When he rejoined them he shook his head, gazing at Alice. "That's what you were looking for, right?"

"Yes."

"Okay. I don't want to wear you out. Can you walk to the stables and show me how you got the zip ties off?"

When they reached the stables, Alice pointed to the office door. Files said, "Wait." Still gloved, he opened the door and walked into the office, followed by Kinsear and Alice. "Show me the lopper you used."

She pointed at the wall. "That one. And those goat clippers."

Then Alice shut her eyes, leaning on Kinsear.

"Let's get her out of here," Kinsear said to Files. Files nodded.

Joske and Silla raced back from the circular pen, both with red hair blowing in the morning breeze.

"Her Discovery's in there. Fob's in it," Joske panted.

"Get prints on everything. Car, outside and in. Steering wheel, ignition, everything. Be sure to get both door handles and the seat belt lock for the driver's side. Let me show you some spots to hit." Files turned to Kinsear. "Stay a minute." He walked Joske toward the pole barn, stopping at the Toyota truck, then moving to the vet stall.

Alice was hugging Silla. "Oh, Silla!" Alice managed. "I probably smell awful."

"A little funky," Silla grinned. She wrapped Alice in another hug.

"But Silla! How did you do it?" Alice asked. "How did you find me?"

Silla's freckled face broke into a vast smile. "When we couldn't raise you, couldn't get you on the phone, couldn't find your car anywhere, I thought it must be that wretched Hutton woman. Of course I knew where her ranch was. But your car?" Alice saw a funny look, proud, guilty, and still amazed, cross Silla's face. "I spotted it—from above!"

Alice's mouth fell open.

"Did you hear any noise yesterday? Up in the sky?"

Alice remembered the faint buzzing that came and faded, and then came back, then faded entirely. "A *plane?*"

Silla nodded, smiling proudly. "That was me. I even used the binoculars to check your license." She gave a little snort. "That made me nervous."

"But—but who was flying the plane?"

"Me." She laughed. "I'm taking flying lessons, Alice! And I flew over and saw the green Discovery! I'll admit the Hutton ranch...wasn't exactly included on the flying plan we filed at the airport in Lampasas, but I told the instructor it was critical."

"Oh, Silla." Alice burst into tears. Then she stared at Silla's face—which held a secret. There was more to this story, she knew. She narrowed her eyes, framing a question, but before she could ask, Files returned from talking with Joske.

"That's how we managed to get a warrant to search this place, Alice," he said. "Based on Silla spotting your car in that pen." He raised his eyebrows. "And now that we've seen this Toyota truck, I need a broader search warrant. I'm looking for evidence showing who drove that truck to the judge's place. Then I've got to find the revolver that killed the judge."

An ambulance, lights on, no siren, rolled down the driveway and stopped.

Files gave Alice an assessing stare.

"Okay, Alice, you need to get going. Hate to ask you to do this, but I need you to climb in the ambulance and go with Joske to the ER and get checked out, then give him a signed statement. We need more photos of your wrists, and so on. I'll stay here and wait for the search warrant for the truck and get the team organized. We'll grab the ranch hands." He looked at Silla. "Can someone take some different clothes for Alice to the ER? After we get the photos, I want everything she's wearing bagged as evidence."

Alice frowned, moved closer to Kinsear.

"No, go in the ambulance," Files ordered.

"I'll ride with you, Alice, while Silla follows in my car," Kinsear added. "Don't worry. I'm not letting you out of my sight. Maybe ever."

Silla nodded. "I'll get some clothes for her and meet you there."

Not what Alice wanted to do. She wanted to go home right now. She wanted to climb into a hot bubble bath in her own bathroom, and stay there for—oh, hours, adding more hot water as needed. With a grilled cheese sandwich. Yes, in the tub, regardless of crumbs. She looked up at Kinsear, who lifted his eyebrows, then gave her the lop-sided smile that meant she needed to do what Files asked.

"Okay, okay," she said. "But...but why is it so quiet out here?" A horrible suspicion hit her. "What about those two men?"

"Don't worry about them," Files said.

She lifted her eyes to Files's face. "I hope you find that damned revolver."

But would they? Was it here?

Chapter Twenty-Five

Back From The Almost Dead

"Almost done," said the ER tech.

"Really, I'm okay!" Alice protested. "I just want to go home. And I need to pee."

The ER tech smiled. "Good. We want to be sure you're hydrating properly."

Kinsear patted her shoulder. Alice felt like a lab specimen herself: photos of bruises and the red marks on her wrists, a look at the nailhead wound, plenty of fluids...a hospital breakfast tray... She'd given Joske the statement he needed to arrest her captors. Including, she hoped, Winifred Hutton.

Alice changed into the clean clothes Silla had brought, dropping the dirties into the bag the ER tech then took to Joske, who stood tapping his feet outside the cubicle. "Tell him those were my favorite jeans," she told the tech. Then she wondered if they'd wind up as an exhibit and if she'd ever dare wear them again.

"Time for that bubble bath," Kinsear said.

*****

Fragrance. Hot water. Bubbles. Kinsear looking around the door. "Want me to scrub your back?"

Yes, she did. And her feet, please. She was too tired to do it herself.

The winter sunset saw Alice in the kitchen in her flannel nightie, barely awake enough for Kinsear to serve her one glass of pinot noir and one bowl of soup. "You're staying, right?" she asked.

"Of course."

She stumbled into bed, her own bed, her own non-concrete, non-hay bed, knowing Kinsear would be there all night next to her. She woke once, at four, groped to find his nearby warmth, and slept again.

*****

On Thursday morning the smell of frying bacon lured her out of bed. Bacon, hot toast, cheesy scrambled eggs (chef Kinsear always included cream cheese as well as cheddar). Espresso in her own favorite cup, with frothed milk on top. She sat on a stool at the kitchen island, watching

Kinsear watching her.

"I'm fine," she said.

He studied her, his eyes narrowed in that dubious way. "And?" he said.

"I am deeply pissed at those two men."

"Because they left you to die?"

"Mm-hmm." She took a breath. "But I'm plotting revenge against Winifred Hutton."

"Good. If Files can find her."

"What?" Alice's insides lurched.

"Ask Files."

Alice hit "Files" on her phone favorites.

"Yes, Alice?"

"Kinsear says you can't find Winifred Hutton! Wasn't she there when you arrived?"

"Nope. Her two bully boys won't talk at all. They're lawyered up. The housekeeper claims she has no idea where her boss is. Any ideas?"

"Did she take her car? Her fancy red convertible?"

"Nope. It was parked under the porte cochère at the side of the house. She didn't take that big black pickup either. The housekeeper said she's got a new Land Rover convertible. We finally found the registration online—it's owned by some entity of hers—and we've put out an APB. But since her employees claim not to know when she left...or where she is..."

"She could've left the first day I was there," Alice said. She tried a couple of deep breaths, trying to calm herself. Murder...by being left alone to die in winter cold, no food, no water...

She made herself think. Where would Hutton go? To someone else's vast ranch in west Texas? To an island in the Bahamas? Would she drive or fly? And if she always carried her revolver...would she need to use a private jet?

Files added, "We're checking private airports, not just Austin."

"Maybe she left the revolver at the house," Alice said slowly. "Well hidden."

"But first I need enough facts for a solid search warrant. I'm waiting on prints from the truck." Files hung up.

Furious, frustrated, Alice slid off the counter stool and stalked around the kitchen. "What if we get the *Coffee Creek Caller* to interview both candidates? And their supporters? Ask a bunch of softball questions about who's supporting their beloved candidate? Silla's got contacts at the *Caller*. It's where we run our probate notices and so on."

"That could be totally non-productive," Kinsear said. "What Files really needs is to place Hutton in the judge's driveway with a working revolver. And as far as I know, he doesn't even have her prints yet."

"You're right. But I didn't know when Dedra Riley came to my office that she was going to volunteer information about Hutton, including that she goes armed all the time and keeps that enshrined Colt on her upstairs wall. Maybe some 'human interest' interview could turn up more info on Hutton, like where she's hiding."

"Maybe," Kinsear said. "You've obviously had two big cups of espresso and are working on a third. Do I deduce you're heading for the office?"

She nodded.

"First, some kissing. We're way behind. Then I've got to meet Javier at the ranch."

*****

When Alice herself finally drove into Coffee Creek, the morning sun was gleaming, the temperature was nearing 60, and she felt wildly alive from her head to her toes. Even my brain's abuzz, she thought. In her jeans and her Goodson Kells boots, a little whisker burn on one cheek, she made it to the office by ten. Silla looked up from her phone, signaled "just a minute."

It felt funny, being back in her own office. She hadn't seen it since Monday, when she took off for Hutton's ranch. The phone message light was blinking...the laptop was closed... already the desk looked faintly dusty. "I'm back!" she whispered to the room.

Back from the almost dead... The deep freeze. She sat down at her desk, looking around.

Silla zipped in, stood in front of Alice's desk, notepad in hand. "The folks on this list need callbacks. But nothing's urgent."

"First things first! I want to hear about your flying lessons!" Alice exclaimed. "Tell, please! And why flying?"

Silence. "You really want to know?" A pink flush spread across Silla's freckled face.

"Look, you're a barrel racer! You're an incredible horsewoman! You can drive a horse trailer all the way to Calgary! But flying?"

"I had this idea," Silla said, "after talking to your archeologist. Bender."

She pronounced his name with a small smile.

Oho, Alice thought. But why flying?

Silla continued. "You know how in *National Geographic* you sometimes see aerial photos that indicate unexcavated ruins?"

Alice nodded, intrigued.

"Well, I thought...I thought if I learned to fly, I could help Bender find some new sites." She paused. "I've gotten really interested in archeology."

Alice couldn't contain the smile on her face. "Archeology?"

"Yes. Deeply interested. You know, from the air I could likely spot early human middens in the Texas Hill Country. Maybe find some unknown rock art sites." Her eyes sparkled.

Tread carefully, Alice thought. "Does Bobby Bender know you can fly?"

Silla broke into laughter. "I'm going to tell him today." Her face got serious. "Listen, Alice, he was really busy yesterday. Last night he said something about a breakthrough. Shouldn't we be checking on the project? So, don't we need to go out there today?"

Alice's heart thumped. "You mean he found something?"

"Don't know. He wouldn't give details. But he sounded pumped." Silla started out the door, then stopped. "Let's leave in half an hour? While there's still sun."

"Deal."

Watching Silla's happy face, Alice couldn't help thinking hard. Silla's plan to win Bender's heart and mind and companionship was all well and good. But what about Bender? He'd better be kind to Silla, better take her seriously, and certainly better not break or even wound her heart—or he'd be answering to Alice.

I shouldn't worry, Alice told herself. How could he possibly resist Silla?

And what was the breakthrough?

Let Me Show You What We Found

"Johnny got out of the hospital yesterday," Silla said, downshifting for Dead Man's Curve. "His dad was there. Eric."

"Tell me!"

"Johnny was talking to him, and he was talking to Johnny—Alice, they seemed really good. I mean, I got a great handshake from Eric. Tells me a lot. I won't put up with a bad handshake from a man."

"So is he just helicoptering in? Or what? I mean, Johnny's the judge's heir, and Eric has no role."

"Nope, Eric's busy with his start-up, but...honestly, Alice, I found myself kind of liking the man."

"Hmmph." Alice was skeptical.

"I know, I know," Silla said. "But he'd gone out for a barbecue sandwich Johnny asked for, and he was bringing Johnny his water bottle, and so on. He's going to stay with Johnny one more day after he's out of the hospital, then fly back to California. I also called Miranda. Johnny's going to stay at the judge's, take care of Charley, and commute to San Marcos."

Lord, thought Alice, I'd forgotten about Charley. "And you really thought Eric was all right?"

"He said over and over how proud he is of Johnny. How mature he is, what a good man, what a dependable person."

"All true," Alice said. "How long did it take his dad to figure that out?"

"Sounds like quite a while. I talked to Eric out in the hall. He said he realizes now he's been messed up. Totally into start-up mentality. Said if Johnny was going to grow up, maybe he could too. He was laughing. Kind of."

Silla turned into the judge's drive, entered the gate code, and deftly angled her truck next to Bender's white camper, where Bender stood waiting in cool sunshine.

An odd bulky electronic device hung around his neck. His face held mingled excitement and anxiety.

"You okay, Alice?" he said. "I heard a wild tale about you escaping from being held prisoner. I thought, that's the Alice I know."

Which made her grin. "I'm fine."

"Well, I want to hear more." He was scanning her face intently. "But maybe over some beers?"

Alice nodded. "Yes, later. What's this around your neck?"

"Kind of a miracle, considering the terrain in this gulch. We've borrowed a hand-held GPR device. Because of the replacement price if anything happens to this baby, I'm the only one allowed to use it. It can detect metal up to thirty feet deep. But given the history of this gulch, geologic and otherwise, I thought the judge would approve." Then he beamed. "So, let me show you what we found down in the gulch. Let's go to the tent so the sun won't interfere."

Under the filtered sunlight in the project tent, Bender set the hand-held GPR on the table, fiddled with knobs, muttering under his breath, then gestured at Alice and Silla. "Look."

The screen showed different colors: red, white, green. Alice saw three small roundish red areas, some red triangles overlapping, and a long red spot. "You're looking at only one layer," Bender said. "The red indicates a divergence in density from the surrounding area. What I'm going to show you now is the adjacent horizontal slices of data."

Again Alice saw similar areas. And again, on the next slice.

"These are at our deepest level," Bender said. "I think we may have three bullets or round balls, a knife blade, and, I believe, possibly some arrowheads. As you know, GPR can detect differences indicating metal and stone in soil."

"I could imagine the Comanche man having some arrowheads in a quiver or bag," Alice said.

"Maybe," Bender said.

"How certain are you those three blobs are bullets?" she asked.

"Metal reflects differently, remember? But certainty would likely require excavation."

"What about bones?"

"It's so long ago, Alice, and the bones mostly dissolve in repeatedly wet materials. But I think we may have a piece of a skull. Hang on." He messed with the controls. A curved red fragment came into focus. Again Bender called up the adjacent slices. "This bit of what I think is human bone lies above the metal and stone bits I just showed you. But below the rubble of rocks and boulders and caliche soil."

Almost like a body was bunched up under rocks, maybe the ones supposedly piled up by the posse, she thought.

Bender went on, "It's a miracle to find anything in that gulch, but I'll tell you what I think happened. I think at some point one of the cedars at the edge of the gully fell over, pinning down the rockpile and entrapping more rocks and sediment, at least for a time. Just speculation, but that may explain why we could find anything at all."

"The blade once had a handle?" Alice asked.

"Probably. But not a metal one."

"What do we do now?"

"Well, this is private property, not tribal land. You can leave the material where it is. But as a professional archeologist, I must document what we've found. In any event as a courtesy we should notify the Comanche Nation. The elders may decide to try to repatriate the remains and any artifacts. If that happens, or if the Comanche Nation isn't interested and you decide to excavate, we'll need to make it, as the judge would say, as unimpeachable as possible, in terms of archeological practice. I feel you should also notify Files. Right now we're making permanent records of this GPR run, including time, date, locations, depths. Those records will be saved and retained where they're as safe as we can make them."

"Online?" That made Alice nervous.

"Not just online. We'll save everything."

"So doesn't this support at least part of Emil Fischer's story?" Silla said. "Part of a body, some arrowheads, a blade."

"We're just getting started," Bender said, turning and ducking under the tent flap. "If you'll just step back outside with me..."

Something Like A Locket

"See that creative outdoor sculpture?"

Bender pointed toward the gap in the rock wall where Alice had speculated the Fischer bodies might have lain, rock-covered, all these years. Two stepladders stood upright about seven feet apart, on the shelf. Another long section of ladder lay horizontally across the two stepladders, resting on the top of each.

"See, you can climb up one stepladder, and lie across the horizontal piece, with the GPR looking down through the surface below. Miserably uncomfortable," Bender announced, "but archeologists are tough. See how it works? You lie on your belly, the ladder rungs prodding your ribs and hipbones, scan an area, move on to the next rung, again sacrificing your ribs..."

"Did it work?" Alice broke in.

"Yes. Back to the tent."

Again in filtered light, he connected the hand-held device to a computer, then twiddled until satisfied. "Here's the view from the north end of our ladder set-up. I'll show you the first horizontal slice... then the next...then the next...then on down...do you see?"

The colored images looked faintly skeletal.

"Is it a skull and ribs?"

"Now we're moving over about a foot." He went slowly through the horizontal slices. "See? It's another skull, smaller, and I believe that's the collarbone below."

On the next slice Alice saw a vivid solid bit of red that repeated as Bender twiddled the dials through slices below. "What's that?"

"It's not bone," Bender said. "I think it will turn out to be metal. Could be something like a locket."

Frieda Fischer, perhaps wearing a locket... "Is it gold?" Alice asked.

Bender's voice: "Excavation needed. Okay, keep looking."

Now she saw a red roundish area, like the three from the gulch. Bender went on through the layers. "Possibly another ball or bullet," he said, "with similar data on the first skeleton."

"A ball? Meaning like a bullet?" Alice whispered.

Bender nodded. "I think it's possible. Now check the metal on the next view."

Prong, curve... She and Silla kept staring at the screen.

"Belt buckle, possibly?" Silla suggested.

"Could be. And the longer object? Maybe a pocketknife. I'm just speculating until we actually excavate."

"What about wedding rings? Wouldn't they last? Wouldn't they show up?" Silla asked.

"Didn't see any rings," Bender said. "They may be nearby and not within this scan. Or someone might easily have taken them from the bodies."

And didn't spot the locket, maybe because Frieda wore it under her dress, Alice thought, imagining Riley stooping over the dead bodies, yanking rings from the fingers.

"So, Alice, your idea was spot on." Bender grinned at her. "A lazy man's solution to a quick burial. Use someone else's work."

Alice was still transfixed by the possibilities held by the images on the screen. People she'd heard about, read about...and there they were...

"If these two bodies had been lying in water or wet soil all these years, I expect the bones would've dissolved," Bender added.

"So now what?" Silla asked, looking first at Bender, then at Alice.

Alice's mind raced. Frohbel was executor. Johnny would own the property. But she herself was charged with overseeing the judge's archeology project. Which involved murder. No, murders.

"Crime scene," she said. "We need to call Files, right away, before anyone moves a single rock."

Bender was nodding. "Strongly agree."

Alice was thinking aloud. "If the sheriff's office or, heaven forfend, the FBI insists on preferred procedures or techniques, we need to know. But in any event, these bodies say murder, which gives a possible motive for another murder—Judge Mahan's. We can't let anything damage the credibility of what you've found."

"Agree."

Alice pulled her phone from her pocket, about to call Files. "Here goes." Then a wave of fear hit her as she remembered Johnny.

"Wait! Anyone who knows about this is potentially in danger! That means you and your team, Bender. So let's keep it quiet. Does Johnny know yet?"

"No," said Silla. "Haven't said a word to him about this project."

Alice called Files and explained. "Can you come out here? Bender's found something—some bodies—very old bodies—you need to see. Just you, if possible, because of the risks involved. Risks to Johnny Mahan...and maybe others." Big Chest, Blindfold Guy—"Are those two men in jail, George? Hutton's ranch hands?"

"At the moment, yes. Awaiting arraignment, maybe tomorrow. On unlawful restraint and unlawful assault under the Texas Penal Code, and possibly other charges. We'll see."

"Good. Can you come out now?"

"Give me twenty minutes." He hung up.

"Give us the rundown, Alice," Bender asked. "And you still haven't told me about being shut up and left for dead."

Alice shivered, remembering how cold she'd been.

"Maybe I'm not being tactful?" Bender asked.

"You're not," Silla retorted. "It's cooling off. Let's go put some sticks on that campfire and get warm."

When the campfire by the big tent was blazing to their satisfaction, Bender, Silla, and Alice dragged camp stools close enough to warm their feet.

"Okay," Alice said. "Richard Riley's running for the Texas Legislature from our district, backed by big dollars from Winifred Hutton. She's determined to suppress the judge's history, in particular the chapter telling that Jasper Riley, kicked out of the Rangers, shot the Comanches who killed and cooked his horse. Then he killed the Fischers."

"Why?"

"According to Dedra Riley—that's Richard's wife—Winifred Hutton indicated she'd researched Richard's family tree and suggested he's related to Jasper Riley. Dedra herself didn't seem too bothered by the Comanche killings but kept insisting there was no proof the Fischers were murdered—that they'd likely decided frontier life was too tough and just run away. The word is that Winifred wants to be a big player in Texas politics. I got an unpleasant visit from Winifred herself. She threatened that the Rileys could sue for defamation."

"Over a story that's at least 180 years old?"

"Yes. But that could get harder if what you find here supports Emil Fischer's story."

Alice glanced at Bender's outdoor sculpture, looming above the rockpile on the shelf next to the gulch. The afternoon sun highlighted in a friendly way the heavily eroded, fossil-bearing burial rocks, piled up nearly two centuries ago...to hide a double murder.

Files arrived, climbed out of his cruiser, and strode to the campfire. "Okay. Show me what'cha got."

Bender led him to the tent, with Silla and Alice following. He reconnected the hand-held GPR to a computer. "Detective, you remember the story about Jasper Riley shooting the Comanches, then the Fischers, who owned the judge's place back then?"

"Yeah, I've seen the judge's draft history."

"First, I'm showing you what we found with the hand-held GPR on that shelf where you see the ladders set up." Carefully he focused in on the slices showing the skeletal remains, then the slices showing the bright red ovoids below the slices showing their ribs. "I think those may turn out to be bullets," Bender said. "Rather, lead balls."

Files took a big breath. "Allegedly from an 1847 Walker Colt."

"That's the tale."

"Any ID?"

"Based on the location, and assuming the Fischer boy's tale is true, it could be Fritz and Frieda Fischer. There may be a locket on the woman's neck, but we'd need to get it in our hands to examine it."

"So you want to excavate this grave?"

"Yes," Bender said. "No coffins, no proper burial, and, so far as we know, the bodies aren't Native American. They're on private property, and the owner could take steps to insure that they're properly and respectfully buried. That's not a legal opinion, just my opinion as an archeologist."

"Could their descendants ask to take charge of the bodies?"

"I don't know," Alice said. "I suppose they could ask." She needed to think more about that. Did Emil Fischer leave any descendants? "But meanwhile, they're on the judge's property. And they're currently unidentified and apparently didn't die a natural death. So I think we need to notify the Justice of the Peace." Might be unusual, but the better part of valor.

"I'll handle that. What about the supposed Comanche bodies?"

Files asked. "You find anything yet?"

Bender smiled, and pulled up on the computer screen the data he'd shown Alice and Silla.

"More bullets?" Files asked.

"Maybe."

"And maybe arrowheads? We could get those roughly dated and identified. Whether they're Comanche or not, when they were made, and where," Files said.

"Well"—Bender looked at Alice. "Counsel objects."

"We should contact the Comanche Nation first. They may have an opinion. But if not, and if we do any excavating of the Comanche bodies, we need to meet the NAGPRA standards and be sure we meet every criterion the FBI or your office has. Just trying to keep whatever we find beyond dispute."

"The feds have backed off. I'm pretty sure neither the feds nor the Coffee County Sheriff's Department would agree to bear the cost of such oversight," Files protested.

"Well, before I do anything, I'll need some written approvals," Bender said. "If we've found evidence of what may be the Comanche bodies and the bones of, probably, the Fischers, I want to be sure that we both comply with archeological standards and don't mess up the validity of any of your investigation."

"Okay. I'll ask the FBI and the Sheriff's Department if they have any objection to your going ahead, at least on the two bodies that might be the Fischers."

"I need an answer pretty fast," Bender said. "I can't keep my team here forever, and I sure don't want any unauthorized digging on the site."

Files nodded.

Alice added, "If Richard Riley is indeed a descendant of Jasper Riley, which Winifred Hutton claimed, we've already found enough to mess up his campaign, which is why Winifred Hutton is so furious about the judge's manuscript. Which may also be why someone tried to kill Johnny, who's the judge's heir. Trying to put an end to the whole Jasper Riley saga. I'm telling you both, I don't want any more attacks on that boy."

Files rubbed his chin, his brown eyes thoughtful. "I see why you want to keep the lid on this. I'll have to inform my federal counterparts. I'll warn them about the risk to Johnny." He gazed at Bender. "Your team—you're in charge of keeping that lid on. No grad student chit-chat, right?"

"Right," Bender growled.

Alice walked Files back to his car. "No warrant yet to search the Toyota truck for fingerprints?"

He groaned. "No. I don't want to blow the case by an illegal search. But we'll get there somehow." As they reached his car he didn't climb in but stood a moment, leaning on the door, looking at Alice. "How are you feeling?" he asked. "Joske said you were tough, at the ER, and kept insisting you were fine. Are you sure about that? Are you really fine?"

Alice started to say, "Oh, I'm fine." But was it true? She paused, wondering. "You know, maybe it's taking a while. Physically, I feel fine. But when I think about those two guys..." She shivered.

He nodded. "Take it easy, Alice. And take good care."

And he got in his cruiser and had driven out the gate before she thought, wait, there was something I wanted to tell you—what was it?

With Silla in the driver's seat, Alice climbed back into Silla's truck. Bender leaned in the open window. "I'll get in touch with the Comanche Nation folks," he proposed, "and see whether they want to repatriate the bones, even though this isn't tribal land. I'll let you know what they say. And then, Alice, you can be thinking about their response, and what the judge would want."

What was the right answer to these questions? They felt like a law school exam...for which she wasn't prepared.

And what was nagging at her, that she needed to tell Files?

Chapter Twenty-Eight

A Proprietary Sort Of Pat

On Friday morning Alice was finishing catch-up calls with clients when Silla popped her head in. "Don't forget you've got a library board meeting this morning! At ten!"

In that instant Alice remembered what she'd forgotten.

At ten minutes before ten she parked at the library, raced in, and cornered Mrs. Gregg, the head librarian, who was standing at the printer pulling off copies of the board agenda.

"Goodness, Alice! Our agenda's not that exciting! Here's your copy."

Alice took it.

"What's up?"

"I need to ask you a question about the reading room."

"Well, follow me."

Mrs. Gregg pushed open the glass-windowed door to the rectangular reading room, the pride of the Coffee Creek Library. The room held the usual rectangular wooden table, surrounded by upholstered chairs, with big windows on the long wall looking over the parking lot. A credenza at one end of the room held a tray with a thermos of coffee and mugs, as well as a bowl of the chocolate kisses Mrs. Gregg always provided.

Above the coffee service hung a large map of early Coffee County.

"Tell me about the map," Alice asked.

Mrs. Gregg laid the agenda copies on the table. She gave a ladylike snort. "It's not what I would have chosen for the library," she said. "And I didn't. The map dates from 1900, and Coffee Creek built its library in 1901. So we're almost as old as the Lockhart Library but not quite. Anyway, do you know Winifred Hutton?"

Alice nodded. "We've met." Her voice was tight.

"Hmm," said Mrs. Gregg. "Well, you know we allow the Historical Commission to meet here, and Tim Johansen begged me to let her put that map on the wall. Apparently she's a big donor to the Commission."

"I've heard."

"But our budget's tight, so I told Tim we'd be delighted to hang the map if she'd donate some money to the library. She grumbled, but she did it."

"How much?" asked Alice, curious.

"A thousand dollars. I bought new computers for the children's section. Of course, as you see, she attached an engraved plaque to the frame indicating it was her gift."

Alice leaned over to read the silver plaque, which hung by short silver chains from the bottom of the frame.

"Were you here when the map was hung?" Alice asked.

"Oh, yes. I mean, when someone's proposing to screw picture hangers into my oak-paneled walls? I was having a conniption."

"Was Hutton here?"

"Of course. Gloating. And honestly, every time she's here—she shows up at their board meetings, even though she's not on the board—I can see her through the door, adjusting the map, like it needs straightening. She nudges it a bit to the left, a bit to the right, cocks her head, scrutinizes the map, then gives it a—oh, I'd call it a proprietary sort of pat."

Aha, Alice thought.

Several board members had arrived and were claiming seats and pouring coffee.

Alice said, "Back in a sec."

She found a quiet corner in the children's section, empty at the moment during school hours, and called Files.

She heard road noise. "Files here."

"George," she said, lowering her voice, "Winifred Hutton gave a framed map to the library. It's hanging on the wall in the reading room. She shows up when the Historical Commission meets in the reading room and reportedly pats the map."

"What? Speak up, Alice."

"Wait, let me go outside."

Once on the porch she said, "Winifred Hutton pats the map. The framed map she gave the library. It's in the reading room."

"Well! That's worth a shot, though who knows who else puts their prints all over it. I'll send Joske over when we get back to town.."

"The library board's meeting in that room right now. We'll be out by one, though," Alice said. "Where are you?"

"I was going to call you with some news," Files said. "I'm on my way to Fredericksburg. The mysterious Winifred Hutton has been found."

"Really? Where?"

"Believe it or not, at the Herb Garden Day Spa in Fredericksburg. My nephew—you remember Adam Files?"

Alice remembered Adam, a young officer with the Gillespie County Sheriff's Department. He and Silla had dated for a while a couple of years ago. Alice liked Adam, but nothing had materialized.

Files went on. "Adam spotted the Land Rover convertible and remembered our APB. She's being detained for questioning and apparently having a fit. I gotta go."

"Wait! When did she get there? To the spa?"

"You guessed it. Last Monday afternoon."

Monday afternoon. When Alice had been thrown into the vet stall...and left in the January cold. No water, no food, no warmth.

"And tell the librarians—hands off that map!" Files hung up.

Alice rushed back into the reading room, tugged on Mrs. Gregg's sleeve, pulled her out into the corridor between YA and Fiction. "Don't let *anyone* touch that map!"

"Why ever not?"

"It's going to be checked for fingerprints this afternoon.

Mrs. Gregg's blue eyes widened behind her glasses. "My, my. I want to watch that! Okay, let's get this meeting done and dusted."

Alice took her seat at the table as Mrs. Gregg convened the meeting. But she couldn't keep her eyes off the map. Finally, Mrs. Gregg said, "Adjourned!"

As the board members left, they blinked at the sight of the three people waiting outside the glass door: Detective Alan Joske, with a police sergeant and a civilian investigator.

"Come in, gentlemen!" said Mrs. Gregg.

Chapter Twenty-Nine

Left On The Doorbell

Alice hung around until Joske emerged from the reading room. "Anything good?" she asked, hoping Files had told him about Winifred Hutton's proprietary pats.

"Plenty of prints," Joske said. "Keep your fingers crossed." He smiled—surprising Alice, who suspected Joske mistrusted her—but maybe he felt differently now that he'd helped rescue her from the vet stall. He and his team left.

Mrs. Gregg beamed at Alice. "What a thrill, to watch actual fingerprinting!" she said. "I'm a mystery nut, you know, but I've never gotten to see the process. Alice, you do add so much to our board."

Alice laughed. But she found herself actually crossing her fingers.

*****

When Alice returned to the office, Silla was gone. She'd left a note: "Back by five. Call if you need me." She didn't say where she was—unusual.

Alice called Bender, who reported that after his call, the Comanche Nation had asked for more time to discuss any proposed change in location for the Comanche remains. Meanwhile, Bender, watched by an expert from the Texas Archeology Society, was preparing to begin the cautious removal of rocks from above the Fischer bodies. "We're videotaping everything. I called Detective Files to say we're about to uncover the bones. He's not sending anyone out but wants copies of the videotapes. The Justice of the Peace dropped by but said it was mostly out of curiosity." And in response to a last question from Alice, "No, haven't seen Silla."

Alice hoped that there was a locket, a gold locket that still bore Frieda Fischer's initials. She sat staring at her computer, where a reminder text from Silla popped up. "Don't forget to finish the outline for your continuing legal education presentation on groundwater issues," she reminded Alice. "Due February 10."

Alice sighed. What she *really* wanted was to see Winifred Hutton locked in the Coffee County Jail. Yes, in an orange jumpsuit, spewing hatred at the guards. And not looking anything like Brandy Clark singing "Stripes." Nevertheless...she started the outline.

At one-thirty her phone rang. She grabbed it.

Files. "Got the warrant for the truck. Winifred Hutton's prints are a match for many of the prints inside the truck. 'Of course they match,' her lawyer claims. 'It's her vehicle! But others drove it. So her prints mean nothing with regard to the judge's death.' That's what her lawyer said. But Alice, here's the great news."

She held her breath.

"Winifred Hutton's fingerprint appears to be one of the last prints left on the doorbell at the judge's house. Maybe the last."

Alice gasped. Suddenly she could see it: Winifred Hutton driving out to confront the judge, maybe taking her ancient Toyota truck to look, oh, less rich? More like a good ol' gal from Coffee Creek? But Hutton didn't have the judge's gate code...so she drove in through the fire gate, stopped her truck in the parking area, then marched up and rang the doorbell. And was furious when no one answered. And maybe then she walked over to look into the garage, saw both the judge's vehicles there, and was even more outraged that no one answered the door. And finally climbed back into her truck...and maybe, about then, the judge quit watching from the ridge and walked down the hill to the parking area...

But what about the gun?

She posed that question to Files.

"Separate warrant," he said. "Now that we've shown she was at the judge's, we're getting a search warrant for her revolver."

"Dedra Riley said Winifred always carries a gun in that hand-tooled leather shoulder bag she wears," Alice said.

"Not at the moment, she doesn't," Files said. "Apparently she didn't bring a gun to the Herb Garden Day Spa."

"But you're searching her Land Rover? And searching her house?"

"Yes."

A wave of blind rage swept over Alice as she remembered Big Chest and Blindfold Guy—grabbing her, tossing her onto the concrete floor in the vet stall, leaving her there to die. "What about those so-called ranch hands? Are those two jerks talking yet?"

"Not yet. They probably still think she'll cover for them. They've got criminal counsel right now, but I don't know who's paying the lawyers."

"Hide and watch," Alice said. "She'll drop those guys in the dirt, say it was all their idea." By four-thirty, she couldn't stand it and called Files again. "Any luck yet on the revolver?"

"Nope." He sounded slightly down. "The team's been out at the ranch for two hours. Still haven't found anything. You know how many closets that woman has?" He sighed. "One for dresses, one for pants, one for formal wear, then there's the coat closet...not to mention shelves and dressers...plus the cabinet with the jewelry, and the safe..."

Closets. Shelves. Boxes.

Alice remembered. And she sat straight up. "Don't skip the hat boxes! Be sure to look in all those hat boxes!"

"*Hat boxes?*"

"Especially the Stetson boxes!"

"Yeah, yeah. Gotta go."

Alice heard the front door open and close. Silla?

Silla was back at her computer, riveted to the screen, scribbling notes on a legal pad.

She turned to Alice. "I've got it. You won't believe this."

"What?"

"Haven't you wondered why Winifred Hutton is so all-fired nervous about Richard Riley being related to Jasper Riley?"

"Not really. I mean, some voters would forgive him for shooting Comanches who were eating his horse. But even with the Fischers murdered—it's 180 years ago! Couldn't Winifred just tell the public it's too old to matter?"

"But Alice—it's about Winifred too!"

Alice stared blankly at Silla.

"I've been poking around the ancestry sites. And this afternoon I drove over to Bastrop County to the old MacTavish Cemetery. Had to climb over the fence. Ripped my jeans." She pointed to a snag at thigh level.

"But look." She pulled out her phone. Alice saw a weathered gray tombstone, inscribed "Jasper R. Riley"—born 1822, died 1910. "And there were two smaller tombstones planted right next to ol' Jasper."

She pulled up a second photo. Alice peered at it: the small tombstone read, "Wife of Jasper Riley, Edith Hutton Riley, died 1870." Silla said, "Remember, the judge found their marriage record in Caldwell County, but it didn't give Edith's maiden name? Well, here it is. *Hutton*. And later on Jasper remarried—a woman named Sylvia Coe." Her next photo showed a small stone: "Wife of Jasper Riley, Sylvia Coe Riley, died 1902."

Alice said, "Interesting. It's also interesting that Riley got married east of Coffee County, over in Caldwell County, and died farther east, in Bastrop County, and never swaggered back to Coffee County."

"But there's more, Alice!"

"What? Where?"

"On the ancestry sites! If you plug in Jasper Riley, you see he had a sister named Carlotta. And once we found the maiden names of Jasper's wives on the tombstones, we could look them up too. So, when you plug in Edith Hutton, who married Jasper Riley in 1863, you learn her brother was Rufus Hutton. Look up Rufus, and you find he married Jasper's sister, Carlotta Riley.

"Then it gets really interesting. And complicated. You need to follow both couples. Edith and Jasper had two children, Chastity and Jethro Riley. Rufus and Carlotta also had two children, Cynthia and Carl Hutton. Got that?

"I'm trying!"

"Okay. After Edith Hutton died, Jasper remarried Sylvia Coe, as we saw from the second little tombstone. Jasper and this second wife, Sylvia, had another daughter, Cora Riley. It turns out—if you look up Rufus and Carlotta's children—that their son Carl Hutton married Cora Riley."

Alice was getting dizzy.

Silla continued, "The son of Carl and Cora Hutton is Henry Hutton. Guess what: he's Winifred Hutton's great-great grandfather. If you look up Jethro Riley, you'll see he's Richard Riley's great-great-great grandfather. Are you following?"

Alice nodded. "Kind of."

"So if you are looking at the Hutton tree and the Riley tree—Richard Riley, several generations later, has two Rileys in his tree—Jasper Riley and Jasper's son, Jethro Riley. And Winifred Hutton also has two Rileys in her tree—Carlotta Riley, who was Jasper Riley's sister, and

Cora Riley, Jasper's daughter by his second marriage. Pretty damn tangled, don't you think?"

"Very tangled," Alice breathed, trying to figure this out.

"I saw Winifred Hutton was quoted in this week's *Coffee Creek Caller* as claiming that, while she's new to Coffee County, she's a sixth-generation Texan. I don't think she's counting right, because Rufus Hutton and his sister, Edith, were born in Tennessee, and Jasper Riley and his sister, Carlotta, were born in Louisiana. But however you look at it, Winifred's as much a Riley as Richard Riley. I'm betting she's desperate for that information to stay out of the news. Especially with the Fischers' bodies being found!"

"But she doesn't yet know they've been found, does she?"

"Come on, she's known for a good while that there's an archeological dig going on, right? Don't you think she sent that guy out to snoop, the first week of the dig?"

"Probably. You're right, she may be terrified that the Fischer bodies are actually there. Silla, do you have this family stuff all sketched out?"

"Yep." Silla handed Alice a carefully drawn and complicated double family tree. "And I've printed out all the backup. It's amazing what you can find online. I'm sure the judge would've gotten there too—but I've messed around with this genealogy stuff before."

"Holy cow," Alice muttered, studying the intricate family tree, and thinking back to Winifred Hutton's furious visit to the office. "Holy cow, Silla. Winifred's thinking the judge's manuscript will link her to the Fischer murders. Of course she would have read the footnotes to Chapter 13. She'd see that anyone could follow up and find those Hutton-Riley connections."

Alice was beginning to understand Winifred's fury. And perhaps her terror. Unless the revolver used in the judge's murder was never found...

*****

At six Alice left the office and stopped at the H-E-B for groceries. She'd put limes, avocados, lettuce, and blueberries in her cart when she spied Rusty James at the nearby meat counter, giving an order to the white-aproned butcher. Alice blocked him in with her cart. "Rusty! Don't you owe me a phone call?"

Rusty turned. "Alice!" Rusty was medium height, getting a little paunch under his polo shirt and fleece, with a big smile and watchful eyes. "Alice, I'm horrified about the judge."

She nodded. "That's what I wanted to ask you about. Last November, when you called him about a, quote, 'highly motivated buyer' for the judge's fifteen acres, who was it?"

He shook his head. "Oh, the buyer wanted to stay confidential."

"Rusty, the judge was murdered. And someone's been prowling that fifteen acres. If you don't tell me who the buyer was, I expect Detective Files will be interested."

A crease appeared between Rusty's eyebrows. "Well...the buyer backed out after making that big offer, when the judge insisted on knowing who it was. I got the impression maybe the buyer needed to put that funding elsewhere. I could be wrong. Anyway..." He seemed to be making up his mind. "Have you ever heard of HFH, LLC? HFH for short?"

"I have. Once. Did you deal with Winifred Hutton?"

"No, it was some employee of HFH. Male. Not a principal, though—I assumed he was taking orders from someone else."

The butcher handed a white-wrapped package over the counter to Rusty. He grabbed it. "Gotta get this home, Alice. Good to see you." He was in quite a rush to check out, Alice thought, and to quit talking about HFH.

Milk, butter, orange juice—she added them to her cart, checked out, and headed for home. Maybe Hutton—or the "principal" at HFH—needed to put that funding toward Riley's campaign?

*****

"Okay, Alice." Files's voice on the cell phone, with car noise. "How'd you know?"

"Know what?"

"Know that Winifred Hutton kept her .38 revolver in a Stetson hatbox underneath her Stetson hat?"

Alice grinned from ear to ear. "Seriously?"

"Dead serious. I got worried after talking to you and drove back to Hutton's ranch. The guys were just about to leave empty-handed, I mean literally. They were halfway down the stairs. I said, 'Did you check the hatboxes? Every single hat box?' They stared at me and turned around, went back upstairs, borrowed a stool to stand on, and opened every hatbox. And there was the revolver, under a lady's Stetson, fedora style, I believe they call it. I'm on my way back to town, and the revolver's on its way to the lab. Maybe tests will show whether it fired the bullet that killed the judge. And we'll check that leather purse for gun residue." He paused. Alice could almost see him, staring out the windshield. "And I'll enjoy watching her lawyer's face when he hears what we found."

"Is she under arrest?"

"Shortly."

Until that happened, Alice knew she would still feel anxious.

"Oh, another thing," Files said. "People are so weird. Know what's displayed on the wall in Hutton's upstairs hall? An antique gold watch. Tell me why? And guess what's next to it, in a big gold frame, label underneath, almost like a shrine?"

"What?"

"An old Walker Colt pistol. The label claims it's one of the original 1847 Walker Colts. The one our governor recently termed the 'State Gun of Texas.' Never heard anything so ridiculous. But here's the thing, Alice. You remember you sent me the judge's history? And you said people were worried about Chapter 13, about the Comanches being shot, and maybe the Fischers?"

"Yes?" She held her breath.

"The label claims this Colt belonged to Jasper Riley. Isn't that the guy whose horse was being eaten?"

"Yes. He'd already been kicked out of the Texas Rangers for killing a fellow Ranger."

"Oops. Well, Winifred Hutton apparently has his original pistol on her wall."

"So did you grab that Walker Colt too, George? Did the warrant cover it, as evidence of her motive for killing Judge Mahan? Because based on work Silla's done, Winifred Hutton has two Riley ancestors in her family tree. She didn't want the judge to publish his history, alleging murder by Jasper Riley, and she sure doesn't want the world to know that the owner of Hutton Family Jewelry is descended from a murderer. The presence of that Colt just highlights her Riley connection." She took a breath. "And remember I told you about some 'highly motivated' buyer trying to buy Jasper Riley's fifteen acres last November? Well, Joske will like this detail: I saw Rusty James at the H-E-B, and he said the buyer was 'HFH, LLC.' Look it up—that's Hutton Family Holdings."

Silence. "Now I see what you're talking about. I'll talk to the DA again."

Chapter Thirty

Her Ancestor's Service

On Saturday morning on her way to the office, Alice called Johnny. "I'm feeling pretty good," he said. "I'm planning to stay at Granddad's place awhile. Dad's going to get me settled before he goes back to San Francisco in a couple of days. It's not a bad commute to school. And I can take care of Charley."

Well, that's an improvement, Alice thought. It felt like a good day to wrap up loose ends. She stopped by Madrone Bank—Miranda, bank manager, was always there on Saturday morning.

Miranda, tall, blonde, wry-humored, dragged Alice into her office, shut the door, and hugged her friend. "That was some adventure, Alice. You realize you missed book group? You scared us all to pieces."

"How was the book?"

"We couldn't discuss it without you, so we just drank wine and wondered where you were. If we'd known Winifred Hutton had you locked outside in the cold, in the dark—" Miranda shook her head. "The irony about that woman—she's so family proud, so sure we should all kowtow to her. She can't have a conversation without mentioning Hutton Family Holdings, the family money. I've always thought it sticks in her craw that her brother managed to multiply his share of the family money, but she hasn't. You probably haven't heard of Hutton Family Jewelry?"

"Not until she mentioned it when she showed up at my office to threaten me."

"Well, it's her baby, and she's trying to expand it. Hoping for an IPO at some point, I bet. So far she's got about six Texas stores in small towns. You know, jewelry for kids, sweethearts, husbands, and wives. Lots of crosses and saints' medals and religious symbols. I got one of her catalogues in the mail—she's spending a bundle on ads and catalogues."

Whew, Alice thought. Winifred might be very worried about the risk of having Hutton Family Jewelry tagged with the Riley heritage. Dead children, dead parents...

"She's having trouble getting outside funding. And you know what else?" Miranda went on, "Her application to join the Daughters of the Texas Republic got turned down."

"Why?"

"From what I hear, because she can't prove any ancestor rendered

'loyal service' before February 19, 1846. That's a membership require-
ment. She tried to claim her ancestor's service in the Texas Rangers, but
there's no record of him before 1847."

"And besides, he apparently got kicked out for deadly assault on a
fellow Ranger," Alice put in.

"Ooh, I didn't know that part. Wonderful."

"Any idea where the family money came from, Miranda?"

"I was talking yesterday with a banker friend who knew Winifred
at Hockaday. She says Winifred bragged to classmates that, back before
the Civil War, her great-great-somebody came back to Texas from St.
Louis with enough money in gold to marry into the Hutton family and
buy some big acreage along the Colorado River. Purest gossip, mind
you."

"The best kind, right?" Alice hugged Miranda goodbye.

Now she was remembering the 1847 complaint filed by Horst
Meyer. What about the gold watches? Was it possible Jasper Riley sold
stolen loot in St. Louis and came back to Texas rich? But how could
that ever be proved? Too long ago for any records...

When she reached the office, Alice picked up the phone to call
David Frohbel. As counsel for the judge's estate, he deserved a status
report on her two assignments for the judge. When she mentioned the
archeology dig, he said, "Alice, may I invite myself over? I so wanted to
be an archeologist. Maybe doing probate work is one kind of excavation—figuring out where the bodies are buried, metaphorically speaking. But oh, man, would I like to see that dig."

Alice laughed. "Wouldn't it be dereliction of duty if you didn't?
Time for a field trip."

"Any possibility we could do it today? I've got a second ulterior
motive," Frohbel said. "Coffee Creek barbecue's better than ours in
Fredericksburg. Can we go to Shade Tree?"

"We can."

"Third ulterior motive. Johnny inherits the judge's place. I'd like to
take him the various keys and documents, if he can be there. He's off
the suspect list, right?"

"Right. I'll call Johnny to see if we can touch base. No classes today,
but if he's started back to work we might have to meet him at the Last

Corral. Want to meet at Shade Tree at eleven?"

"Great."

*****

In the big grove outside Shade Tree, a light wind rattled the leaves on the sinuous branches of the old live oaks. Alice lifted her face to the sunshine—it was unseasonably warm for the end of January, warm enough for her to carry their beers to a picnic table and wait for David Frohbel to collect their chopped brisket and grilled Czech sausage. David, short, with his starched blue shirt, sharp blue eyes, and sandy hair, was born and bred in Fredericksburg. During her first year at law school, Alice had made friends with David and his brilliant wife, Isabel, who memorably closed down Scholz Garten in Austin, dancing on tables in the outdoor biergarten, after final exams.

Now, sipping a draft beer in the sun, she remembered how a couple of years ago she'd been sitting in the sun in Fredericksburg, with Frohbel and a cold beer, when Ben Kinsear had walked up to their table—tall, dark-haired, in his jeans and cowboy shirt with the sleeves rolled up. It was Alice's first encounter with Kinsear since law school; since then her husband, Jordie, had disappeared, and Kinsear's wife, Betsy, had died. How skittish she'd been that day in Fredericksburg, how nervous about reconnecting with this man. But his persistence— and, she had to admit, the undeniable chemistry between them—had won out. She looked down at the ring on her left hand.

David's sharp eyes had noticed that ring. "Kinsear, right?"

"Mm-hmm."

"Good man. I knew he'd win you over."

Between bites of brisket sandwich, Alice and David gossiped about small-town law practice, their children, and the peccadillos of certain members of the judiciary. Wiping the orange sauce from the corner of his mouth, David said, "Fill me in on the murder investigation. Any news?"

"Nothing definite. Winifred Hutton's a suspect. The investigating detective has placed her at the judge's house the afternoon he died. He's waiting for test results on the revolver found at her ranch. Her daddy's

.38, apparently."

"She didn't throw it in a river?"

"Sentimental value, is my guess." Alice served herself more of the grilled sausage slices, added a little German mustard, took a bite. "Mmm."

"Agreed." Frohbel closed his eyes. "The owner makes this sausage himself?"

"Yes."

"There should be a Nobel Prize for Peace through Barbecue," Frohbel said. "If people in the Middle East could just sit down together over some Texas barbecue..."

"Beef," Alice added.

As they finished the last bites, Alice's phone beeped. Text from Johnny: "I'm at the judge's place but need to be at work by four."

"Great," said Frohbel. "I'm in a highly benevolent state of mind, post-barbecue. Eager to meet Johnny. Let's roll."

*****

When they reached the judge's place, Johnny answered the front door, accompanied by Charley. Alice introduced Frohbel, Then she gave Johnny her maternal once-over stare—his bruises were mostly gone, his eyes were focused. "You look—recovered."

Johnny put up with it, smiling. "I'm fine."

Frohbel shared information on the probate process and how to manage utility bills and other house expenses before the assets were distributed.

Johnny thanked him, then grabbed his jacket. "Got to get to the Last Corral on time," he said.

Outside, Bender stood waiting near the gulch. Alice introduced Frohbel, who shook hands and asked for a status report. Bender explained that the Comanche Nation representatives would be arriving soon to confirm proper removal of the Native American remains and artifacts under the Native American Graves Protection and Repatriation Act and to take them back to Oklahoma. Then he showed Frohbel the GPR data, explaining how archeologists had to interpret the multiple horizontal slices to zero in on possible bones and artifacts.

"By the way, has anyone identified the Fischer cabin site?" asked Frohbel.

"It's not our task, but we've found what we think are traces, just up the west ridge"—he pointed—"about a hundred yards from the creek."

"Last question: what's the plan for the Fischers' remains?"

Bender looked at Alice. "Counsel hasn't told us yet."

"You could bury them here, of course," said Frohbel. "Assuming Johnny wants that. But have you checked with family members? I mean Fischer family members?"

"I need to research Emil Fischer," Alice blurted, remembering his letter to his Aunt Jutta about his father's pocket watch. Lizzie Bond apparently died before tracking down family members as she'd intended.

She turned to Frohbel. "If you've got your questions answered, let's get going." She was suddenly desperate to look for Emil Fischer, the boy who started medical school at Tulane, served as a medic during the Civil War, then finished medical school with the Meyers' help. Where did he wind up? Did he have descendants? Where was the pocket watch?

Chapter Thirty-One

What Justice?

When she got back to her empty office—so quiet on Saturday afternoon she could hear the hall clock ticking—Alice dived into the Texas Code of Criminal Procedure, searching the statutes of limitation for theft of property. But as she remembered, the statute for criminal theft would have run out well before 1859, when Emil left for medical school. Murder? While traces of DNA could be used to convict a murderer years after the victim's death, that didn't work if the murderer was also dead. And while descendants of victims of Nazi war crimes could sue decades later to retrieve stolen artwork, she thought Texas civil procedure wouldn't entertain suits filed for theft of pocket watches and gold coins—180 years later. Maybe if Emil Fischer had tracked down his parents' killer after the Civil War? Maybe then he could have obtained some restitution, some satisfaction, for years of heartache, for being orphaned, for never having his parents see their grandchildren...if they had any.

But now? What justice for the Fischers?

As the saying had it, justice delayed is justice denied.

Maybe, though, some closure?

According to Jutta Meyer, Emil had traveled to Baltimore for med school. She called the University of Maryland Medical Center, where even on a weekend a helpful voice answered. "I wonder if you can confirm whether a student named Emil Fischer graduated in 1866 or 1867 or 1868?" The helpful voice promised to get back to her.

Why would Emil have gone to Baltimore rather than to med schools farther north? Penn? Yale? Harvard? Dartmouth?

After serving in the Confederate army as a medic? She wondered how welcome he'd be. Maybe a border state felt...safer. But if and when Emil finished—where did he go?

On a whim she searched property records in Taylor, Texas, for the current owner of the property at the address the judge had scribbled for Lizzie Bond. Someone named Judith Bond now paid taxes on that property. Lizzie's relative? Alice picked up her phone—nothing ventured, nothing gained—and called. No answer; she left a message, hoping it didn't sound too weird—"I'm trying to locate descendants of Emil Fischer, whose aunt was Lizzie Bond's great-grandmother. My client owns land once owned by Emil Fischer's parents. An archeological dig has found what may be his parents' remains, and we want to talk to the Fischer descendants about whether the remains should be buried on the property. Please call..." She left her number, feeling pessimistic.

Saturday afternoon. Pink and gold clouds gathered in the western sky. No dinner with Kinsear tonight—it was "Dad night," and he was in Austin, taking his daughters, Isabel and Carrie, to dinner. Both were UT students—Carrie a freshman, Isabel a senior. Alice had asked him for an update on both girls. How was Carrie doing? How serious were Isabel and her beau, Sam Brody?

Alice wished her own kids were home, but they were far away in Boston, Edinburgh... That was the problem with encouraging your children to flap their wings and fly, she thought: they did. She wished they were with her right this minute.

The phone rang. Her best friend, Red. "Are you free for dinner? I haven't seen you since your escape from that Hutton woman."

"Yes, indeed! Anywhere you choose!"

"Jobell's in Wimberley? I'm craving the ahi tuna salad. I'll drive. See you in ten."

*****

Riding shotgun in Red's red (of course) pickup, Alice felt a bubble of delight, felt her face breaking into a smile. What could restore the soul better than riding shotgun in her best friend's pickup, heading to dinner down the curvy road to Wimberley while facing no immediate threats from Hutton or her ranch hands? She heaved a sigh of contentment.

She and Red chatted all the way to the restaurant—about Red's adventures at her rescue ranch for abused horses and Silla's amazing flight to find Alice's car. When they were settled at their table, each with a glass of prosecco, Red said, "Let's get serious."

"Serious?" Alice flinched.

"Yes. Am I a bridesmaid or not?"

Alice stared blankly.

"Of course!" Then she wondered—and also Ann? Who else? Carrie? Isabel?

"When? A girl's got to plan, you know. This year? Next year? The year after that? And what are we going to wear?" She leaned forward, holding her glass in the air. "Have you and Kinsear even set a date?"

"Ummm..."

"I thought not. Come on, Alice. Time's a-wasting. Just tell him you've decided he can move in with you. Or that you'll take turns, one week at his place, one at yours. Is that all that's holding you up?"

Alice nodded. "I think that's what it is."

"Well, get on it! You can always adjust the location decision after you get married. Glad that's settled." She picked up her glass. "Here's to setting a date."

Alice lifted her glass, clinked Red's, took a sip. The prosecco tickled her tongue. She settled back in her chair, basking in the pleasant restaurant atmosphere—warm lights, the low voice of a waiter, a soft laugh from a table in the corner.

"And moving on," said Red, "let's think about the wedding. Weather, first. Bluebonnets?"

Alice nodded. "Yes. And also, if possible, prairie celestials and winecups."

"End of March or early April, then," Red announced. "At your place? Or his place? Or are you getting married at church and having a reception at the Beer Barn? Or doing the whole thing at the Beer Barn?"

"Oooh. I don't know!" Alice tried to imagine the possibilities.

"Hold that thought. Let's get down to brass tacks. What are you going to wear?"

Alice's first thought was not about her own outfit, but what about Kinsear's? If it was an evening wedding, maybe Texas tux—the tux jacket with jeans and a fancy tux shirt. A bolo tie. He'd look stunning. And his boots.

That settled at least one aspect of her own wedding garb.

"Boots."

Red nodded. "Good. You're finally putting your mind to it. And let's get that date *nailed down*. I need to help you pick the bridesmaids' outfits!" She grinned, saluting Alice with her glass. "Okay. Now I've got to hear every lurid detail of this murder investigation and Winifred Hutton. A friend of mine who lives out on Middle Creek says she had some pricey horses but sold them off. Also says she's a poisonous neighbor to have."

"I understand the crime scene team found her fingerprints at Judge Mahan's place and in the truck that was apparently at his property that afternoon. The detectives also found a revolver at her house that may turn out to be the one that killed the judge. But it's still early days, Red."

"But *why?*" Red pressed. "Why in the world would she kill the judge?"

"She doesn't like his draft history of Coffee County. There's a story about a shooting back in 1847 on Judge Mahan's property that may involve a relative of hers. The judge wanted his manuscript to be accurate. Until we're pretty sure it is...I can't tell you anything more."

"Oh, Alice. This is why lawyers are so frustrating. You get access to these juicy stories, and then you just draw a finger across your lips."

"Well, what if I knew a secret *you* wanted kept quiet, Red? Wouldn't you want me to?"

"Huh. Isn't that what best friends are for? Besides, my life's an open book." She smiled and waved two fingers at the bartender, who walked over with the prosecco bottle. Behind him came the waiter with their ahi tuna tacos, sending irresistible smells into the air.

"Oh, boy," Red said. Momentarily silence prevailed.

After a moment, Alice asked, "What if your secret was that 180 years ago some ancestor, a great-great-grandfather, say, had murdered some folks?"

"That long ago? Come on, what would happen now? The sins of the fathers are not visited on the heads of the children, or great-great-grandchildren, are they? If so, we're all in trouble."

"What if you're so proud of your family name you don't want anyone to know about the murders?"

"I know people like that. But doesn't every family have branches they don't want talked about? Or at least twigs? Besides," Red said, "haven't you noticed sometimes that there's loud silence about the family sinners? We joke about the scamps—but villains? Written out of the family story." She took another bite, closed her eyes. "Mmm. Listen, how's Silla?"

"Fine," said Alice. And maybe it was the mention of a bluebonnet wedding, but really, what about Silla and Bender? Where was that going? She needed to know. He'd better treat her right...

"Come on, Alice, we're celebrating! Let's have dessert. I'm going for chocolate." Alice watched the animated face of her best friend, thinking how Red had encouraged her to make the big move to Coffee Creek. And how had that turned out?

Pretty damn well.

Red dropped her off in town at the office. Alice climbed into her car for the drive back up the creek road to her donkeys, her house, to what she now thought of as the bounds of her habitation. But not bounds in a limiting way...

Her phone beeped. She peeked at the screen. Kinsear, texting so late? "Had dinner with the girls. I'm driving back from Austin. May I spend the night with you? Got some news. I'll fix breakfast..."

A quick yes, but what was his news?

*****

Fiddling with Alice's sound system, Kinsear said, "How about some blues guitar? Jimmie Vaughan?"

Alice laid another log in the fireplace, watching the orange sparks fly, feeling the irresistible slow beat of the music.

Then Kinsear said, "The news is that Isabel wants to marry Sam this summer."

"Oh, that's wonderful!" Alice loved Kinsear's elder daughter and thought Sam Brody was terrific.

"I want us to get married before she does. I don't want you distracted." He smiled, watching her, but Alice knew he was serious.

"So does Red. She wanted to talk about that at dinner. Wanted to know if she'll be a bridesmaid!"

"Are we going to have to have bridesmaids and all that?"

That made Alice think about her children. "I should ask Ann how she'd feel. And I don't know the answer. What will your girls think?"

"Same. I'm not sure. I guess we need to ask. Hey, come dance with me. I love how Jimmie Vaughan slows this version down." He took her hand, singing along with on "I Ain't Never..." The new version had a heavy slow beat that captured Alice. Kinsear slowly spun her away, then back, then took her again by the waist, holding her close, his baritone voice emphasizing every syllable— "I ain't never...I ain't never..." He held her tight, no longer dancing, but swaying back and forth to the compelling beat.

Alice loved the way Kinsear smelled. She buried her face in his neck, inhaling the whiff of clean cotton and the salty sweet smell of his skin. "I ain't never..." he crooned, swaying.

Now he was kissing her with intention, his face lit by firelight. "One thing I am sure about, and that's you," he murmured. He slow-danced her down the hall to her bedroom. Jimmie Vaughan was still singing.

Chapter   Thirty - Two

What An Interesting Call!

On Sunday morning, armed with a cup of espresso topped with foamed hot milk, Alice took a deep breath and said, "What about a bluebonnet wedding?"

Kinsear nodded. "Great."

"And will you move in with me here? At least at first?"

"If that's what you want, yes!"

"I'll ask Laura at church this morning, about the end of March."

Which she did. Laura's response: "Finally! I was beginning to think you'd never ask!"

Alice found herself singing along to Sun Radio on her way to the office—Lukas Nelson and Sheryl Crow singing "Midnight Rider." No, no one was gonna catch her now, or ever again, and especially not Big Chest and Blindfold Guy. She was emerging from the stifling fear that had blanketed her.

At the office she found an email from the Medical Center in Baltimore. "Ms. Greer, your request about Emil Fischer was so intriguing I took the liberty of emailing on Sunday. Yes, Dr. Emil Fischer graduated in 1869. Our information is that he later practiced in Annapolis. Although you did not ask about any others with that surname, I want you to know that Professor Dr. Maria Fischer has recently retired as professor of endocrinology. I believe they are related. My understanding is she plans to contact you. With best wishes..."

Interesting response.

But right in the middle of her desk lay the unfinished draft of Alice's outline on groundwater issues. Sticky note on top, from Silla: "DUE FEBRUARY 10."

Alice sighed, sat down, pulled up the draft on her computer, and got to work. She finished the legislative review, looked up the relevant new cases, and began analyzing them. Feeling a desperate need for caffeine, she started toward the kitchen. Her phone rang.

Alice stood rooted to the floor, amazed at the screen name that appeared.

"Dr. Fischer?"

"What an interesting call I had from the Med Center, Ms. Greer!"

"Please call me Alice."

"Is it correct that you represent the owners of the property where my ancestors were killed? The property on Blue Creek?"

"Yes, it is."

"And that archeologists have found remains that may be the parents of my great-grandfather, Dr. Emil Fischer?"

"Yes."

"I would very much like to visit the property. And since I'm in my seventies, times a-wasting. In short, I managed to get a reservation on a flight from Dulles airport, leaving shortly and arriving in Austin at six this evening. I have made a room reservation in—is it Coffee Creek?—somewhere close, and I will just take a Lyft out."

On impulse, Alice said, "Let me pick you up! Call me at this number when you've got your bag."

"Very well. Most kind of you. I'll be standing outside Exit E, I believe. My suitcase is bright pink."

She hung up.

Holy cow, thought Alice. And I forgot to ask if she's got the pocket watch. She called Bender. "How would you like to meet the great-granddaughter of Emil Fischer tomorrow morning? She wants to see Emil's parents' bones."

"Perfect timing. We'll be ready for her."

*****

At 6 p.m., Alice sat in the cell phone lot, thinking what an unusual legal project the judge had handed her: taking to dinner the distant descendant of two German immigrants murdered 180 years ago, whose remains had now been found. Keeping tabs on an archeological dig. As to the judge's history? That was more in the legal line, because it was all about facts. And Alice was all about facts. Once you had the facts, and particularly once you'd acquired the key facts, you were locked and loaded.

Which is precisely how she wanted to feel about the judge's history.

Her cell rang. "I'm here! In front of Exit E!"

"I'll be right there."

The sunset must have looked lovely from the air—purple, gold, pink. But Alice's eyes were glued to the entrance ramp. Always a trick, negotiating the crowds waiting for rides at the Austin airport. She spotted a bright pink suitcase, accompanied by a white-haired smiling woman in a pink suit. No way to miss Dr. Maria Fischer.

The woman in pink lifted her suitcase into the back seat and climbed in front and stuck out her hand. "Maria Fischer. Please call me Maria. I'm so glad to meet you, Alice! Thanks for picking me up!"

"I'm delighted you called. Unless you object, we'll have dinner and get you settled and then go first thing tomorrow morning to Judge Mahan's property. Dr. Bobby Bender's the archeologist leading the dig, and he'll show you what we've found. First, though, we've got to make it out of the airport and head west toward Coffee Creek." Alice threaded her way into the exit heading west, grateful that it was Sunday night, with lighter traffic than usual.

Once on the highway, she asked, "How do you feel about Mexican food for dinner? A place called Hecho en Mexico?"

"Sounds great."

Driving west, she asked Dr. Fischer about her career. It turned out she'd graduated from the Maryland med school, specialized in endocrinology, and later returned there to teach. Dr. Fischer was eager to hear about Judge Mahan, horrified by his death, and intrigued by the projects he'd hired Alice to bring to fruition.

Alice couldn't help feeling happy when she walked through the restaurant door. Colorful décor, colorful food, cold cerveza. After they ordered—*cochinita pibil* for Dr. Fischer, ceviche for Alice—she gazed at Dr. Fischer and said, "Now I can ask. I've seen the letter from Emil Fischer to his aunt Jutta Meyer, about his father's pocket watch. Do you—does anyone—still have that pocket watch?"

Alice held her breath, waiting.

Dr. Fischer unbuttoned the top button of the cream silk blouse under her pink jacket. She tugged at a sturdy gold chain.

And there it was. An antique gold pocket watch, its case burnished for 180 years by pockets, by human skin. It hung several inches below her chin. Dr. Fischer snapped open the case and held it up. "Keeps perfect time," she said. "Right now, Eastern Daylight Time."

"May I see the back of the case?"

Dr. Fischer turned her wrist so Alice could see the back. Two tiny linked letters, fluid and perfect: *FF.*

"Emil Fischer was my great-grandfather. I am honored to wear this watch. Knowing what he went through, it's been meaningful. When I'm down, when something's tough, I just touch the watch and think—I can do this." She looked at Alice, her gray eyes shining. "When I die, my daughter will wear it. Dr. Annette Fischer. She's a surgeon—pediatric endocrinologist."

Alice sat spellbound. What had that watch been through? Where had that watch been? How many times had it brought comfort to a Fischer descendant reaching inside a shirt, inside a pocket, to touch it?

And what happened to the other four watches? The ones in Horst Meyer's theft complaint?

"Dr. Fischer, I'm going to email you a folder titled 'Fischer Family Docs' that the judge compiled for his draft history. Will you have time to take a quick look at those documents? And I'll also email Chapter 13 of the draft history, including the footnotes."

"I'll read whatever you send!"

After dinner she delivered Dr. Fischer and her pink suitcase to the Tea Garden House B&B, run by Alice's friend and client M.A. Ellison, a couple of blocks from Alice's office, promising to pick Dr. Fischer up the next morning at eight sharp. On the way home, Alice couldn't stop wondering what they'd see when Bender lifted the last rocks from the Fischers' bones.

And maybe it was the bluebonnet wedding discussion, but—what about Silla and Bender? She had never heard Silla even mention the possibility of getting married. So where was that going?

Chapter Thirty-Three

Bones Are Facts

That night it poured, rain drumming on Alice's metal roof. At dawn the rain stopped. Before Alice finished making her espresso, she heard the donkeys outside, braying for carrots. "Hush, burros," she muttered, frothing the hot milk for her coffee. "Give me a minute."

After the requisite two cups of coffee, she marched outside in her winter robe and her flip-flops to give them their carrots. "I know, I know, I missed yesterday," she said, walking them to their traditional snack area under the towering cedar elm. She handed Queenie, then Princess, then Big Boy their carrots, then stroked Big Boy's neck, leaning against him. As always—even after coffee—she felt her breathing slow, felt her heart slow, felt herself breathe in morning air, gazing across the wet meadow. The bounds of her habitation. And the bounds of the burros' habitation.

"Okay, guys." She knew that by the end of the day they'd have explored their habitation for a muddy area and covered themselves with mud, rolling in the pasture. She headed inside for one more cup of coffee and a shower.

At eight Dr. Fischer met her in the entry hall at the Tea Garden House, with its faint scent of lavender and–what? Something toasty from an oven?

"What a place!" Dr. Fischer exclaimed. "The biscuits! Incredible! My egg! Perfectly done! The orange juice! Freshly squeezed! And did I say homemade Mexican plum jam? Who knew? I could stay for a week!"

Alice laughed. "It's the best."

They drove south toward the judge's property. Thank goodness it's not raining now, Alice thought. Sixty degrees—at least we won't freeze.

Dr. Fischer sighed. "This feels so weird. You're driving me to the home of a man I don't know but to a place I feel I *should* know...where my great-great-grandparents were murdered by some—oh, should I call him a sociopath? Someone who just killed, and took, right?"

"Yeah. I'm guessing his parents back in Louisiana said 'Don't come back!' when he left. But who knows?"

"There's no indication he ever went back home, is there?" said Dr. Fischer. She gazed out the window as they topped the hill overlooking the Blue Creek valley. "Oh, what a view."

After a moment, she went on. "I read those documents you emailed me. And Chapter 13 of the judge's history. I was intrigued by Horst Meyer's 1847 complaint about the theft of the four watches that were in a case. I looked online and saw each one would have been quite valuable, both then and now. Of course they'd have been wonderful models for Fritz Fischer, who must have dreamed of making watches like that. But those watches and the gold coins would also be, forgive me, a gold mine for the thief."

Could set you up in business, Alice thought. Buy you a big chunk of river bottom land when you got married. Start your family fortune. Maybe Files needed to check out that gold watch in Winifred's upstairs hall. Winifred might not give a rat's ass about Riley shooting six people...but she might not want to have it known that the family fortune was based on stolen goods, stolen by a murderer and common thief...

Dr. Fischer's voice softened. "At least Fritz wore his beloved pocket watch in his waistcoat. At least Emil got to keep it and to pass it on to his descendants." She switched gears. "So, Alice, tell me more about this GPR technique."

Alice tried to explain that the radar picked up differences in reflectivity, so that practiced users could interpret different slices at different depths to identify varying materials.

"The important thing about the Fischers' bodies is that they weren't left in the creek bed," Alice said. "Not left sitting in water. So their bones are more identifiable."

"Tell me about the judge. How did he get so interested in this? Why did he hire archeologists, for goodness' sake?"

"I knew him," Alice said. "He was a good man." She thought for a moment. "He was a stickler for accuracy, for facts. I mean, without accurate facts, the justice system would come tumbling down. At least in his courtroom. And the story's about the land he lived on... I think he wanted to pursue the truth about the gulch that runs across his property, the same way he pursued the truth about birds. He was an inveterate birdwatcher, bird lover."

"Oh!" exclaimed Dr. Fischer. "So am I!

"He took a picture of an American kestrel the afternoon he died."

"How I wish I'd known him," said Dr. Fischer. "How I wish he hadn't been shot."

Me too, Alice thought. Me too...the piercing blue eyes, the small smile, the fierce intelligence, the tenderness for his grandson. The dignity of his courtroom, and the insistence on truth.

*****

The sun was out by the time they drove down the judge's driveway and stopped in the graveled parking area. Alice didn't tell Dr. Fischer that she never reached that spot now without remembering Silla, standing in tears by the judge's body. As they climbed out, Alice heard the rush of water from Blue Creek, running merrily at the bottom of the slope.

The archeology team had shrunk now that Bender had acquired GPR data for the entire gulch, leaving only Bender and the two original grad students, Gordon and Wayland, to greet them. Alice introduced Dr. Fischer. "Dr. Fischer is the great-granddaughter of Emil Fischer, the little boy who saw his parents shot here."

Dr. Fischer shook their hands, then turned to survey the gulch. "Where are they?"

Bender walked her along the side of the gulch to the gap in the rock wall. "Alice pointed out that the gap might've been made when the rocks were moved to cover their bodies. And indeed we've found two skeletons."

Beyond the gap, on the shelf, rocks surrounded a large area covered by a tarp, elevated on stakes, and firmly anchored to the ground.

"Are the bones complete? Articulated?" asked Dr. Fischer.

"The larger bones are still present." With Wayland and Gordon helping, Bender folded back part of the tarp. A small plastic table stood at one corner.

Dr. Fischer walked forward, slowly bending to look at the ancient bones before her.

Alice followed. She felt a bit like an intruder—these weren't her relatives—but the judge had charged her with finding facts. Bones are facts.

Before her on the rocky ground, white with its load of lime-stone rock, lay two skeletons, overlapping at the shoulders and feet, as if they'd been dumped in a pile. But both skulls stared at the sky. I couldn't have borne that, Alice thought. If I were a killer, I'd have put them face down. Wouldn't want to see their dead faces staring up at me.

Bender might've read her mind. "They were probably dragged over to the shelf one at a time by the feet," he said. "See how the foot bones overlap?"

Dr. Fischer nodded.

"We haven't yet removed any artifacts," Bender said. "So far we've photographed and videoed the uncovering of the bones and their positions *in situ*. But that's all. Dr. Fischer, are you the appropriate person to make decisions about what we've found here?"

She raised her eyebrows. "Hadn't thought about it that way. Well, Emil Fischer was the only child of Fritz and Frieda. At this point I believe that I'm the only remaining great-grandchild. But I do have a daughter." She frowned for a moment. "I should poll any cousins, don't you think? But I believe my daughter and I can decide what to do about the remains."

Bender said, "I know you'll need to decide that, but first we need to document very carefully what's here and what we do here today. I want to show you what artifacts remain."

He motioned to Wayland and Gordon, Wayland holding a camera, Gordon holding a video camera.

Bender knelt near the skulls. "First, you can probably tell which is male, which is female."

Dr. Fischer nodded.

Using a laser pointer he sent a red beam below the female skeleton's jaw. "Can you see that—that bit of metal?"

Alice spotted it. The locket?

With Gordon and Wayland filming, and using his gloved hands and some tongs, Bender gently retrieved the object from below the skull. "This is what we spotted on the GPR," he said. He laid the object on a piece of glass and put it on the table. Old, partly gold, but with its hinge rusted away, and minus its chain, the locket was still heart-shaped.

With tweezers Bender gently turned it over. On the back Alice saw two entwined initials—*FF.*

Dr. Fischer unclasped the pocket watch from her neck and held it close to the locket, slowly turning it to show the same entwined cursive double "F" on the back.

Alice took pictures with her phone.

Wayland leaned over to see, eyes wide.

"For Fritz and Frieda," whispered Dr. Fischer.

Alice shivered. The dead couple suddenly felt very close.

With his tweezers, Bender slipped the locket into a labeled bag, which Gordon deposited into a metal case. "Alice, you'll let me know when I can give the locket to the right person." He smiled at Dr. Fischer.

Then he said, "On the GPR we also saw two roundish objects. The Walker Colt was a big heavy revolver, weighing four-and-a-half pounds. It was .44 caliber, fired lead balls, took a heavy powder charge, and was designed to be powerful enough to kill a soldier or even a horse with a single hit. Of the two roundish objects we identified with GPR, we believe one is lying just below the female skeleton's bones, covered with soil or caliche dust. On the GPR it's adjacent to the left side of the spine, below the sixth rib. Alice, you want all this documented for the judge's history, correct?"

She swallowed. "Yes."

Carefully, Bender, talking quietly into the video camera as he worked, used a long narrow brush to uncover the area between the ribs. A pitted ball appeared, about thumbnail sized.

"Wow," breathed Gordon.

"The other's in roughly the same position, near the vertebral column, but apparently nicked a front rib on the way in." Bender maneuvered carefully to the side of the male skeleton. "See the nick?"

"Yes," said Dr. Fischer.

Again with his brush, Bender delicately uncovered another pitted ball, next to the thoracic vertebrae.

"Got it," said Gordon, holding the video camera.

"I don't want to move these bodies until we know further plans," said Bender, "But we absolutely need to document the existence and locations of the revolver balls." He looked up at Alice. "Agreed?"

"Agreed."

He turned to Dr. Fischer. "One more artifact that showed up on the GPR. We thought it might turn out to be a pocket knife. Can you see the object below the crest of the male skeleton's right ilium, not quite level with the pubis?"

She nodded. "Carried it in his right pocket, I see."

Alice said, "Bender, I'll need copies of all this data. Every bit, please. And also for Dr. Fischer. And Frohbel."

"Sure. Files wants it too."

The five stood, staring down at the bones. A breeze ruffled Alice's hair. Overhead a heron cruised by, then swooped low over Blue Creek.

Okay, Judge, thought Alice. We've got you some facts. About Fritz and Frieda, the watchmaker waiting to open his shop, and his wife, with her butter and cheese, making a new life in the New World— until they were shot down by Jasper Riley. With their son watching in horror from the cedar scrub.

Gordon and Wayland helped Bender replace the tarp.

"Do you want to see where we think the Fischers lived?" Bender asked Dr. Fischer.

"Of course."

He turned and started up the slope toward the ridge, angling toward the creek. He stopped at a level area. "We think it was about here. This square of ground's more compacted. We haven't done any GPR here—that wasn't part of what the judge asked us to do."

"I feel oddly at home, like I've been here before." Dr. Fischer gazed out at Blue Creek, the wind riffling the water as it curved around a bend. "What a lovely place. No wonder they chose it."

She turned to Alice. "All right, my dear. I can't tell you how much this means to me. And thanks, Dr. Bender, for your kindness. And for sending me the data. For letting me see the locket. And yes, I will want to take possession of that locket at some point."

Alice pulled her phone from her pocket and took pictures of Dr. Fischer standing by the tarp with Bender, Gordon, and Wayland. Then Bender walked the two women back to Alice's car. After Dr.

Fischer was settled, he closed her door. He turned to Alice, walking her very slowly around to the driver's side. He stopped, holding the door handle. "Silla's at the office this morning, right?"

Alice nodded, waiting.

"She's really something, you know."

Alice nodded again. "She sure is."

"Well...umm..."

She'd never seen Bender so tongue-tied.

"I think she likes you, Bender."

"You do?"

"Mm-hmm."

"I think she's awesome. *Awesome!*" He blushed beet red and said, "Okay, later."

Well!

As she drove Dr. Fischer back toward Coffee Creek, Alice was wondering how to ask what Dr. Fischer wanted to do with the family bones. Dr. Fischer beat her to it. "Fritz and Frieda were members of the local Lutheran church, I believe. That church is apparently still here, is it not? I checked online."

"Yes."

"Could we stop by there? Do you have time? Let me see if the office is open." Dr. Fischer checked her phone, then called. "You're open this morning? Oh, lovely. May I stop by? Dr. Maria Fischer is the name."

*****

Whew, thought Alice, waiting in the car at the Coffee Creek Lutheran Church. I'll want an agreement from the Fischer family members—at least Maria and her daughter, Annette——that they will hold harmless the judge's estate if there's ever any dispute from any relative about these bones being moved and re-buried at Coffee Creek Lutheran Church. And we'll need to document absolutely everything. Weirdest legal assignment I've ever had, Judge!

When Dr. Fischer returned, she was smiling. "Lovely spot in the far back corner. The church would be glad to handle a service, too.

And thanks for sharing the Bond woman's contact information. I'm eager to meet another cousin."

Alice still felt anxious. And Dr. Fischer seemed restless. "Tell me again," she asked, "about why Winifred Hutton wanted to kill the judge."

"She doesn't want the world to hear that her ancestor Jasper Riley killed the Fischers," Alice said. "He's part of this mythic heritage she claims. When she shot the judge, she didn't realize that his death wouldn't prevent his county history from seeing the light of day. Now that we're tracking down the facts, she'll be looking for anything she can to prove he didn't kill the Fischers."

"But you've found me! And I've got Emil's pocket watch!"

"Yes..." And, Alice thought, that fact was enough to give her sufficient confidence to let Dr. Fischer bury the bones. But wasn't it all circumstantial? Sure, Dr. Fischer had a pocket watch with the double F engraved on the back. Sure, she could show Emil Fischer was her great-grandfather. But...

Dr. Fischer turned to Alice. "Here's my plan. I'm going to ask that we test for DNA using either the petrous part of the temporal bone, or a molar, from the skeletons to show that Annette and I are descendants of the very skeletons buried on the property. I think the petrous bone is useful for autosomal DNA. I've always wanted to be part of a study like that, and we have a terrific forensics lab in Baltimore. I'm sure there's one here as well. What do you think?"

Why not? Why ever not? It might hold up the burial of the remains...but they'd been waiting a long time. Those bones could wait a little longer. Couldn't they?

Chapter Thirty-Four

May I Wear Boots?

"Autosomal DNA?" Silla asked.

"Yes," said Alice. She'd dropped off Dr. Fischer at the Tea Garden House, where she'd told Alice she intended to arrange immediately for samples from both skeletons "just in case."

Alice had driven straight back to the office. "I see no reason she shouldn't be allowed to do that. After all, she's entitled to be sure the people she's burying are her relatives, right?"

"Right," Silla said. "And wouldn't it be one more nail in Winifred Hutton's legal coffin?"

"I think it's good for Dr. Fischer to make the arrangements and get some expert out here to take whatever samples are needed before those bones disappear into the Lutheran Church cemetery." Alice paused. "As long as she'll hold the judge's estate harmless if anything goes awry. So I'm working on a hold-harmless draft."

"So," Silla asked, "Only Wayland and Gordon are still out at the judge's place with Bender?"

She flushed pink as Alice grinned back at her. "You know what Bender said? He took me aside just before we left. And he said—about you—'I think she's awesome! *Awesome*!' Just like that. Twice."

Silla stood stock still. "He did?"

"He did."

Silla whirled out. Alice heard her humming in the hall.

*****

Alice called Frohbel in Fredericksburg and told him what she'd seen beneath the tarp—including pistol balls and the locket with its initials—and what Dr. Fischer proposed to do about ancestry testing. "My thought is, before we get samples from the skeletons or release them to Dr. Fischer for burial, we get a hold-harmless agreement from her for the estate."

"I agree," Frohbel said. "Send me a copy."

Next, Alice realized she'd promised to call Laura at church this morning. But she's off on Monday, she thought. Still, maybe she wouldn't mind being called at home? Alice found her number. "Umm,

Laura. I was wondering—could you possibly perform a wedding cere-mony on the last Saturday in March?"

"Hallelujah!" Laura said. "I have been waiting for this. Yes, I can perform a wedding ceremony on the fourth Saturday in March. I've blocked it on the calendar. May I wear boots?"

"Absolutely! Thank you!"

Alice hung up to see Silla's face peering around her office door. "Did I just hear what I think I heard?"

Alice felt her face go bright red. "Yes. Believe it or not."

Silla beamed. "You'll need my help planning this, Alice. I hereby undertake that task."

"Really? That would be fabulous!"

"I'm on it. But at the moment?"

"Yes?"

"Dr. Fischer called to say she's located a DNA expert who's in touch with Bender about getting the requisite samples from the skeletons. She's arranged for our office to get copies of everything and notice be-fore the skeleton samples are taken. Right now, she's taking a Lyft to the expert's lab to give her own sample and then coming back to the Tea Garden House. I told her I'd take her to the airport to catch her flight back to Baltimore at five."

"Great. Let me finish this hold-harmless agreement to protect the judge's estate, and let's get her to sign it before she leaves."

"Okay. But don't forget you still need to finish that outline on groundwater issues so I can get it to the legal education people. It's due February 10th, remember."

Alice drafted madly, emailed the draft agreement to Frohbel, got his "looks good," and printed out copies for Silla. "You'll notarize it after she signs, right?"

"Of course. Got my seal. See you later."

As Silla disappeared out the door, Alice thought, she *is* awesome. Really.

Dutifully she turned to the dratted groundwater outline, finished the case analysis, and forwarded it to Silla.

*****

By six that Monday evening, she felt brain-fogged and exhausted. "A sinking spell?" she asked herself. Hutton had so much money...she'd doubtless claim Alice was trespassing on her property...the "hands" would say whatever they had to about the trespassing woman they'd caught...Hutton would blame the "hands;" and the hands—well, who knew what they'd say. One might say—"just a mistake! I thought *he* was taking her food and water and a blanket!" Finger-pointing at each other.

What about Hutton's fingerprint on the doorbell? Winifred could just say she'd rung the doorbell, waited, and left when no one answered.

The revolver in the Stetson hatbox? Maybe it hadn't been fired.

Her phone rang. Files. She grabbed it. "George?"

"You still at your office? Can you come by for a sec? Got some news."

His voice had that "I've got a secret" timbre. Possibly a *good* secret...

"On my way, this instant."

Too excited to walk, she locked the office and drove the two blocks to the Sheriff's Annex, screeched into a parking spot, and raced in. The desk sergeant recognized her and pointed toward Files's hall. Files stood waiting, with a lopsided smile.

As they walked into his office, he said, "Ballistics results. The .38 caliber revolver in the hatbox? Positive ballistics test. Appears to match the bullet that killed Judge Mahan."

Alice sighed, let out a long breath. Another fact for the judge. She settled into the chair across from Files's desk, too relieved to complain about the hard metal seat.

"So we've charged her with murder. But wait, there's more," said Files, riffling through papers on his desk. "And it relates to you. Joske remembered a missing persons case and did some digging. Do you remember when the heir to a Brenham jewelry store disappeared, about three years ago?"

Memory stirred. "Yes. Wasn't the family trying to sell their business?"

"Full marks. The family owned a small-town chain in East Texas called Paschal Family Jewelry. They were approached by none other than"— he glanced up at her—"HFH, LLC. Apparently, that's short for Hutton Family Holdings. The son who ran their Brenham store, Dan Paschal, was a tough negotiator and wanted to keep a piece of the business. Then he disappeared, in January, during that big ice spell we had. Months passed. The Paschal family finally sold out to HFH."

"Yikes."

Files went on. "Joske can be a pain in the butt sometimes, but he remembered that later on, during the last drought, some kids spotted a submerged car in the LaGrange reservoir. When the city towed the car out of the water, they found a body in the driver's seat. Guess who?"

"Dan Paschal?" Alice breathed.

"Yep. Sitting in the driver's seat in his own car. They managed to identify him—dental records, healed wrist fracture. But here's the weird thing. The pathologist couldn't find a mark on him—no sign of being shot, stabbed, strangled. Skull intact. Could've been smothered, maybe. Or drugged. But the pathologist insisted he'd been dead awhile before the car went into the reservoir."

"In January. During a deep freeze," Alice said. "That's what Big Chest and Blindfold Guy called it, putting me in the vet stall. 'Deep freeze action.' Sounded like they'd done it before."

Files's eyes rested on hers. "Those guys have worked for Hutton for several years. Joske's checking their whereabouts around the time when Paschal disappeared. Haven't got that nailed down yet."

"Will you be able to keep them locked up? No bail?" Alice asked.

"I'll keep you posted. At the arraignment hearing, the judge ordered them each to post $500,000 in bail. That hasn't happened yet. I'm guessing Hutton's may be a million."

"I've thought of one more thing," Alice said. "Can you get someone to check the antique framed watch you saw on the wall in Hutton's upstairs? On both front and back?"

"Why? What does that watch have to do with anything?"

"The documents the judge kept in his footnote folders include a copy of a theft complaint filed in 1847 on behalf of the dead Fischers by their relative, Horst Meyer. It lists the stolen items as including some gold coins and four antique pocket watches belonging to Fritz Fischer. Those watches are still quite valuable. The one on Winifred Hutton's wall may be one her ancestor stole from Fritz Fischer in 1847. It may have the double cursive capital Fs on the back, like the initials on the back of the locket found on Frieda Fischer's skeleton, and the initials on the back of the one surviving pocket watch, which Dr. Fischer inherited. If so, its presence at her house may explain part of Hutton's motivation for killing the judge, and going after Johnny, and trying to get rid of me." She shifted on the metal chair. "Hutton might gloss over having an ancestor who killed Comanches who were eating his horse. But she'd find it a little harder if that ancestor was not only a murderer but a common thief."

"I'll talk to the DA. Again." He shook his head, made a face. "Explaining why I need a warrant to look at a watch...nearly two centuries old."

Which is about how old I feel, Alice thought, walking back to her car. But her eyes were drawn to the sky, now pink and violet. Sunset was coming later every day. Weren't those pale green buds on the cedar elms on the courthouse lawn? As she neared the car her arm brushed a straggly shrub and she stopped, surrounded by the loveliest scent. Honey? Jasmine? Lemon? She looked up to see, on the untidy branches, the tiny yellowish blossoms of wintersweet—*chimonanthus praecox*, spring's rare and secret gift. She closed her eyes, taking a deep breath, then another. Whatever else spring might bring, she'd remember this.

Chapter Thirty-Five

Conference Call At 10:00 a.m.?

On Tuesday morning Alice punched Kinsear's number into her office phone. "Did you just get this email from Isabel? Setting up a conference call at 10 a.m.?" she demanded. "On Zoom?"

"Damned if I know," Kinsear said. "I just saw it too."

"Did you talk to your girls yet about the wedding?"

"Not yet," he confessed. "You talk to Ann and John?"

"I was so tired last night," she said. A silence. "Well, the truth is I hadn't come up with my opening line."

"Same." He started laughing. "Let's see what they have in store."

*****

When she entered the computer link at ten, Alice saw faces of not just Kinsear plus Isabel and Carrie, but also her own John, looking very grown-up, and Ann, sparkly as usual.

"We're gathered together," intoned Isabel in her deepest voice, "to give you the news."

"Right," said John. "At the upcoming wedding on the fourth Saturday in March, the authorities have announced the designated roles for the participants."

"Alice, Dad, your roles are to stand quietly and answer each question properly," said Carrie.

"And our roles are as follows," said Isabel. "Dad, Carrie and I will stand up with you as your best persons. You can add some guy if you want."

"Furthermore," said Ann, "Mom, you know that juvenile moment when the officiant says 'who giveth this woman to be wed'? We're having none of that. Instead, Reverend Laura will ask, 'Who presents this man and woman to be married? And we'll all say, 'we all do!'" she added, with that irrepressible smile. "And don't worry, you can have another attendant or two. I know Red's dying to be up there with you."

"You all..." Alice began, torn between laughter and tears. "How did you find out?"

"Silla alerted Ann. It's gonna be fun," John announced. "Now let's get down to brass tacks. Barbecue, right? A decent band? I need a new tux jacket and some new boots. These Edinburgh streets—mine are worn out."

"You wear them in Edinburgh?" asked Carrie.

"Part of my identity," John retorted. "The bold invader from across the Atlantic."

"Silla's already in charge of the wedding," Alice warned.

"We know that!" said Isabel. "Of course we've talked to Silla. She's treating this as practice for my wedding, which she's already agreed to plan."

Before Kinsear could ask a question, Isabel said, "Okay, guys, we've all got classes. Thanks, peeps! Love you!"

In a chorus of "goodbye!" and "love you!" the kids' faces disappeared from the computer screen. Alice called Kinsear on her cell.

"Kidnapped!" he said. "The pirates have us! Whose wedding is this, anyway?"

"Unless we elope, it's clearly theirs. But you know..."

"Yeah. It's wonderful that they plotted this, that they're together. I'm feeling kind of soppy about it," Kinsear said.

After they hung up, Alice went to Silla's worktable. Silla's smile was innocent, but she'd raised one knowing eyebrow. Alice put her arms around Silla and hugged her, then leaned back, shaking her head. "Oh, Silla, you knew all about this!"

"We had our own conference call, the kids and I."

"Aha." All those secret machinations! "Thank you so much for taking charge of the wedding and getting these kids on board. What a joyful relief!"

"It'll be a blast. I've always wanted to tackle a wedding. Can't be any harder than a rodeo...or flying a plane."

"How are the lessons going?"

"I love it. I'm gonna solo this weekend. But you didn't tell me Bender hates heights!"

Alice remembered Bender telling her about taking a bad fall on a climb to see rock art out at Big Bend. "Does that mean he won't fly with you?"

"We'll just see."

*****

Alice returned to her desk, trying her best to settle her mind and prepare for a client call on a new project—a conservation easement for a family who owned acreage out along Middle Creek. Which inevitably reminded her of Winifred Hutton.

As she finished the call, Silla stuck her head in the door.

"Files called while you were on the phone. Winifred Hutton's arraignment's at 1 p.m., here in Coffee County. State court jurisdiction, per the feds, on the judge's murder. Files says she'll also be charged with unlawful restraint. Still looking at the Paschal death as well."

"I'll be there." Promptly at one, as she slipped into the back row of the courtroom, Alice got her wish. Winifred Hutton didn't look that good in orange. If looks could kill, the Coffee County judge on the bench would be dead. So would the *Coffee Creek Caller* photographer, who got a stunning picture of Winifred's face when the judge set her bond at a million dollars.

*****

Two weeks later Dr. Fischer was calling, her voice triumphant. "Got the preliminary DNA results back! Annette and I are clearly descendants of Emil Fischer and his parents! I'm sending you a copy!"

"Wonderful! Send the results to Bender and Detective Files and David Frohbel, too, will you? I'm going to add this to the judge's manuscript!" Then Alice asked, "How does this feel?"

A pause, different from Dr. Fischer's usual brisk decisiveness. "You know that phrase, justice delayed is justice denied? But the thought of having the facts of our relationship laid out for history—so that the story of Jasper Riley's murders is out there for all to read—confirmed by DNA results—is unimaginably satisfying. Our story is *true*. No, there was no justice in 1847. But now? Now we feel there's some justice in at least having our story confirmed." Another pause. "It's hard to explain. Not knowing the truth of what happened felt like a gap, a hole in our being! Like the world didn't think our great-great-grandparents were worth remembering. But now—the chopped-off branches of the family tree have been restored. Leafy and green. I feel—vindicated. Thank you!"

Vindication, at last.

That didn't bring back Judge Mahan. But in a way he'd been vindicated as well, in his search for the truth. She sat, wondering what he'd say if he were here. If he could read the DNA analysis. If he'd stood at the side of the gulch, leaning over to see the pitted lead balls, to watch Bender lift out the locket, to see Dr. Fischer turn over Emil Fischer's pocket watch to compare the initials.

"We got your facts, Judge," she whispered. "I hope you're seeing lots of birds, hearing some new birdsongs, out there."

Chapter Thirty-Six

Rest In Peace

Just after Valentine's Day, Dr. Fischer and her daughter flew back to Texas for a quiet graveside service at the Lutheran church in Coffee Creek. "Please come," Dr. Fischer had said. "We aren't asking anyone else except you and Silla."

Alice took a bunch of early daffodils to lay on the grave. The gray granite stone read, "Here lie Fritz and Frieda Fischer, husband and wife, murdered in September 1847 at their property on Blue Creek. *Requiescant in pace.*"

"I started to add 'murdered by Jasper Riley' to the gravestone, but it didn't seem appropriate for this peaceful corner," Dr. Fischer told Alice. "May they rest in peace, as long as the judge's history sets forth the real story."

*****

On a cool sunny Saturday afternoon in the fourth week of February, an overflow crowd showed up for Judge Mahan's memorial service at Coffee Creek Presbyterian Church. Alice recognized at least five judges and thirty lawyers in attendance. The service itself was simple, with familiar readings from Psalms and the New Testament and a short homily from Laura McDowell. The choir sang again the anthem Alice loved, about the "bounds of their habitation." The judge's habitation—the land on Blue Creek, the ancient live oaks, the murmuring water, the gulch, the stone walls, the old house that felt like a library, with its fragrance of old books—filled her mind, along with her awareness of Johnny and his father, Eric, sitting on the front row.

After the service, the crowd adjourned for refreshments in the community hall, and Johnny, Eric, Alice, and Silla slipped off with David Frohbel and Laura, still in her black robe, for the private inurnment. Alice had been surprised and touched when Frohbel called and told her the judge wanted her and Silla to join the small group at the columbarium. "He felt you were part of his family."

In the cool sunlight, Alice, Silla, Frohbel, and the two Mahan men followed Laura into a walled garden adjacent to the sanctuary, before the wall of columbarium niches. The day before, in the church office under Frohbel's watchful eye, some of Muriel's ashes had been mixed with the judge's, as he'd requested.

Laura led them in a brief prayer. Then she nodded to Eric Mahan. He opened the door to the niche. Frohbel handed the heavy burgundy velvet bag holding the ashes to Eric and Johnny. Standing side by side, father and son placed the velvet bag inside the niche. Frohbel stepped forward and said, "Eric, Johnny, the judge left you each a letter in the niche and would like you each to read your letter here, while we're together."

Eric's face was a stiff mask. Alice wondered if he feared a final scolding. He reached deep into the niche and pulled out two white envelopes. He handed the one labeled "Johnny" to his son. He stared down at his own envelope, clearly not ready to open it. Johnny looked at his dad, then gently lifted the flap, pulled out a card, and read. His nose turned pink, and he grabbed a tissue from his jacket pocket, then looked at his dad.

Frohbel closed the niche. Then he nodded at Johnny, who began to read aloud his card from the judge. "Johnny, I have watched you grow into a man of courage and vision. You already have the mind of a scholar who can pull together different disciplines and offer new ideas to our world. And you are made of, and for, love. Extend your ideas, as well as your love, to the world and to those who love you, for this world needs your courage and your vision. I love you. Thank you for taking care of Charley."

Eric opened his envelope and read the enclosed card, then looked at Frohbel, face bemused. He cleared his throat. "Eric, I don't know how to write a note that contains all the love and admiration I feel for you. I'll never forget your unfailing tenderness and love for your wife in her last illness and your courage in caring for her as she died. Such a demonstration of love! I regret my own inability to show love as fully as you do, so, in cowardly fashion, I'm writing you this letter. I love you; I so admire your drive, vision, and imagination as you create new enterprises. I hope you'll seek out someone who not only needs your love and imagination, but will also give you the love you so richly deserve."

Eric looked up, eyes wet. "I never knew..."

Frohbel said, "He wanted you to hear the letters he wrote to each of you. He told me he'd never been good at telling people—except

Muriel—how much he loved them."

After a pause, Laura led them in a closing prayer and benediction.

Then Alice and Silla glanced at each other, eyes wide. Nothing to say. They hugged Johnny, shook hands with Eric, slipped through the gate, and walked toward the parking lot.

Neither said a word as they climbed into Alice's Discovery.

Silla said, "It's true, some people have trouble saying 'I love you.'"

"But not Bender?" asked Alice.

Silla's face was pink. "Not Bender."

*****

The following Monday Alice stopped at the grocery store to pick up some staples for the office kitchen—especially coffee. On the way back she drove past Coffee Creek Elementary, slowing to a stop at the crosswalk. School had just let out; a flood of kids with backpacks, waving and calling to each other, streamed toward the line of parked cars where parents waited. Alice was thinking of Dedra Riley and her children when she spotted a trio of kids racing for a silver mom-mobile, where a woman in pink scrubs bent down and picked up the youngest, then hugged the two older kids. Dedra, in nursing garb...

Alice thought about the judge's comment that love was irrelevant in a criminal court.

This wasn't a criminal court.

When she walked into the office, Silla handed her a note to call Tim Johansen. "Also," Silla said, "I heard this morning at the diner that Richard Riley's pretty much out of the race. Ran out of money. I think Gracie'll be a shoo-in."

Alice stood at Silla's desk to call Johansen, putting him on speaker. He answered immediately. "Alice! How are you? I heard about this awful mess at Hutton Ranch."

She waited. What could she say? "Yes?"

"Well, I just wanted to check. How's the judge's manuscript coming?"

"Silla and I are working on the footnotes. We expect to have them done soon." She paused, but he was silent. She glanced at Silla. "We're adding a footnote reporting that the results of the archeology study confirm Emil Fischer's story, that the Comanche Nation is retrieving the Comanche remains, and that the archeologists found the remains of Fritz and Frieda Fischer."

"Ah," he said. "Sounds good."

"I think we'll include information about Emil Fischer's life and work. But I expect we'll omit the full genealogy of Jasper Riley's descendants."

Another pause. "Well, the Historical Commission looks forward to getting the finished manuscript. We're thinking of publishing it as a special edition in the judge's honor," Johansen said. "Will June work?"

"Yes. We'll keep you posted," said Alice. She hung up, looking at Silla.

"You know, I always hated those Bible verses about the sins of the fathers being visited on the children," Silla said. "Don't we all have some scallywags up in the branches?"

Alice nodded. "But remember Ezekiel 18:20. 'A child shall not suffer for the iniquity of a parent.'"

*****

Johnny called a week later. "Can you and Silla come by this afternoon? Something I want you two to see..."

It was a blue sky afternoon, with wispy white cirrus clouds high above and some cumulus clouds piling up in the west. About five, Alice and Silla drove down the judge's driveway. Johnny met them on the front porch, holding a bottle of champagne. Next to him stood a young woman with a freckled face, intense brown eyes, and brown braids. "This is Lisette," he said. "She's an art major at Texas State."

Lisette smiled, revealing dimples. She offered a strong handshake.

"We need to walk up the slope," Johnny said. He set out, carrying the champagne, while Lisette brought the four champagne flutes.

Alice and Silla followed Johnny and Lisette uphill toward something tall and bulky, covered with canvas, tied with a rope. Alice asked, "Isn't this close to the area where, according to Bender, the Fischers' cabin stood?"

"Yes indeed."

Alice had thought it was the loveliest spot for a cabin. Downhill to the south, Blue Creek's rapids sparkled as the water ran over limestone rocks, the ripply sound filling the afternoon air. Downhill to the east, the gulch cut across the pasture, with thick cedar scrub on the other side. She turned west to see the live oaks atop the ridge, where Judge Mahan had finally photographed his kestrel.

Johnny popped the champagne. Lisette handed around the empty flutes.

"Are we ready?" he asked.

Lisette nodded. With one hand she pulled off the rope around the canvas-covered lump, letting it drop on the ground. Then she leaned over and tugged off the canvas.

There stood a four-foot-tall chunk of pink granite, rough except for the polished flat oval surface facing them. Carved in the middle of the oval was a wide-branched live oak, its branches curving in welcome. Up from the branches flew birds—tiny songbirds, crested titmice, cardinals, then an owl, and finally, at the top, a kestrel with elegant outspread wings.

Letters carved into the granite at the bottom read, "For all who have sojourned here—and now are free as any bird."

Alice stood speechless. The Comanche family, the Fischers, little Emil hiding in the scrub...sojourners. Free.

"Do you like it?" Johnny asked.

Alice could only nod, not trusting her voice.

"It's beautiful," Silla said.

"Lisette made it," Johnny said proudly. "I wanted a memorial for Granddad, and I thought he'd want one for—for everyone. The Comanches, the Fischers..." He poured champagne into the four flutes.

"To all the sojourners," Alice said.

"Hear, hear," said Silla. They sipped the champagne. "And to Judge Mahan, and his boys."

"Hear, hear!" said Lisette.

They lifted their glasses in the March sun. Alice felt a soft breeze touch her cheek. Was it the judge, stopping by?

✕

Chapter Thirty-Seven

Definitely A Good Idea...

"Which do you prefer, France or Big Bend?" asked Kinsear. He'd cornered Alice on the couch, where she was reading a mystery by Andrea Camilleri.

"Or Sicily?" she asked. "The way this man describes Sicilian seafood, I'm ready to go right this minute."

"But what about the Dordogne? A little town by the river...croissants for breakfast...hiking in the cave areas...duck confit...markets...?"

"Not bad. But we had such a nice time in Marathon, and hiking in Big Bend..."

"Well, don't worry your pretty little head about it. I'm in charge of the honeymoon."

"Sounds good."

"And Silla's handling our wedding, starting with the rehearsal dinner, plus dancing and ribaldry, and the wedding, with you looking lovely in your great-grandmother's dress..."

"Assuming I can still get into it," Alice said.

"You, on the other hand, are in charge only of getting a new tux jacket for your son and choosing appropriate finery for the feminine side of the wedding."

"Right."

"Just one more week," said Kinsear, looking down at her and snatching her mystery, which he tossed onto the coffee table.

What's it going to be like, being married to this man? she wondered. Then she wondered if he was wondering, is this a good idea? Or not?

"Oh, yeah," he said. "This is definitely a good idea..."

THE END

I live and write north of Dripping Springs, Texas, in the stunning Texas Hill Country, loosely supervised by three burros, with occasional visits from other inhabitants: foxes, jackrabbits, deer, armadillos, skunks, raccoons, owls, hawks—and porcupines. The harsh but beautiful landscape, with its limestone-bottomed creeks and springs, won my heart years ago. I left Texas for Wellesley College, then entered graduate school at UT Austin and later the University of Michigan Law School where I grew intrigued by dirt and water law. Current preoccupations: human prehistory, water issues, boogie-woogie piano.

HEARING FROM YOU

Thank you for reading *Ghost Bones*! If you enjoyed meeting Alice and her Coffee Creek companions in *Ghost Bones*, please consider rating or reviewing it. You can stay in touch with Alice and her adventures at www.helencurriefoster.com, and sign up on the email list there for updates and news about upcoming books. Future events as well as pictures of the burros and various aspects of the Hill Country also appear on Facebook at https://www.facebook.com/helencurriefoster.

Check out my blogs at https://austinmysterywriters.com and https://inkstainedwretches.home.blog.
Happy reading!

Thanks to family and friends for their generous help—Charles Scott on aviation issues, Grace and Bill Bradshaw, Keith Graham, Dr. Megan Biesele, and Kay Holladay, as well as fellow writers Kathy Waller, Dixie Evatt, Kathy Gresham, and Francine Paino, and, always, Larry, Sydney, and Drew Foster. Any errors are mine. Many thanks to Susan Wittig Albert for her kind comments.

Finally, to Judy Cohen for superb copy-editing, and to Bill Carson for cover, design layout, and sheer professional brio, thanks and more thanks.

9 781732 722934